*The*

FINAL VOW

A *Living History Museum* Mystery

AMANDA FLOWER

MIDNIGHT INK
WOODBURY, MINNESOTA

First Edition
First Printing, 2017

Cover design by Kevin R. Brown
Cover illustration by Tom Jester/Jennifer Vaughn Artist Agent
Map by Llewellyn Art Department

Midnight Ink, an imprint of Llewellyn Worldwide Ltd.

Library of Congress Cataloging-in-Publication Data

Names: Flower, Amanda, author.
Title: The final vow / Amanda Flower.
Description: First edition. | Woodbury, Minnesota : Midnight Ink, [2017] |
    Series: A living history museum mystery ; #3
Identifiers: LCCN 2016056327 (print) | LCCN 2017002178 (ebook) | ISBN
    9780738745923 | ISBN 9780738751832
Subjects: LCSH: Murder—Investigation—Fiction. | GSAFD: Mystery fiction.
Classification: LCC PS3606.L683 F567 2017 (print) | LCC PS3606.L683 (ebook) |
    DDC 813/.6—dc23
LC record available at https://lccn.loc.gov/2016056327

Midnight Ink
Llewellyn Worldwide Ltd.
2143 Wooddale Drive
Woodbury, MN 55125-2989
www.midnightinkbooks.com
Printed in the United States of America

The
FINAL VOW

For Sherry Bixler and Charlotte Spitali

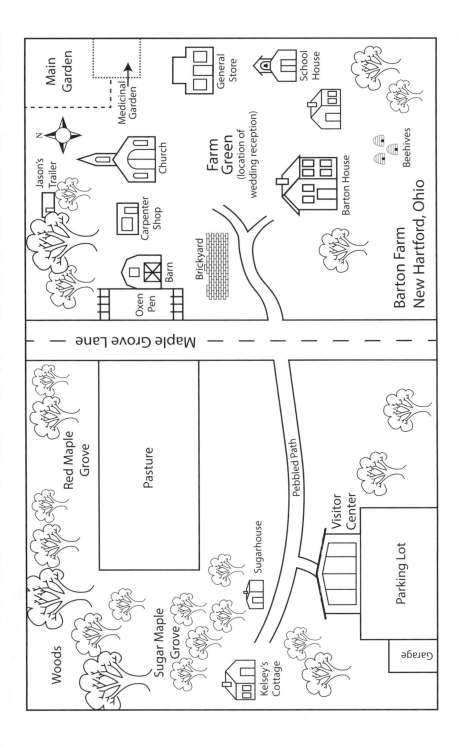

Barton Farm
New Hartford, Ohio

The vow that binds too strictly snaps itself.
—Alfred, Lord Tennyson

ONE

KRISSIE PUMPERNICKLE DREAMED ABOUT being a June bride, and Krissie Pumpernickle got what she wanted. Or so I was learning in short order. As a rule, I was a quick study, but apparently to Krissie my learning curve was on the slow side.

In the perfect movie starlet pout, she stuck her lower lip out at me. "Kelsey, you said the Civil War reenactors would be here for my wedding. I'm expecting a full-scale reenactment. You promised me. You promised me Lincoln!" She brushed her blond hair over her shoulder. When I'd first met her a year ago, her hair had been styled into a delicate pixie cut. Over the past twelve months, she'd been growing it out for the wedding. Everything that Krissie Pumpernickle had done since the day we met had been for the wedding.

I gripped my ever-present notebook that detailed all the things I needed to do in every aspect of my life, from running Barton Farm, a living history museum tucked away in Ohio's Cuyahoga Valley, to raising my six-year-old son, Hayden. I took a deep breath before speaking. I'd learned, in the last three months planning Krissie's wedding, that it was always better to collect myself before I responded. I had to be careful. Krissie had me in a vulnerable position, and we both knew it.

"Krissie," I began. "I never promised you the reenactors would be here, and I told you from the start that there wouldn't be a reenactment battle during your wedding. That just isn't possible. Unfortunately, I don't know if there will be any reenactors here at all. There's a big Civil War event happening in southern Ohio this weekend. Most of the reenactors will be there."

"That's not acceptable. My family has donated a lot of money to the Cherry Foundation so you can keep this Farm open. Should I tell my parents they wasted their money?" Her bottom lip popped out for a second time.

Again, I took a second, but the urge to tell her where she and her parents could go with their donation was on the tip of my tongue. It was going to take me more than one breath to respond to this one.

Thankfully, my assistant Benji jumped into the fray. Cocking her head, she sent her braided ponytail decorated with purple and green beads swinging over her shoulder. "Miss Pumpernickle, there will be at least a dozen Civil War reenactors here the day of the wedding. As friends of Kelsey and Barton Farm, they graciously agreed to skip the other reenactment to attend your wedding instead. We may not be able to provide you with a full-scale battle, but there will be enough men in uniform here to charm your guests. Be sure of that."

Krissie narrowed her eyes at Benji, and my assistant smiled brightly in return. I knew when Benji smiled like that it was time to take cover, but Krissie was clueless when it came to Benji's facial expressions, which was for the best.

"What about Lincoln?" she snapped. "I said that I want Lincoln there and I meant it."

I opened my mouth to tell her that my Abraham Lincoln reenactor, who was the best in the business, was among the group going to the reenactment near Marietta, which was over three hours away. It was his biggest gig of the season.

"Honest Abe will be there," Benji said without batting an eye. "You can count on that, and thank Kelsey for making it possible."

I stared at Benji. She knew as well as I did that Lincoln wasn't coming to the wedding. I opened my mouth to correct her, but Benji stepped on my foot with her red Doc Marten boot.

I swallowed a yelp of pain. She'd put a lot of force behind that stomp.

Krissie adjusted the shoulders of her cardigan. "There had better be. I don't want to have to be the one who tells the Cherry Foundation that my father has removed his funding. My wedding planner will be along shortly to talk over the last-minute details. I expect that between the two of you, Kelsey, you can do everything I need for my wedding."

Out of the corner of my eye, I saw my gardener Shepley's flock of free-range chickens marching across the village green toward us. I groaned internally. In a moment of weakness, I'd let Shepley talk me into acquiring the chickens. His theory was that if the chickens were free to roam the Farm at night, then the Hooper boys—the Farm's closest neighbors and utter teenage delinquents—would be less likely to bother us with their childish pranks. As it turned out, Shepley had been right; we'd heard very little from the Hooper boys or their just-as-unpleasant mother, Pansy, so far that summer. The chickens patrolled the village side of the Farm like an inner city gang, not a brood of hens. Benji called them our attack chickens.

There were four of them in all. Each bird was a different color. There was a black chicken, a black-and-white chicken, a blond chicken, and a red chicken. The red one, Gertrude, was by far the biggest and the leader of the brood. Everyone knew who the top hen was.

Krissie shook with indignation. "And those chickens have to go. I will not have chickens at my wedding!"

Gertrude ran toward the bride at full tilt. Krissie yelped and backed down the path at the edge of the green. I can't say I blamed her. I'd fled from Gertrude's advance more than once. The hen stopped and smoothed out her feathers.

At that, Krissie spun away, sending her skirt swirling around her legs as she marched across Maple Grove Lane toward the other side of the Farm.

"Remove the funding?" Benji said crossly. "You can't ask a non-profit for money back after giving a one-time monetary gift, no matter how large the gift is. She's such a b—"

"I know." I interrupted Benji before she could get the full word out, despite how I may have agreed with the sentiment. We had children's summer camps in session, and there were families visiting the Farm and milling around the historic village. The last thing I wanted was for word to reach Henry Ratcliffe and the other members of the Cherry Foundation board of trustees that visitors had overheard Farm staff swearing. "And what are you doing telling her that Lincoln will be at the wedding?" I added. "You know that Darren can't make it." Darren was Lincoln's real name, or at least the one he went by sans top hat.

Benji grinned. "I found another one."

My brow knit together. "How did you find someone? Usually those guys are booked all summer long."

"Umm . . . " She paused. "It turns out he had an opening. He must have had a cancellation or something. Pretty fortunate, right?" She smiled cheerfully at me. "He's going to come by today so you can meet him."

I squinted at her. There was something my assistant wasn't telling me about Abe, and I had a sneaking suspicion I wouldn't like it when I found out. I decided to let it slide for the moment. "I was impressed that you called her Miss Pumpernickle. It was a nice touch."

Benji shrugged. "I took one for the team. I still can't believe that—"

I gave her a look.

She frowned. "I still can't believe that *person* tricked us into hosting her wedding. It's a slap in your face, Kelsey. I don't know why you put up with it."

I scanned the village around me. It was a collection of mid-nineteenth-century buildings that Cynthia Cherry—the beloved and, sadly, deceased director of the Cherry Foundation—had moved from other parts of Ohio to save from demolition. Cynthia's father had made a fortune in the tire industry when it was booming in nearby Akron, and he'd created the foundation that supported Barton Farm. His daughter had been the Farm's benefactress for decades, reconstructing the imported buildings on the Farm land piece by piece. The village was arranged in a circle around a wide green, and it featured the original Barton home, another Civil War-era home, a one-room school house, a carpenter shop, and our crown jewel, a large white wooden church with a steeple built in the classic Western Reserve style. It was the church where Krissie was to be married that upcoming Friday evening.

It was the church where Krissie was going to marry my ex-husband.

Children and adult visitors smiled as they chatted with my historical interpreters, who were dressed in nineteenth-century garb. In the middle of the green, a young boy wearing cargo shorts and a Captain America T-shirt walked on stilts like it was an Olympic sport. This scene, and all it meant, was why I put up with the challenges of being the director of Barton Farm.

Benji sighed, because she knew what I was thinking. My life's mission, other than raising my son, was to save Barton Farm and all it taught to the public about the past. Benji knew this. There was no reason for anyone to say it aloud.

I sighed too. "Let's just survive until the weekend. After the wedding is over, we'll be free of Krissie and her demands."

Benji shook her head. "That's not true, Kelsey. After Friday, you'll never be free of Krissie again."

I knew that to be the truth too.

Gertrude and her gang had moved around the side of the church. "I actually do need to talk to Shepley about those chickens," I said. "Gertrude is out of hand."

Benji nodded. "But don't do it today."

"Why not today?"

She dug the toe of her Doc Marten into the ground. Doc Martens were her footwear of choice; she had at least five pairs, all in varying colors and patterns. "It's the anniversary."

"Oh," I said, knowing immediately what she meant.

When it came to Shepley, there was only one anniversary that mattered: the anniversary of the day that his family—his wife and daughter—had died in a fire. The accident had happened over twenty years ago, but for the gardener it was like yesterday.

The radios hanging from both of our belt loops crackled at the same time. I removed mine and held it to my mouth. "What's up?"

Benji gave me a forlorn look. I rolled my eyes and said, "What's up? Over."

She grinned. It was her personal goal to make Farm staff use "over" to end radio calls. I was the worst at it.

"Kelsey, we need help over at the visitor center. A young boy lost his lunch in the cafeteria, and no one is free to clean it up." Judy's voice came over the line. She was in charge of the museum gift shop and ticket sales. "I can't take care of it myself. A busload of day campers just came in."

Benji groaned. "I'll go."

"Benji is on her way. Over," I said.

"Great. Over and out," Judy replied with obvious relief.

I arched one of my dark brows. "Taking another one for the team?"

"You bet. I'm always on your team, Kelsey. And I'll always have your back even when I think you're making a huge mistake, like allowing Krissie Pumpernickle to get married on our Farm." She spun around and jogged toward the other side of the Farm.

I watched her go. A feeling of gratitude washed over me. I knew Benji was sincere in her promise. She'd been loyal to me and the Farm for many years, having worked at the Farm every summer through high school and college. She'd just graduated from college and would be starting masters work in history that coming fall.

When I'd needed a new Farm assistant last year, she'd jumped into the role despite it being the middle of her senior year. Selfishly, I was happy Benji was headed straight to grad school at a local university because I knew I'd be able to keep her on as my assistant for a few years more. I didn't have any illusions that she would stay my assistant at Barton Farm forever—she was too smart, too ambitious, and too talented. Someday she would be running the Smithsonian.

Why Krissie wanted to have a Civil War-themed wedding was still a mystery to me. My best friend and Farm employee, Laura Fellow, insisted it was because history was my occupation. Since Krissie had already stolen my husband, she was now after my life's work. That was Laura's theory, at least. Laura could be a tad dramatic at times. Scratch that. Laura was always dramatic. I think she should have been a drama professor like my father instead of a high school history teacher.

And I should add that it's not completely fair to say that Krissie stole my husband. My marriage to Eddie was over long before Krissie Pumpernickle bounced into his life—just after our son Hayden's second birthday, Eddie had started an affair with a married woman. With a toddler, it had taken me a little while to catch onto what he was up to, but when I did, I didn't hesitate to file for divorce.

That new relationship of Eddie's ended soon after our divorce, but it wasn't long before he hired Krissie as a physical therapist at his PT practice and the two of them started dating. Since Krissie was eight years younger than Eddie, I'd thought she was harmless, although maybe a little annoying. How wrong I'd been. Krissie had a mission, and that mission was to steal my son's affection to win Eddie over, marry Eddie, and make my life as difficult as possible.

I would be lying if I didn't admit that she was succeeding, at least at the marrying Eddie part. As far as I was concerned, she could have him. However, I would have been a little more enthused about their wedding if it wasn't going to happen on my Farm.

I spotted Laura, in full period dress from her petticoats to her hoop skirt, speaking with a visiting family just outside the Barton house. I hoped that she wasn't telling them anything inaccurate. Despite being a high school history teacher, my best friend was loose when it came to historical detail. If she knew the right answer to a question, she would readily share it, but if she didn't, she wasn't above giving a visitor the wrong information. Once I'd heard her tell a group of schoolchildren that Benjamin Franklin wore eyeglasses because he invented them.

"Kelsey, yoohoo!" a high pitched voice called from the edge of Maple Grove Lane.

I cringed. There was only one person I'd met in my entire life who said "yoohoo." It was Vianna Pine, Krissie's wedding planner.

Vianna was someone I disliked even more than Krissie herself. And considering that Krissie was spearheading a custody battle between Eddie and I over Hayden, that was saying something.

TWO

"Kelsey, I'm so glad I caught you. I wanted to talk again about the lights in the bell tower." She smiled as if we were the dearest of friends, which we were not.

This conversation was exactly why Vianna Pine put my teeth on edge. For weeks, she'd hounded me about every last detail of the wedding, and she did it all with a cheery smile on her lips and a wide-eyed, almost stunned stare, as if she were in perpetual wonder about how she'd gotten here and what she should be doing. Her heavy-handed use of the eyelash curler and mascara only made her look of surprise that much more pronounced. Despite being petite, like me, and probably about my age, Vianna and I couldn't be more different—and not only because I'd never wear such a confused expression plastered on my face.

When I was in graduate school, one of my classmates said he felt like he was under a microscope whenever he met my penetrating gaze, like I was always trying to figure him out. This was probably a more accurate description than I was comfortable admitting. I was, in fact, continually trying to figure people out. Yet Vianna Pine remained a mystery to me. Every so often, her wide-eyed façade seemed to slip, and I would see her scanning her surroundings with calculated precision.

"Vianna, we already went over this," I said. "There will be no alterations to the church for the wedding."

"But—"

I held up my hand to stop her. "No alterations means no alterations. There's no electricity going to the building, so stringing lights would involve alterations, and that's against the Farm's building use policy. Krissie and Eddie agreed to this. It was plainly written into the contract that they signed. I can provide you with yet another copy of it if you've lost the five I've already given you."

A college-aged girl stood behind Vianna, making notes on a clipboard that had a thick sheath of paper attached to it. I suspected the papers were just a small sample of Krissie's demands for the wedding. Piper Clark was Vianna's intern, and she wore a tea-length, swirl-covered dress with wide gauzy sleeves that looked as if it came straight from my mother's 1970s summer wardrobe. Her blond hair, streaked with blue highlights, was pulled back from her face in a silver clip, and razor-thin eyebrows hovered over her dark eyes.

Like Piper, Vianna wore a dress, but hers was cut like a suit and had a matching jacket topped by a pale pink scarf around her neck. In the three months that I'd known her, I'd never seen her without the scarf. She fidgeted with it constantly, and she was tucking at it now.

"But Krissie and Eddie didn't *read* the contract when they signed it," she said. The loose waves of her dark blond hair bounced on her shoulders as she spoke.

Piper made another note. I wondered if she was recording this conversation so that Vianna could look back at it later and tally up what I promised to do. I'd already promised much more for the wedding than I'd ever wanted to; I certainly wouldn't promise her this. Hanging lights on the church steeple not only could damage the two-hundred-year-old structure but was also a safety issue. The floor at the top of the bell tower was unstable and brittle, half rotted away from the elements that had made their way into the tower through its slatted windows over the last two centuries. No, I couldn't have another accident on Barton Farm. In the last year, I'd faced enough safety issues to last me two lifetimes.

Vianna dropped her hand from her scarf. "Eddie and Krissie trust you, as a member of the family, to give them the wedding of their dreams."

I scrunched my eyebrows together. A member of the family? Really? I supposed that as Eddie's ex-wife and the mother of his child, I was family, but certainly even Vianna could see that I wasn't the kind of family who would want to give them a wedding of any kind.

"My decision is final," I said.

Vianna pressed her pink lips together so hard that they turned white. Maybe I'd pushed her too far.

I closed my eyes for a moment and reminded myself that most of the irritation I felt about the wedding wasn't Vianna's fault, no matter how annoying she was. My frustration came from the custody battle that Eddie and Krissie continued to threaten me with if I didn't do their bidding. The problem was that if I gave into the lights-in-the-steeple request, which I had no intention of doing, it would then be one threat after another from them about Hayden. I had to put my foot down. My line in the sand was here, and I wasn't moving it a little farther down the beach.

I took a breath. "I'm sorry, Vianna. I know you're under a lot of pressure from Krissie over the wedding. I know from firsthand experience that she's not always easy to work for."

Vianna's face brightened, as if she had the tiniest spark of hope that I would change my mind. I was almost sorry to crush it. Almost.

"But that's not going to change anything," I continued. "We do not allow alterations to our historic buildings for anyone. The governor of Ohio was here two years ago as part of his reelection campaign and wanted to move the brickyard. We wouldn't do that for him, and we won't do this for Krissie. I'm sorry."

"But Krissie wants this." Her tone was plaintive, almost panicked.

And Krissie gets what Krissie wants, I thought, although I didn't say it aloud. I wouldn't want to be Vianna when it was time for her to deliver my decree to Krissie. I didn't envy her job one bit.

"There has to be something we can do. Can't you run an extension cord up to the steeple? Or there must be battery-operated lights we can use." She grabbed at her scarf again. "I'm sure there must be something."

I shook my head. "It's too risky. As I told you, it's a safety issue, as well as violates the contract they signed. No one has been up in the bell tower for years. I don't know if it's stable enough to hold someone's weight. The last thing we want is for someone to get hurt." As I said this, I thought of the murders that had occurred on the Farm grounds in the past year. I didn't want to be in a situation like that again. Ever. I'd almost lost the Farm and my son over them.

Tears welled in Vianna's eyes. Was she seriously about to cry? I gripped the edge of my notebook a little bit tighter. "Vianna, I know that Krissie can be difficult to work with, but she can't have every single thing she wants. No one can."

Vianna stepped back and wrinkled her tiny nose. "No, Miss Pumpernickle is fine. She's a wonderful client."

Even to her own ears that statement had to have sounded false. I raised one eyebrow.

Behind Vianna, Piper rolled her eyes. I guessed she wouldn't say the same about Krissie.

"She is," Vianna insisted. "She's a client who knows what she wants. Trust me, that's a much easier person to work with than an indecisive bride. I had a bride last month who changed her cake selection four times before the wedding, including on the day of the wedding." She stood a little straighter, looking me squarely in the eye. There was new resolve in her expression. "But I was able to give her what she wanted even at the very last moment because I'm the best and I *always* deliver. Everything I touch turns out perfectly." She said her last statement with such ferocity that again I wondered if her sweet and helpful wedding planner persona was just an act.

"I can respect your determination to do a good job," I said, softening. Vianna was a perfectionist. It was something I could relate to, or at least I could up until the point Hayden was born. After having a child, I'd became a lot more flexible for survival's sake.

She wiped at her eyes. "And I understand. I really do. It's your job to worry about the safety of everyone at Barton Farm, but there must be a way we can make this work. What if I climb up there to install the lights myself? Could I do that? I'm happy to sign a waiver or something. I promise not to sue the Farm or the Cherry Foundation if I get hurt."

"No." My tone left no room for argument.

She bit her lower lip as if it was the only way for her to keep herself from crying. I felt a twinge of compassion for her. I'd been on the receiving end of Krissie's orders more than once and they were admittedly hard to take, and I was made of much sterner stuff than Vianna Pine.

She straightened her shoulders as if she'd come to some kind of decision. "Fine. We won't put any lights in the steeple."

Piper looked up from her clipboard as if the pronouncement surprised her.

"Really? You're okay with my decision?" I knew I shouldn't be questioning her, but her change in attitude was so abrupt that I found it a wee bit suspicious. My mom-radar was activated. When Hayden changed his mind about something he wanted that quickly, I knew that could only mean trouble.

She nodded curtly. "Really. I'll tell Krissie about your decision."

"Oh-kay." I was still dubious.

"But there's another matter I want to speak with you about."

I sighed, suddenly feeling impossibly tired. The sooner this wedding was over the better. "What is it?"

"When I was on my way over here I received the most disturbing text message from Krissie. She said there won't be a Civil War reenactment on Farm grounds on the day of the wedding. That simply is unacceptable."

"Krissie was just here complaining about that. Didn't you pass her on your way in?"

"No, but even if I had, there isn't time to chat. Poor thing. She's stressed out to the max over this wedding, which is why we, as her planners, have to make this as effortless as possible for her, even if we ourselves are working like dogs behind the scene."

"We?" I asked.

She wrinkled her tiny nose a second time. "You're one of the planners, as the wedding host."

Wedding host? I didn't like the sound of that.

"The client must always, always come first," Vianna went on. "Now tell me what the problem is with the reenactors and we'll get it fixed, lickety-spilt."

Lickety-split? Was this woman for real? Or did she make it her personal mission to be annoying?

Secretly, I was relieved the reenactment in Southern Ohio conflicted with the wedding. The last thing I needed was a second full-scale Civil War reenactment when we already had one on the Farm every summer. The event was the biggest the Farm hosted every year and it took a year's worth of planning. This summer's event was less than a month away as it was; there was no way I could have handled two full-scale reenactments in that short a period of time, even if the other details of Krissie and Eddie's wedding hadn't been a factor.

"Vianna, there's nothing that can be done, as I told Krissie. There's a huge reenactment happening three hours south of here that day. It's even bigger than the annual reenactment we hold here on the Farm. Almost all our reenactors will be there. I can't ask them to miss it for the wedding. It's their biggest event of the season."

She looked miffed. "If you knew that event was happening on this particular weekend, why on earth did you put the wedding on that day?"

"This was the only Friday in June that worked both for the Farm and for Krissie. As you'll remember, Krissie very much wanted to be a June bride." Now I was becoming irritated. "And besides, she came up with this reenactment idea long after the wedding date was set. She only asked about it three weeks ago. I told her then that it wasn't going to happen and that's still true."

Vianna's eyes, so expertly lined with eyeliner, widened. "But this is what Krissie wants for her wedding. She *wants* a Civil War battle. Krissie will get what she wants."

I had every reason to believe that she meant what she said.

THREE

"She'll get Abraham Lincoln and a small band of soldiers," I explained. "That will have to be enough." I hoped I was telling the truth about Honest Abe, and that Benji would come through in that regard. It was too late to take the promise back now.

Vianna wrinkled her small nose as if she smelled something sour.

I remained amazed by the number of people who were so determined to give Krissie exactly what she wanted. Her parents, Vianna, Eddie. I wondered what kind of hold she had over them all. Despite our custody issues, she didn't have that kind of hold over me and never would. I may have been unable to give her what she wanted, but sometimes I wished I could give her what she deserved.

"Abe and a few soldiers is the best I can do," I repeated, holding up my hand when I saw she was about to protest yet again. "There will be no battle. But perhaps the reenactors can do some drills or something to entertain the wedding guests."

I winced a little as I said this. I wasn't sure what my boyfriend, Chase Wyatt, who was one of those reenactors—a reluctant one at that, who was drafted into the pastime by his overzealous uncle—would say when he heard I signed him up for a drill. Then again, I knew exactly what he'd say, and it was going to cost me.

"This is not what Krissie wanted." Vianna was like a broken record.

"Like I said, it's the best I can do." I shrugged.

She winced, and I felt a twinge of sympathy. It was hard enough being the wedding host for Krissie's wedding. I couldn't imagine what it must be like to be her wedding planner. Sounded like torture to me.

An elderly couple toddled out of the church. The man held the handrail on the side of the steps, his other hand firmly tucked under his wife's elbow. Seeing the couple, who were a decade older than my parents, made my heart constrict. My mother died when I was a teenager; she and my father never had an opportunity to grow old together. They'd been cheated. I'd been cheated.

Vianna's shrill voice broke into my thoughts. "Why are people still able to go in there? Shouldn't it be roped off in preparation for the wedding? We don't want anything ruined by these people."

Piper's gaze dropped back down to her clipboard, as if she thought that if she didn't make eye contact we would forget she was there.

I stared at Vianna for a long minute, hoping my staring would deliver the message that she was being ridiculous.

"Well?" she demanded. Her hazel eyes were wide as she waited for my response.

Clearly, my pointed stare hadn't worked. "Vianna, first of all, it's Tuesday. The wedding isn't for three more days, which gives Farm staff time to clean the church in the very unlikely event that something is disturbed by the tourists. Second of all, the Farm is a museum. Its primary purpose is to be open to the public so that the community can learn about Ohio history. The buildings, especially the church, have to stay open so visitors can see them. That's why they're here. All the buildings will be open all week. And," I said in my best director-of-a-museum voice, "the church will be open on the day of the wedding too."

She opened her mouth as if to argue.

"The wedding isn't until seven in the evening. We'll close the church to prepare at two in the afternoon. That should give you and your team plenty of time to set up."

"But the reception tent," Vianna gasped. "That takes hours to set up."

"You can start setting up the tent in the morning, but be aware that there will be tourists milling about the green while your people are working."

"That's unacceptable." Vianna's cheeks turned pink. "I have to have time to build the wedding of Krissie's dreams."

"And I have to run my museum." I narrowed my eyes.

"The museum is not as important as this wedding. Not this week. You have to know that." Her eyes pleaded with me.

I snorted. "Obviously, you don't know me at all to think I would believe that."

She threw up her hands. "You leave me no choice but to talk to the Cherry Foundation about how uncooperative you're being." She spun around. "Let's go, Piper."

The young woman pressed the clipboard to her chest and hurried after her boss without giving me a second glance.

I hesitated for half a second, then I jogged after her. "Vianna, wait!"

She turned around to face me and folded her arms. Piper stopped too, clipboard out, pen in hand.

I skidded to a stop on the grass. "Let's compromise. We'll close the church at noon on the day of the wedding, and you can start setting up on the green the evening before. That's my best and final offer."

She considered this for a moment. "I'll take it. But this doesn't change the fact that I might have to talk to the trustees about how uncooperative you've been. If I ran this Farm, things would go much differently, I can tell you that." With that, she spun on her heel and stomped toward the church. She almost knocked into the elderly couple I'd seen a moment ago. "Hey!" the man cried. "Watch where you're going!"

Vianna glared at them down her button nose before continuing on her way. Piper scurried after her. Her flowy dress fluttered behind her.

The older man shook his head at me. "I feel sorry for you, sweetie. She looks like she's a real pill."

She was that.

FOUR

I BRUSHED MY HAND across my forehead and checked the time on my cell phone. It was almost noon and lunchtime. Hayden, who'd spent the morning in the visitor center while I met with Krissie, would want to eat soon. I'd promised my son we'd have lunch together. It was no easy feat to spend time with Hayden in the middle of the day during the season, but I was determined to keep my promise to him.

I was about to head over to the visitor center on the other side of the Farm when someone else called my name. My shoulders sagged. As usual, it was nearly impossible for me make my way across the grounds without being stopped half a dozen times. Always being in demand was the price I paid to be the director of Barton Farm.

"Kelsey!" the gruff voice called again. Even though the speaker was behind me, I knew who it was before I turned.

Shepley was my gifted but disgruntled gardener. He wore his long gray hair pulled back from his face in a ponytail tied with a piece of garden twine. He had dirt perpetually encrusted under his fingernails from digging in the Barton Farm gardens, which were his personal sanctuary. The only happiness in Shepley's life were the gardens, and he cared for them with affection that leaned toward obsession. If Shepley had his way, the gardens would always be pristine and no one, not even me, would ever see them. And woe to anyone who disturbed his beloved plants. I'd witnessed Shepley make grown men cry after they accidently tromped on one of his precious flowers.

I would have fired him years ago if it weren't for the fact that the Farm's gardens were some of the most beautiful in the county, if not in the state. They were a showpiece that had won countless beautification and heirloom plant awards. They attracted visitors from all over the country, even people who had no interest in the history aspect of Barton Farm. A superstitious part of me thought that Shepley was right—that all of his flowers would shrivel up and die if he ever left the Farm. It was a tiny part, but apparently strong enough to force me to let him keep his job even though he was a difficult employee at best.

Then I reminded myself that today was the anniversary of his family's death. This wasn't the day to become embroiled into an argument with my gardener.

He waved a piece of paper at me. "What is this?" He waved it again.

I grimaced. I'd hoped Shepley would never see that piece of paper. I rubbed my forehead, feeling a migraine forming just between my eyes.

I decided that playing dumb was the best tactic. "What do you have there?"

He crumbled the piece of computer paper in his hands and threw it at my feet. "Take a look at it for yourself."

I stared at the piece of paper in the grass. There were so many things that were on the tip of my tongue as I stared at it, the most prominent being "You're fired." I took another deep breath—I found I was doing a lot of that lately—as I bent down and picked up the piece of paper. I smoothed it out on my thigh. I could feel Shepley grow more agitated by the second.

Finally I read the heading at the top of the paper. *Directions for gardener for the Pumpernickle-Cambridge wedding.* Number one on the list was *Remove all plants that may attract insects.*

I had to look at my shoes to hide my smile. My shoulders began to shake, which unfortunately gave me away.

"This is not funny." Shepley glared at me with dark eyes that were barely visible, even when he wasn't squinting, because of the many hours he'd worked in the sunlight. "I see nothing about this that is funny."

I folded the piece of paper. "You have to admit, the fact that it says 'remove all plants that attract insects' is a little bit humorous."

He scowled a little deeper, and I couldn't see his eyes at all at that point. "Is it funny that that woman"—he pointed in the direction Vianna had just gone—"wants to put lights up in the church steeple? Yes, I overheard her telling you that. Do you think making changes to the church are funny? It's just another example of how these people think they can do whatever they want to this Farm just because they have money." He spat on the ground about a foot from my toe. "That's what I think of all those people who donate money. Barton Farm doesn't need them."

His question sobered me up. "No, none of that's funny," I said.

When would I ever learn that Shepley had zero sense of humor? Was it any wonder that the two of us didn't get along? And Shepley was wrong. Barton Farm *did* need donations like the one from the Pumpernickle family. All nonprofits needed donations. It was how we kept our doors open.

"So, why did you approve the plant removal?" His scowl deepened and his wrinkled skin seemed to fold farther into his face.

I chuckled, trying to calm him down. "I didn't approve it. Vianna told me weeks ago that Krissie wanted this, and I said there's no way we're altering the gardens or any aspect of the village for the wedding. People who want to get married on the Farm have to want to because of what Barton Farm *is*, not what they wish it to be. Krissie and Eddie signed a contract. Vianna can't make us do anything."

Shepley pointed at the piece of folded paper in my hand. "It says right there that you approved this. You signed it."

I opened the piece of paper again and noticed for the first time a handwritten note at the bottom with a very poor imitation of my signature. I felt my face grow hot. "I didn't sign this."

"That's your signature," he protested.

"That's my name but not my signature. It's not even close." I tilted my head to the left. "Shepley, even you have to be able to recognize that's not my signature. Whoever signed this left the second 'e' out of Kelsey. Do you really think that I would misspell my own name?"

He folded his arms. "Maybe you were in a rush when you signed it."

"I'm telling you, I didn't write it, agree to it, or sign it. Vianna shouldn't have done this." I folded the piece of paper a second time and stuck it in the back pocket of my jeans. "I had no idea she would go to such lengths to get what Krissie wanted for the wedding."

I resolved to have a little talk with the wedding planner about this. How dare she give directions to my staff without my consent?

How dare someone forge my signature? I could feel myself growing angrier by the second. "Just ignore this, Shepley. Act as if you never saw it."

"How can I ignore it? It was in my mailbox in the visitor center."

"If I really had approved it, it wouldn't just be sitting in your mailbox. When have I ever told you to do something that way? I know you hardly ever check your mail. I always talk to you in person when I have a new project."

He sniffed. "How am I to know what you'll do when you make so many changes to the Farm? We were just fine here until you came along and started messing with things."

Again, he was wrong. When I'd taken over the Farm, it was just months away from closing its doors forever. The previous director had been more concerned about preserving the history than the practical side of running a nonprofit. I'd brought the Farm back from the brink of ruin, with the help of Cynthia Cherry and her foundation, of course. I'd been the director now for four years. It was true that in that time, I'd made many changes to keep the Farm afloat, but I hadn't made nearly as many as I'd planned. The Farm had so much potential. I wished Shepley could just see that instead of hating every little change or improvement that I made.

I didn't say any of this to the gardener. It would be a waste of time and breath. He was happy living in his illusion of times being better in the good old days.

Shepley nodded, slightly less angry at least. "Yes, you usually do talk to me in person." Then he scowled. "But why would I think of all that? You've been so preoccupied with this wedding. Because of that, many things have fallen to the wayside around the Farm. The staff has been talking about it."

"What things?" It was my turn to scowl.

He frowned, but he didn't answer. It didn't matter. I would talk to Laura about it when she had a free moment. If anyone knew about grumblings happening on the village side of the Farm, it would be her. I was surprised she hadn't said anything to me about it before now if it was really a problem, which told me that Shepley was most likely making much more of it than it was.

"I don't change my gardens for anything," he reiterated. "What's in the garden is up to me and me alone."

That wasn't exactly true either. Ultimately, what happened on the Farm, including in the gardens, was up to the Cherry Foundation's trustees. I wasn't happy about the arrangement myself.

A thought occurred to me. "You got this list from your mailbox? What made you go into the visitor center and check your mailbox? You never go into the visitor center."

Shepley crossed his arms. "I just happened to be passing through and saw it sticking out of my box."

I couldn't think of a single time that Shepley "happened to be passing through" the visitor center, especially in the middle of the season. He hated the visitor center, mostly because it was overrun with visitors, whom he hated.

My doubt must have been written all over my face because he said, "I'd be careful if I were you, Kelsey. If you're not careful, you'll lose control over more than this wedding."

That made two threats within fifteen minutes of each other. In a way, I was impressed with myself. It was a new personal record.

FIVE

By the time I made it to the visitor center, Hayden was already in the cafeteria. Judy sat across from him, in her proper blouse and long khaki skirt. The pair ate peanut butter and jelly and shared a bag of Oreos. I shivered to think how many of those cookies my son had downed in the time it took me to walk across the Farm.

I took a seat next to him. His soft brown hair was mussed, and there was dirt on his X-Men T-shirt and his khaki shorts. I didn't bother to ask how he'd gotten his clothes dirty so quickly. He was a six-year-old boy. Six-year-old boys were known to be dirt magnets.

I kissed him on the top of the head.

He beamed at me. "Hi Mom."

My heart melted looking at that smiling face, especially now that one of his front teeth was missing. He'd lost it last week. Krissie had not been pleased that he'd lost a tooth this close to the wedding and wanted him to wear a flipper for the wedding photos. Thank God, even Eddie put his foot down about that.

Judy slid the bag of Oreos toward me. "You're going to need these."

I took two from the bag. I might not want Hayden to eat them, but I wasn't immune to their chocolate comfort, and whenever Judy said I needed a cookie, I took it. Judy wasn't one to push sugar unless it was an absolute emergency. "Was that kid getting sick to his stomach worse than we thought?" I asked.

She took a swig from her bottle of water. "No. Benji took care of it like a champ." She held up her water bottle in salute to my assistant. "You might want to think about giving her a raise."

"I think about that every day, and I would if I had the funds," I said. Lack of funds was always my number one concern at Barton Farm. "So if that's not the problem, what is?'

She adjusted one of the barrettes that held her silver hair out of her face. "I noticed something unusual in storage."

"What do you mean, something unusual in storage?" I lowered my voice. We weren't the only ones in the cafeteria. Families and day camp groups were starting to file in to eat their picnic lunches or purchase something from our snack counter in the back of the room.

Hayden pushed what was left of his PBJ aside and watched the campers.

Judy leaned in closer. "I went down there to look for the Christmas lanterns. You know, the ones that we use for the candlelight tours of the Farm in the winter?"

I nodded. The candlelight tours, which we'd hosted for the first time last December, had been very popular. We'd decorated all the buildings in the village in Christmas greenery. I hoped to do it again this Christmas. I popped an Oreo in my mouth.

"Krissie wants us to use them for the wedding reception," Judy explained. She rolled her eyes. "Anyway, when I was down there, I noticed something was off."

"Off? Off, how?" I asked, nearly choking on the Oreo lodged in my throat.

Hayden slid his water bottle across the table to me. He was a good son. I'd raised him right.

I downed half the water and repeated my question in a rasp.

Judy eyed me over her wire-rimmed glasses. "I think some things have gone missing."

"What?" I asked.

Judy put the cap back on her bottle of water. "I don't know for sure, but it just seems like things aren't where they were, and some are missing. I don't know what's down there well enough to know what's actually gone."

I stood. "I need to go down there and check it out."

"Mom, aren't you going to eat lunch?" Hayden asked, staring up at me with his bright blue eyes.

I took two more Oreos from the bag. "These will work."

Hayden frowned. "How come you can just have Oreos for lunch, and I can't?"

I smiled at him. "It's an age thing. When you're over thirty, you can do it too."

He gave a long-suffering sigh. "There are so many things I can't do until after I'm thirty."

As his mother, that sounded just fine to me.

The Barton Farm storage room was in the basement of the visitor center. The stairs, which led to the basement, were at the back of the cafeteria, off a small hallway by the kitchen. I opened the door to the stairwell, and Hayden and Judy followed me down the stairs.

The basement was unfinished, with gray cinderblock walls and a concrete floor, but it was cool and dry. It was the perfect place to store costumes and supplies for the Farm. The storage room was the first door on the right. It was twice the size of the lower floor of my cottage—maybe even twice the size of the cottage altogether, including the square footage of the second floor. The room's size and cool temperature was all it had going for it, however, because unfortunately it was a mess. Metal racks of period clothing butted up against boxes of candlemaking wax and enormous containers of mustard, a donation from a local grocer that I'd regretfully accepted. We had more than enough mustard to survive the zombie apocalypse twice over.

Organizing the storage room was on the list of things that I needed to do at the Farm. I should have hired someone or paid one of my employees to do it a long time ago, but being the control freak that I am, I wanted to do it myself. Most of the things in storage were period replicas, but occasionally I'd run across a true artifact from the Barton family that had been misplaced. A volunteer or even most of my staffers wouldn't be able to tell a replica from a real artifact. I could, and I didn't want anything thrown away or lost that might have some historical ties to the Barton family and their life on the Farm.

It seemed I needed to make this room a priority, but after the wedding. Everything in my life lately was getting filed under "after the wedding." The To Do list was growing quite long in my notebook.

"Mom, what's this?" Hayden picked up a saber that thankfully was still in his sheath.

I took it from him and put it on a high shelf. "No knives or swords, okay?"

He sighed, as if I'd said that he wasn't allowed to play with his iPad for a week.

"So what's off?" I asked Judy as I glanced around the room. "This place is such a mess. How can you even tell that something is wrong?"

"It was the trunk that got my attention." She pointed at the concrete floor. "See the dust. The trunk has been moved. Look how the dust has been disturbed."

My eyes fell to where she pointed. Judy was right; the dust did look like it had been disturbed. I bit the inside of my lip. I didn't have a good feeling about this. The trunk had to weigh at least 150 pounds and was a three-by-three-foot cube of iron. Why would anyone move it?

The trunk had been discovered during the renovation of the Barton House, when I first started at the Farm as museum director. That was four years ago. At the time, I'd been overwhelmed by the massive restoration. It was my responsibility to make sure the project went smoothly and was true to the historical integrity of the large brick house. At the same time, I'd been just getting my bearings in the insurmountable task of bringing Barton Farm back from ruin, so I'd ignored the trunk. But when Benji came on as my assistant, I asked her to inventory its contents. She did it in short order, documenting each piece and putting them into our artifact database. The trunk held some of our most valuable artifacts from the Barton family, and when I say valuable, I mean that most of the items' value lay purely in the historical significance to the Bartons themselves and the region. Monetary value was not as important to me as the history of the artifacts and what they could tell us about daily life on the Farm.

Even with Benji's careful cataloging, I had yet to come to a decision as to where to put the items, so here they and the trunk remained until I could make up my mind. The visitor center was the most secure place on the grounds, I figured. No one would walk out unnoticed with a trunk that heavy, and it was locked up tight to boot. The key was in my office. The trunk wasn't hurting anyone or anything in storage. Deciding what to do with it and its contents could wait—or at least that's what I thought. How wrong I'd been.

"We'd better open it to make sure that everything is there," I said.

Judy stuck her hand into her pocket and came up with the small key. "I knew you were going to say that, so I'm already one step ahead of you. I took the liberty of grabbing this."

I forced a smile. "I'd say you're more than just one step ahead of me." I took the key from her and knelt in front of the trunk. Hayden squatted beside me. I fit the key into the lock and it turned easily.

Using the key was only one way to open the iron box. The top could also be opened by pulling on the many levers decorating the front of the trunk in the proper sequence. I never remembered the precise combination of levers to pull, so I was happy Judy had had the foresight to bring the key.

I opened the trunk and swore under my breath.

"Earmuffs, Hayden," Judy ordered.

My son dutifully covered his ears with his small hands.

The trunk was empty. Completely empty. Not a scrap of cloth or a single dust bunny had been left behind.

I rocked back on my heels. "This is bad." I felt sick to my stomach. One of my most important jobs as Director of Barton Farm was to preserve history. One of the ways to do that was to protect the Barton family's possessions, and I'd failed miserably at that.

"Do you think it's some type of mistake?" Judy asked. "Maybe someone took the artifacts out of the trunk for safekeeping or to inventory them?"

I looked up at her. "I would be the only one who would do that, or maybe Benji, but she would never do it without telling me."

"Then say," Judy began, "that someone took them. Would they be valuable? Could they make money from selling them?"

I stood up, my knees cracking as I moved. Hayden remained squatting in place, staring into the empty trunk. "Not much, not really. The real value of the things inside there was to the Farm. Why bother stealing them at all?"

Judy frowned.

I sighed. "I should have decided what to do with the artifacts years ago."

She patted my arm. "Don't worry, Kelsey. We all know you've had a lot on your plate. You saved Barton Farm almost single-handedly. You worked a miracle. No one would blame you if you didn't have time for one small project."

I wished I could say I believed her, but I didn't. I knew that Henry Ratcliffe and rest of the Cherry Foundation's board of trustees would blame me and hold me accountable for the loss. As much as I hated the thought of it, I had to tell the Foundation and report the theft to the proper authorities. I couldn't pretend the artifacts had never been there. "I have to report this to the police," I said.

"Are you sure you want to do that?" Judy asked.

I frowned. "No, but I have to. I'll have to check the artifact database, but I know for sure that Jebidiah Barton's gold watch was in there." I paused. "And his revolver."

Remembering the missing revolver spurred me into action. I removed my cell phone from my pocket and called the New Hartford police station. Unfortunately, it was a number that I now knew by heart.

After I ended the call, I asked Judy to take Hayden to the gift shop while I dealt with the police.

"I want to see the cops catch the robber," my son protested.

"They aren't going to catch him here," I said. "The robber is long gone."

Hayden sighed. "I miss all the good stuff."

If I had anything to say about it, he always would.

"Come along, Hayden," Judy said, wrapping her arm around my son's thin shoulders. "We got a new shipment of penny candy to sell in the gift shop. If you help me fill up the candy jars, I'll give you a piece or two."

Hayden jumped up and down. "Really?"

"Sure thing," she replied.

Hayden pumped his fist and ran for the door.

I mouthed "thank you" to Judy as she turned to leave. In this case, I thought bribing my child with candy was one hundred percent acceptable.

I followed them upstairs at a much slower pace and radioed Benji. "Benji, meet me in the lobby of the visitor center. I have a situation. Over."

"Already there. Over," she said. "And I think I have an even bigger situation. Over." She ended radio contact.

Great.

SIX

WHEN I ENTERED THE lobby, I blinked three times and pinched myself for good measure to make sure what I was seeing was true. Benji stood a few feet away from Abraham Lincoln. Truth be told, it was not unusual to see a deceased president wandering about Barton Farm. The unusual part about it was that this president was plastered and could barely stand upright. He leaned on the wall, and it looked like he was starting to drool.

I turned to my assistant. I didn't even need to say a word.

She shrugged. "You know how I said that I found another Lincoln reenactor to step in for Darren?" She gestured at the man leaning against the wall. "That's him."

"You're joking, right?"

She grimaced.

"Four score and seven years ago ... " Lincoln hiccupped.

I covered my face with my hands. I didn't know if it was better to laugh or cry. I felt my shoulders move up and down. Apparently, my gut reaction was laughter. It was a good coping mechanism.

Benji cocked her head, not looking the least bit amused by my sudden mirth. I couldn't help it.

"Are you done?" she asked, sounding annoyed. "I mean, I'm giving you a Lincoln, and he did show up for his appointment today as promised, even if he's a little tipsy."

I considered "tipsy" a euphemism in this case.

She glanced at Honest Abe. "He might not be perfect, but he'll work in a pinch."

I chuckled and placed a hand to my stomach. "I—I—" I said breathlessly. "I don't think so."

Benji rolled her eyes. "Obviously, I've told him he can't have the gig because he showed up sloshed. I know we can't have a drunk Great Emancipator."

I shook my head. "Okay, okay, I know it was hard to find someone. I really appreciate that you tried."

"I was born in a log cabin," Lincoln muttered to himself. That set me off again.

The glass front doors to the visitor center, which faced the parking lot, slid open, and that sobered me up. I turned, expecting to see the police. Instead, Krissie floated in, her pink patent-leather purse, which I suspected cost twice my monthly salary, hanging from her delicate arm.

"I thought she left," Benji hissed.

"She did," I hissed back.

I needed to tell Benji about the police coming, especially since they'd be asking her about the contents of the trunk, but before I could get the words out, Krissie crowed, "Kelsey, I'm just making a quick stop before my dress fitting to tell you about the situation with the florist."

"There is a situation with the florist," Benji whispered under her breath.

I elbowed her in the side, hoping it would be enough to shut her up. I wanted to usher Krissie in and out. I didn't want her to be around when the police arrived. It would be another thing she could hold against me in the Hayden custody battle. Much like her must-haves for the wedding, Krissie had decided that she wanted a "traditional family"—and, with that in mind, she'd inserted my son into it. Unfortunately for her, I wasn't giving him up without a fight. Krissie didn't even know what she was asking for. Raising a child was a full-time job, and Krissie was too selfish to take care of a goldfish.

"The florist?" I asked.

"Yes. I asked for two hundred roses." She shuddered. "And he's giving me one hundred roses and one hundred carnations. Carnations? Can you believe that?"

Benji again looked as if she wanted to say something again, but I made a motion to step on her foot. She closed her mouth and sidled away.

"Did he say why?" I asked.

Krissie waved her hand. "He said something about a beetle infesting the rose farm's garden. Like that's my problem."

I winced.

She widened her eyes. "You have to talk to him."

"Me? Why not Vianna?" I asked.

"You know him. You can make him fix this."

My brow wrinkled. I did know the florist, Armin Coates, but I didn't know how Krissie got it in her head that I could fix this. People didn't mess with Armin. I certainly didn't.

She adjusted the strap of her purse on her arm. "I told Armin he'd be hearing from you."

Great. "Krissie, I can't—"

Krissie clapped her hands. "I can't believe it! You came through." She held her hands to her chest. "Abraham Lincoln!"

Lincoln pulled on his beard and squinted at her. "Do I know you, ma'am?"

Krissie stopped just short of jumping up and down. "OMG! OMG! Kelsey!"

Benji clamped a hand over her mouth to hold back the laughter that I knew was there.

"Krissie, he isn't for the—"

She hopped in place. "He's for the wedding." She turned to me. "You really did it!"

"Yes." Lincoln pushed off from the wall. "I am at your service."

Benji grimaced. I suspected that my face appeared much the same. "Krissie, this Lincoln," I said.

"Four score and seven years ago…" The reenactor again launched into the Gettysburg Address, reciting it word for word. It was moderately impressive considering his condition.

"He's perfect." Krissie beamed and adjusted her purse on her arm. "If you can find Abraham Lincoln, you'll have no trouble talking to Armin."

Through the glass doors, I saw a police cruiser pull up in front of the visitor center.

"All right, Krissie. I'll talk to Armin. Now don't you have a dress fitting to get to?" I asked, walking her toward the door.

She peered at the slim gold watch on her wrist. "I do. I knew I could count on you, Kelsey." She shook her head. "I should have put you in charge of this entire wedding instead of hiring Vianna." She lowered her voice as we reached the doors. "She's been such as a disappointment."

I wanted to ask her what she meant by that, but Officer Sonders, a young cop from the New Hartford Police Department, was getting out of his cruiser. It was time for Krissie to go. I ushered her to her convertible, and if she saw the police officer, she made no mention of it. She climbed into her sports car and peeled out of the parking lot.

Officer Sonders watched her go with a scowl. I was certain I had the same expression on my own face.

An hour later, Sonders closed the notebook in which he'd been itemizing the missing artifacts. He, Benji, and I stood in front of the visitor center next to his cruiser. I was much relieved that he was the one who'd come to investigate the trunk situation rather than Detective Brandon, the lone detective on the New Hartford police force. I'd have thought Brandon would jump on the case in the hope of making my life a little more difficult. Brandon and I had issues, to put it mildly.

Benji stood beside me, fiddling with her radio. The movement was distracting, but I stopped myself from taking it from her hands.

"Can you describe the gun that's missing, again?" Sonders flipped through the spreadsheet that listed all the artifacts in the trunk. "That might be the easiest piece to track down."

I pulled my smartphone out of my pocket and did a quick Google search, coming up with hundreds of antique flintlock pistols just like Jebidiah Barton's. I showed Sonders the images and enlarged the one that most resembled what I remembered Jebidiah Barton's looking like.

"Does the pistol work?" he asked.

I shrugged. "I never tried it, if that's what you're asking. From what I remember, it appeared to be well cared for. It was wrapped in a cheese cloth. It was on the very top of the trunk's contents, along with Jebidiah Barton's watch, which is why I think I remember it so vividly."

Sonders eyed me. "And you just left it there in the trunk?"

"The trunk was locked," I said a tad defensively. "It was heavy, difficult to move, and a good place to store valuables. It's where the Bartons kept their things a hundred years ago. It was secure."

"Not as secure as you thought." He folded the spreadsheet by quarters and put it inside the breast pocket of his uniform. "Was the gun registered?"

"It was a museum artifact, so, no."

He frowned. "I'll file a report and start to see if anything comes up online or if the local antique shops have been approached with anything that might fit what you've described. Maybe we'll get a hit on the watch, since it's engraved with Barton's initials ... that will make it a little more unique." He walked to the driver's side door of the cruiser and opened it. "Let me know if you think of anything else, or if anything else goes missing."

I promised him I would.

Benji looked as if she might be sick. I felt much that same. Officer Sonders' tone was judgmental, blaming me and the Farm for the theft of the artifacts. The problem was, he might just be right. I was at fault. If Benji's expression was any indication, she felt much the same. Even worse, I still had to admit what happened to the Cherry Foundation, especially since it would come up in our small town's police blotter. I might not be able to recover what was lost, but I vowed to never let it happen again. There would be new protocols and procedures in place. Things around the Farm were about to change.

But first, I reminded myself, I had to survive Krissie and Eddie's wedding. After the wedding, I would be better equipped to deal with the repercussions of my carelessness and the fallout from Henry Ratcliffe at the Foundation.

The police officer got into his cruiser and drove away.

Benji sighed. "I can't believe this. This is all my fault."

I looked at her. "Why?"

"Because the contents of that trunk were my responsibility. I should have taken better care of them."

I shook my head. "Stop right there. This is more my fault than yours. I should have made a decision about where to display the artifacts months ago."

Benji hooked the radio back onto her belt. "It's not your fault, Kel. Trust me on that." She turned and walked back inside the visitor center.

I had that sinking feeling that the missing revolver would come back to haunt us both.

SEVEN

BEDTIME IS ALWAYS A struggle when you're six, a fact that my son reminded me of on a daily basis.

"Why can't I stay up and watch a show?" Hayden asked in a sleepy voice that night. We were finally alone in my little cottage on the Farm grounds, tucked away behind the sugar maple grove on the western edge of the Farm. His eyes were half closed, but he was determined to stay up as late as possible because he was six. That was explanation enough.

"Buddy, we agreed that you would go to sleep after one show. You need your rest so you can have even more fun tomorrow." I tucked his sheet in around him.

He sighed deeply and his eyes fluttered open. He was trying so hard to stay awake. I had to look away to hide my smile. His heart-shaped face was so angelic when he was tired. But I knew better than to say that aloud. Superheroes didn't wish to look like angels, or so I'd been told.

Frankie, Hayden's grumpy, one-eyed tabby cat, watched me from the foot of my son's bed. Frankie and I had an unspoken agreement: I fed him and kept his litter box nice and tidy, and he didn't claw my face off in the middle of the night.

Hayden yawned. "I don't need as much rest as I did when I was in kindergarten. I'm a first grader now," he said proudly. Ever since the school year ended, he'd been playing the first grader card hard. "First graders shouldn't have to go to bed so early."

"Early?" I asked. "It's after nine. You should have been asleep ten minutes ago."

He sighed. "Nine is an early bedtime for summer, I think. My friend Tim doesn't have a bedtime in the summer, and he's a first grader too."

"Buddy, but even first graders need sleep. Moms need sleep too." I felt a yawn of my own coming on.

He shook his head and his white-blond bangs fell across his smooth forehead. "Not you. You're Super Mom. Super Mom doesn't sleep."

I bit my lip to hold back a whimper. I didn't feel like Super Mom on most days. I was just doing the best I could, juggling my responsibilities on the Farm and raising Hayden. More often than not he spent the majority of his summer days either with my father or with one of the members of the Farm staff. Not with me. I told myself I did this because I had to, which was true—not working wasn't an option. But I also had to do it because I wanted Hayden to be proud of me, to say that his mom had taught him what it was like to work hard for something she loved. I didn't care what his passion would turn out to be someday. It didn't have to be history. But when he found it, I wanted him to give it his all, like I'd given my all to Barton Farm.

Hayden's eyes closed a final time. He could no longer fight the exhaustion as much as he wanted to. First graders did need their sleep. I brushed his bangs out of his eyes and kissed his forehead before standing up from his bed.

As I turned off the light, Frankie settled his chin on his paws and closed his one good eye.

I walked down to the main room of my cottage. When I'd first taken the position as museum director, Cynthia Cherry had paid to have the old caretaker's cottage transformed into a home for Hayden and me. The main floor consisted of one large room that encompassed the living room, kitchen, and a small dining area. Behind the kitchen there was a full bathroom and a large pantry. We'd converted the pantry into a tiny bedroom, and this was where my father slept when he was with us. There wasn't much space in there for more than a single bed. Dad piled his clothes and things on the old pantry shelves.

My father stayed with us during the summer months when he wasn't teaching. The rest of the year, he lived in campus housing at the local college, where he'd been a drama professor for over thirty years. Despite the close quarters of the pantry-bedroom, Dad never complained. I knew he loved the time he spent with Hayden and me during the summers.

At the moment, his bedroom was empty. My father not only taught drama, but he was also a stage actor. For the first time since I'd graduated college, he'd joined a touring Shakespearean theater group that performed all over the state, so we weren't seeing him as much as we usually did during the summer. I was happy for him, but

45

it made the child care situation a little more difficult for me, which was something I didn't need now that Eddie was threatening to go back to court to increase his custody of Hayden. Currently, I had primary custody, and Eddie got Hayden three weekends a month plus alternating holidays. But he wanted shared custody, or at least that's what Krissie kept telling me. Eddie was far less direct.

Happily, my father had a break in the tour starting tomorrow, so he would be home for a few days, through Eddie's wedding. That was when I'd really need him.

I went to the refrigerator and pulled out a bottle of wine. I wasn't much of a drinker, but the wedding had me on edge and I needed to find a way to unwind so that I could get some sleep.

If Chase Wyatt had been there, he would have made me laugh with some ridiculous story about his day, and that would have relaxed me immediately. I had a sneaking suspicion his funniest stories were embellished for maximum effect, but I didn't mind. I smiled as I thought of him. He was so different from Eddie. Maybe that was his greatest appeal. Chase couldn't be there that night to make me laugh, though, since he was on call as an EMT.

I'd always considered myself self-sufficient, maybe even more so since I divorced, but I found myself missing Chase at times like this. That worried me. I took pride in my independence. Laura would say I took a little too much pride in it.

I was about to take the first sip from my wineglass when someone pounded on the cottage door. "Kelsey! Kelsey! Are you home?"

I set the glass down and ran to the door. I threw it open. "Jason, what are you doing? You're going to wake up Hayden." I said this in a harsh whisper.

My farmhand's thin face flushed red. "I—I'm sorry, Kelsey. Something is wrong." The thin-as-a-beanpole twenty-year-old boy shook from head to toe.

I put a hand on his arm and pulled him into the cottage. "Are you okay? Are you hurt?"

He shook his head but continued to shake from head to toe.

"Are the Hooper boys back? Did they do something to you?"

The closest neighbors to the Farm were the Hoopers. The mother had inherited the home from her father, who'd never complained about living next to Barton Farm. His daughter was a different story. Since day one, she'd been a thorn in my side. She constantly complained to the New Hartford city council about noise and disturbances on the Farm. There wasn't much that the Hoopers could do about it, because the Farm had all the necessary permits for all our activities. At times, the Hooper boys, as they were known on the Farm, had resorted to vandalism. To keep the peace, I hadn't pressed charges, but if they'd hurt Jason, my forgiving nature would change in an instant.

Jason shook his head.

I led him over to the dining room table and he fell into one of the chairs as if a great weight had forced him down. "No, not the Hooper boys. At least I don't think so," he said. "There's a woman in the village."

"She's trespassing?" I started to gather up my radio and cell phone. I knew I'd have to go over to the village to check this out. "Is she a hiker who's wandered off?"

It wasn't unusual for hikers to wander onto Farm grounds when they'd lost the trail in the state park that surround the museum. Technically, the park closed at night, but there was onsite tent camping to the south and sometimes people wound their way to us from there when they lost the path. The Farm was a good place for hikers to come when they were lost, as it was one of few wide open spots in the dense forest and a landmark for the area.

"I don't know if she was trespassing or not." His face appeared pinched, as if it was all he could do to hold tears at bay.

"Was?" I caught the past tense, and something about it felt deliberate. The hairs stood up on the back on my neck. "What do you mean *was*?"

He licked his lips. "Can I have some water?"

Without a word, I went over to the cupboard, removed a glass, and filled it with water from the tap. I handed him the glass and watched as his guzzled it down as if he'd been lost in the desert without water for days. I waited. He set the empty glass on the table, and I asked him again, "What do you mean *was*?"

He looked up at me from the chair. When Jason was sitting, it was the only time that I, at five one, was taller than his six-foot lanky frame.

He swallowed and his Adam's apple bobbed up and down. "She's dead."

"What?" I yelled, completely forgetting my earlier warning about waking up Hayden. "Who?"

He began to shake again. I had to remind myself to be gentler where Jason was concerned. He was a sensitive kid. After working with him the last couple of years as my farmhand, I suspected that he had Asperger's or something close to it, although this had never been confirmed. Normal social interactions were a challenge for him. I did know that he'd had a terrible childhood in the foster system and was sent around from house to house. Barton Farm was the first place that felt like home to him, and Hayden and I were the closest thing to family he'd ever had.

I took a breath. "Jason, I'm sorry. Can you start from the beginning? Tell me everything from the start."

He nodded and closed his eyes for a moment, as if he was trying his best to remember everything perfectly. "I was in my trailer for the night. You know I get up early to take care of the animals."

I nodded but did my best not to look impatient. I knew he would only shut down if I rushed him.

"Through my window over my bed, I can see the church, and I saw lights in the steeple."

"Lights? What kind of lights?"

"I don't know, but I knew they weren't supposed to be there. I got out of bed and went to check it out. When I was almost to the church, I heard a scream and crash. I ran around the barn to the church and saw her there on the ground. Dead." He lowered his voice. "I think she fell out of the window."

My chest tightened. This was bad. This was very bad. I hoped that Jason had been dreaming and imagined all of this, but for all his oddities, I'd never known him to make up a fantastical tale. "Why didn't you call me on the radio when you saw this?"

His face turned bright red. The radio and Jason's lack of use of it had been a hot button issue between us for months. It seemed he always forgot to carry it or charge it or something. I suspected that mostly he didn't want to be found, even if that want was subconscious.

"I guess I forgot," he said. "I'm sorry. I'll try to remember to carry my radio from now on."

It was a promise that he'd made many times before, so I had my doubts he'd be able to follow through with it even though I knew he wanted to. I sighed, and at the moment, Jason's lack of radio use was the least of my problems. I had to run to the village and see for myself what he'd described. I prayed that Jason was wrong and what he was telling me was just a terrible dream.

"Mom?" Hayden appeared on the stairs, holding Frankie in his arms. He appeared sleepy, and Frankie looked angry. That didn't mean much, though, because Frankie always looked angry. Hayden was the only person the cat tolerated, and he was certainly the one person that Frankie would let carry him around like a ragdoll. I wouldn't even attempt it. There was too great a risk of losing a limb.

"What's going on?" Hayden blinked at me. "Why's Jason here?"

"Hey, sweetie," I said in my best let's-pretend-everything-is-all-right-for-the-kids voice. "I have to go out for a little while, and Jason is going to stay here with you while I'm gone."

Jason opened his mouth, and I gave him a look. He shut his mouth.

Hayden's face brightened. He liked Jason almost as much as he liked Frankie. My son had an open heart and an affinity for people and creatures that others might be more likely to ignore. "Can we watch a show?"

I sighed. I couldn't see any way out of this, and I had to get to the village as soon as possible to see what was going on. "Sure, honey, you and Jason can watch a show."

"Yea!" Hayden bounced down the rest of the stairs and ran straight for the TV cabinet, where he began rifling through the DVD collection.

Jason stood up. "Shouldn't I go with you?"

"No, someone has to stay here with Hayden."

Hayden already had a *Veggie Tales* episode up on the screen. It was an old one but a current favorite of my son's.

"Did you call the police on your way here?" I asked in a low voice, so that Jason was the only one who could hear me.

His eyes went wide. "The police?" He shook his head.

I wasn't surprised. After his difficult upbringing, Jason was afraid of most authority figures, especially the police.

"Don't worry. I'll call them on the way to the village," I told him. "Just stay here with Hayden and don't leave until I get back. I don't care who comes to the door. Do you understand?"

He nodded.

"And bolt the door behind me when I leave."

I poured my glass of wine into the sink, grabbed a sweatshirt from the coat closet, along with my radio and cell phone, and ran out the door. At the last second, I called Tiffin, my corgi, to come with me. I thought that I might need my dog for backup.

Tiffin and I ran through the maple grove. In the winter months, when the trees were bare, my cottage could be seen, but in the height of summer, where we were now, the foliage hid it from view. This was good, because most visitors came to the Farm in the summer, and I liked to have at least a little privacy even though I was a permanent resident of the Farm.

Tiffin ran ahead of me on the pebbled path as I dialed the police.

"911, what's your emergency?" the officious-sounding female voice said over the line.

"Hello. This is Kelsey Cambridge. The director of Barton Farm." I rattled off the address of the Farm. "There's been an accident here on the village side of the Farm."

51

"Another one?" she asked.

I grimaced.

"What happened?"

"One of my employees reported that he thought someone fell out a window and is seriously hurt." I couldn't bring myself to say dead, not yet, not until I saw the dead body for myself. Maybe it was wishful thinking on my part to want to believe the person could still be alive after a fall like that. I prayed that Jason had been wrong and the person, whoever is was, was still alive. Most likely seriously hurt, but alive.

"What's the name of the person who fell?" the dispatcher asked.

"I don't know yet. I'm on my way there to see for myself. My employee said it was a woman." I was out of breath from talking while running. I reached Maple Grove Lane. Tiffin was waiting for me at the edge of the road.

I looked both ways and the two of us sprinted across the street. "Please send EMTs and police as quick as you can," I said. "The woman needs help. Tell them she fell near the church on the green."

"They're on the way. Please stay on the line," the voice said calmly.

"I'm sorry, I have to go." I ended the call. I knew I'd hear about hanging up on the dispatcher from the police chief, but the phone call was slowing me down and I had to beat the police to the scene. I had to assess the situation for myself before they did.

It was close to nine thirty, and the sun had dropped below the horizon. Barton Farm was devoid of street lights, so the night always seemed much darker than in town. I wished I'd thought to bring a flashlight. I fumbled with my phone and turned on the flashlight app. It wasn't as strong as my trusty Maglite, but it worked in a pinch.

As I reached the green, the moon moved out from behind a cloud and the village was awash with moonlight, which seemed jarring after the solid darkness. My eyes traveled up the church's steeple, and I knew right away that something was wrong. A string of twinkle lights hung from a broken window. The lights were lit and looked like a line of listless fireflies floating in the breeze. Most of the wooden slats that had once been the window in the bell tower were gone. All that was left were jagged pieces of wood that resembled shark teeth. The moonlight reflected off the shards that had managed to hang on.

With my eyes, I followed the string of twinkle lights down. They only dangled a couple of feet below the window, but they seemed to point downward to a heap at the foot of the church steps. My stomach turned. It was a body.

I ran to the crumpled form and knew within five feet of it that the person couldn't still be alive. And I had a sinking feeling I knew who it was, even before I saw her face. The face of Vianna Pine.

I dropped to my knees beside her. Her neck was clearly broken. No one's neck should bend that way. I had to look away, and my eyes traveled up to the dangling twinkle lights again. A shadow moved in the steeple above.

EIGHT

I BLINKED, CONVINCED THAT I'd imagined what I'd seen. Then I saw it again. There was someone looking down at me from the bell tower's broken window. "Hey!" I cried, jumping to my feet. "Hey!"

The shadow jerked back from window and disappeared. But it had been there. I was sure of it. In the distance, I heard the approaching sirens. I had a couple of choices. I could stay with Vianna, who was clearly beyond help, or I could find out who was in the bell tower. The police would arrive in a matter of moments—I would be safe, or so I told myself.

Before I could change my mind, I ran to the back of the church, Tiffin on my heels. I figured that if *I* had just killed someone, I would be much more likely to run out the back door than the front door, especially if I heard the sirens of oncoming police.

I was right in my guess. I rounded the back of the church just in time to see a dark figure sprint into the woods. I ran after the shadow. "Hey! Stop!"

Tiffin barked.

The shadow kept running. I didn't know why I thought yelling "hey, stop" would help. It never works in cop shows, so why did I think it might work for me? "Stop!"

The shadow melted into the trees. The weak light from my cell phone was my only guide as I followed. "Wait!" I cried. I could see the shadow just out of the range of my light. "Wait. Ahhh!" I cried out as the toe of my shoe caught on a tree root and I fell to the ground face-first.

After a moment, I rolled onto my back and caught my breath. I felt on the ground around me for my phone but couldn't find it anywhere. Great. It was almost pitch-black in the forest. The dense canopy of trees barely let any moonlight peek through.

A twig snapped somewhere in the forest and my heart skipped a beat. What was I doing lying here like a sitting duck? What was I doing chasing a possible killer into the woods in the first place? I could be murdered myself and then what would happen to Barton Farm? More importantly, what would happen to Hayden? I struggled to my feet.

Tiffin whimpered and dropped my phone on top of my shoes. I scooped it up and scratched him between the ears. "Good dog."

He barked agreement.

"Let's get out of here." I turned the flashlight app back on and made my way out of the trees with Tiffin on my heels. I was surprised by how far I'd traveled before I took that tumble.

Tiffin stopped in the middle of the path and whimpered. Every fiber of his being still wanted to race after the culprit. I understood. I felt the same way, but I wasn't going to risk it in the dark.

I slapped my thigh. "Come, Tiffin." The corgi dropped his head and galloped to my side. Together we shuffled out of the woods and back around the side of the church. We'd almost reached the front when another figure jumped in front of me. I screamed.

"Police!"

"Geez, Detective!" I cried, placing a hand to my chest. "Are you trying to give me a heart attack?"

Detective Candy Brandon lowered her gun and shined a flashlight in my face. "Cambridge. I could have shot you."

"I know. But there's no time for small talk." I pointed into the trees. "That way! Someone ran that way! I saw them! Hurry!"

"Who was it?" she demanded.

"I don't know, but I think whoever it was might have been inside the church and pushed that poor woman out the window."

Without questioning me any further, the detective took off into the trees. A moment later two more police officers, one of whom was Officer Sonders, raced across the village green and into the woods. I hesitated, unsure as to whether or not I should follow them or stay behind to guard Vianna's body.

Before I could make up my mind, Detective Brandon reappeared. Although she'd been running, she wasn't the slightest bit out of breath.

"Did you find them?" I asked.

She shook her head. "I radioed for backup. My officers will keep looking while I check out the scene."

I nodded. I could hear the two police officers crashing through the trees like a herd of bison.

She shone the flashlight in my face for a second time that night.

I raised a hand to block the flashlight's beam. "Is that necessary?"

She lowered the flashlight, but I noticed that she had her finger on her gun's trigger.

"Can you put the gun away too? You're making me nervous."

She grunted but finally, after a long beat, holstered her gun.

"About time," I grumbled.

She scowled at me. As usual, her dark red hair was pulled back into a bun on the back of her head and she wore a loose-fitting suit to hide her figure. Despite her efforts, the detective couldn't hide the fact that she was a striking woman. I could see why Chase had been drawn to her. The two of them had once been engaged, which went right to the heart of why Detective Brandon wouldn't have minded shooting me.

"What do you know about the body?" she asked, getting down to business.

"She fell out the church window." I decided to stick to the facts.

"How do you know that? Did you see her fall? Were you in the church when she fell?" Her questions came in rapid succession.

"No. I just inferred it based on where she's lying and the broken window in the church steeple." I tried to keep my voice calm. The detective was just doing her job. I had to remind myself of that and push all the personal stuff aside. What was most important here was to find out what had happened to Vianna. Even though I hadn't cared for her, she didn't deserve to die, and certainly not in such a horrible way.

"It's not your job to infer *anything*, Ms. Cambridge. This is a police investigation. We don't need any of your assistance." Brandon took a step closer. Her five-nine height loomed over my small frame. What I would have given for eight more inches so I could look her in the eye!

I wanted to take a step back, but I held my ground. I wasn't one to back down, and heaven knows, Detective Brandon was the last person I would back down from—I'd dealt with more formidable opponents than her.

"You and I both know what another death on Farm grounds will mean for your little museum," she added. "More bad press. I'll be surprised if you're able to keep your doors open at all."

I felt a flush start at my neck and run up to my hairline. What the detective said was true, but I certainly didn't want to hear the thoughts already running through my head spoken aloud. Even more, I didn't want to hear them from her.

"Maybe you should focus on Farm safety so that people stop dying here." Her lips curved into a mocking smile.

I would have loved to do that, if I knew how. Things kept happening at the Farm that were completely out of my control. But what if the Cherry Foundation removed their support or funding? I closed my eyes for the briefest of seconds. I couldn't think about that right now, not with Detective Brandon staring down at me. The detective didn't miss a thing, and I didn't want her to know I was worried.

The sound of footsteps running across the loose stones on the pebbled path distracted her and she looked away from me. I took the opportunity to step out of her looming range.

"That will be the EMTs," she said with not a little bit of disgust in her voice. I knew she must be thinking of Chase. Their breakup had gone as well as my split with Eddie. Hard feelings on both sides remained.

"Kelsey!" Chase sprinted toward us. His equipment bag beat a rhythm on his thigh as he ran. "Kelsey!"

Detective Brandon's lips curled into a sneer.

Behind us, one of Brandon's officers popped out of the trees. "Detective, whoever it was got away. Sonders and I lost them."

The detective scowled and went over to confer with the officers.

My shoulders slumped. If I'd kept going, would I have caught a glimpse of whoever it was? If I had, I might have seen who'd done this to Vianna. Assuming, of course, that she'd been pushed.

Chase pulled up short when he saw Detective Brandon. Then he saw Vianna's body on the ground. He shot me a look and went straight toward Vianna. His job came first. I recognized the two other EMTs from events I'd gone to with Chase at the fire station, and also, unfortunately, from scenes with other dead bodies on Barton Farm.

I swallowed. It sounded so much worse when I considered "bodies," plural. Brandon was right. It would be a miracle if the Farm continued to stay open.

I forced the thought aside and stepped back as the other EMTs joined Chase, kneeling on either side of the body.

Detective Brandon told her officer to keep searching the trees for any sign of the person and then joined the EMTs at the body. I followed her. I was sure she noticed, but I didn't care. I had to know what was going on too.

Chase looked up at her and shook his head. "She's gone."

From the odd angle of Vianna's neck, her death was obvious from the start, but at the same time, it was almost merciful to have it confirmed. Her body was so broken; I couldn't imagine the pain she would have endured had she survived. She might have wished she were dead.

It was true that I hadn't liked Vianna much. She was like an annoying fly that I couldn't shoo from the house. But I didn't want this to happen to her. I wouldn't want this to happen to anyone.

I turned away just in time to see a wide man shuffle up the pebbled path. He wasn't in a hurry. The beam of his flashlight bounced against the ground as if he were out on a quiet evening stroll. As he approached, I could see his luxurious mustache and sideburns, grown in the style of the Civil War's General Burnside, whom he portrayed on the battlefield more often than not. In reenactments, Chief Duffy played both Southern and Northern generals based on the need, but Burnside was his favorite.

Brandon noticed him coming, too, and her face fell into an even deeper scowl, as if that were possible. The chief was her boss, but she wasn't happy about the arrangement. Everyone knew this, even Chief Duffy, who I suspected didn't much care what Brandon or anyone else thought of him. I mean, the man had colossal sideburns. He had to have some serious self-confidence to pull that off in the twenty-first century.

Brandon removed her cell phone from the pocket of her shapeless suit jacket. "I'll call the medical examiner."

The EMTs backed away from the body and collected their equipment. There was nothing more they could do. It was up to the police, the medical examiner, and the crime scene techs now. Unfortunately, from past experience I knew the drill.

"Kelsey," Chief Duffy said, lowering his flashlight so that the beam wouldn't hit me in the face. He was much more polite than his detective. "Dispatch said that you called in about another accident. This is turning into a bit of a trend, isn't it?"

"Not on purpose," I said.

"Dispatch also said you refused to stay on the line." He waggled his busy eyebrows.

"I wanted to get to the village as fast as possible," I replied. "I called on the way."

He turned the flashlight off and slid it back into his duty belt. Unlike Detective Brandon, the chief didn't mind wearing his uniform. I thought that it must remind him of the many period uniforms he wore during reenactments. "Isn't there a big wedding on the Farm this weekend?" he asked.

I raised my eyebrows, surprised that he knew this. Then it suddenly occurred to me to wonder whether the wedding would go on as planned under the current circumstances. The venue was vandalized and the wedding planner was dead. It couldn't get much worse than that.

The surprise must have shown on my face because Chief Duffy added, "Chase mentioned the wedding to me."

I glanced over at Chase, who was in what appeared to be a deep conversation with his EMT colleagues. I supposed that I shouldn't be surprised that he'd told the chief about it—the chief was his uncle, after all. New Hartford was a small town, and everyone was related to everyone else somehow. It was the town's most endearing—and aggravating—quality.

Brandon nodded at Chief Duffy. "The techs and the ME are on their way. They'll get here as quickly as they can. There was a shooting in Akron earlier tonight."

"You're always on the ball, Candy." The chief smiled.

I was certain he was the only one on the force who could call her by her first name without getting punched in the mouth.

"I'd like to interview Kelsey if I could," she said.

The chief took a step back. "You go right ahead. I'll check in with Chase and the boys." He strolled over to the EMTs, leaving me alone with a very irritated-looking detective. Lucky me.

NINE

Detective Brandon narrowed her eyes and removed a small notebook from the inside pocket of her jacket. "So let's go over everything from the top."

"All right," I agreed. There was no point in arguing with her. She was just doing her job, and she was very good at it. I was willing to give her that.

"Tell me exactly what brought you over to this side of the Farm so late at night. Did you just happen by when the victim fell from the window?" She sounded dubious.

I frowned. The last thing I wanted to do was embroil sensitive Jason in this police investigation. He'd been in others with Detective Brandon at the helm, and they'd not gone well for him. At the same time, I couldn't lie. "Jason, my farmhand, lives in a trailer on this side of the Farm."

She made a note in her notebook. "I remember that."

Of course she remembered that. She forgot nothing. I'd give her that too.

"Anyway," I went on, "he saw a light in the steeple from his trailer and decided to check it out. By the time he reached the church, Vianna had fallen out of the window. He ran to my cottage to tell me."

"Why didn't he call the police first? That's what he should have done."

"He panicked. It's not often you find a dead body."

She arched her eyebrow. "That's not the case for you, though."

I pressed my lips together. I didn't see any reason to reply.

"Where is he now?" she asked after a beat.

I shivered and crossed my arms over my chest. It was a warm summer night. I guessed that it was close to eighty, which was hot for this late at night in northeast Ohio. I suspected my proximity to Vianna's broken body was making me cold. Then again, the chill could have been from Brandon's icy stare. "He's at my cottage with Hayden," I said. "I told him to stay there while I went to see what was going on."

She made another note. "I'm going to have to speak to him."

I nodded. I knew there was no way around it. Jason would just have to be able to handle the detective's questions. Maybe she would allow me to be there when she questioned him. I wasn't holding my breath that she would.

"Chase"—she said his name with something close to resentment—"identified the victim as Vianna Pine. He said she was a wedding planner." Her jaw tightened and she was barely able to get out the words.

I wondered if she thought that Chase knew the wedding planner's name because he and I were getting married, which we were not. We'd only been dating for a few months, and after my disastrous divorce, I was taking this new relationship at a snail's pace.

"Do you know the victim?" she asked.

I nodded. "She was planning a wedding that's supposed to be in the church here on Friday." I glanced up at the broken window and the strand of glowing twinkle lights that swung lightly back and forth in the breeze. "It was Eddie and Krissie's wedding."

She looked up from her notebook. "Your ex-husband's wedding?"

I nodded.

"Your ex-husband was getting remarried here on Barton Farm?"

I nodded again.

"And you were okay with that?"

No, I wasn't okay with it, and Detective Brandon must have known that. Instead, I said, "It's what the Cherry Foundation wanted."

"Ah!" A smile curled on her lips. "And what was the wedding planner doing in the church's bell tower at night?"

I pointed at the dangling string of twinkle lights. "Putting up those lights, I would guess."

"Why? And why was she doing it in the middle of the night?" She made more notes.

"It's a long story."

She glanced up from her notebook. "A woman is dead, Kelsey."

"I know. I'm sorry." I dropped my arms. "Krissie wanted lights in the steeple for the wedding. I said that we couldn't do it because it was a safety issue. The bell tower is old and unstable. Candles are also out of the question due to the fire hazard. I wouldn't let her install the lights and reminded her that the contract both Eddie and Krissie signed stated that no changes could be made to the historic buildings."

"But she went ahead and did it anyway." Brandon tapped her pen on the edge of her notebook.

I nodded. "From what's happened, I can only assume that's the case. I'm sure that Krissie wouldn't take no for an answer from Vianna about the lights, and Vianna thought it would be better to break the Farm rules than to face Krissie's wrath."

"Krissie's wrath?" Brandon arched one of her perfectly formed eyebrows. Given that the detective went a long way to hide her natural beauty when she was on the job, her perfect eyebrows must have been her one vanity.

I rubbed my own brow, knowing that I might have just made a mistake. I didn't want Krissie to sound vindictive. At least, I didn't think I wanted her to sound like that. I didn't want Krissie to be considered a suspect, not really. "Maybe wrath was a poor choice of words. Krissie knows what she wants, and she gets what she wants."

"Including Eddie?" Brandon asked.

I frowned.

"So your theory is that Vianna busted through the window when hanging lights and fell to her death?"

"That's one theory," I said.

"You have others?"

"Or . . . " I paused. "Or she was pushed."

"By the person you saw running into the woods?" Her eyes narrowed.

"Yes," I said. "I think that person was up in the bell tower. I saw movement in the tower right after I found the body."

"What kind of movement?" Her voice was sharp.

"A shadow that was certainly big enough to belong to a human. I called out to the person, or whatever it was, and he ran off. I took off after him, but realized that might not be a good idea." I saw no reason to tell the detective that I'd fallen while in pursuit of the shadow. "Then you and your officers showed up."

"*Him?* Did you get a look at the individual? Was it a man you followed into the woods?"

I shook my head. "I didn't see the person at all other than the shadow of him or her. I'm using 'him' in the generic sense."

"Can you describe this *shadow* you saw?" she asked.

I shook my head again. "I've got nothing. It was just a shadow."

"Like Peter Pan's shadow?"

"I didn't imagine it, if that's what you're getting at."

"It very likely was the killer. You do realize how stupid it was to run after a possible killer." It was a statement, not a question.

"Candy, can you come here a second?" Chief Duffy called her over to the body.

In the time that we'd been talking, the medical examiner and the crime scene techs had arrived. One of the techs set up floodlights on tripods. The bright lights washed Vianna's body and face in a garish yellow glow and made her injuries appear even more gruesome.

"Wait here," Detective Brandon ordered me. "I have more questions for you."

I had no doubt that she did. As I watched her and the chief consult with the medical examiner, I felt that knot in my stomach tighten a little bit more. Another death had happened on the Farm. Another murder, most likely. I knew it was murder from the top of my head to the soles of my feet. I knew it. What would it mean for the Farm? I'd been lucky so far with the other murders. The Cherry Foundation had been very forgiving about those crimes, but looking at Vianna Pine's crumbled and broken body under the lights, I couldn't help but think that this just might be the death that would close Barton Farm for good.

Chase and the other two EMTs were walking in my direction. Chase headed straight for me. One of his colleagues said, "Don't be long, Wyatt."

Chase gave his friend a thumbs-up sign and then took my hand. "Are you okay?"

"I'm fine," I said automatically.

He cocked his head. "Is that true? Or is this Kelsey trying to be tough?"

"I have to be tough," I said, allowing my gaze to meet his warm brown eyes.

He smiled, but it was a smile with a hint of sadness in it. "Not with me you don't. I wish you'd remember that."

I opened my mouth to say something in return, but nothing came out. I couldn't be vulnerable, not even with Chase. My life had made me tough, and it was who I was. My mother's death and my divorce had formed an impenetrable wall around my heart, which Chase had diligently been chipping away at over the last year, but the wall was still there. I doubted it would ever disappear completely.

"Wyatt!" one of the EMTs yelled from the pebbled path.

"I have to go. My shift ends at midnight. I'll come to the cottage as soon as I get off."

"You don't have to do that. I'll be—"

He cut me off with a kiss, and it wasn't a peck on the mouth either. I pulled away.

"Chase," I hissed. "You can't kiss me in the middle of a crime scene, and you're on the clock."

He grinned. "Why not? My uncle is chief of police, and he doesn't care."

I looked over his shoulder and saw Detective Brandon glaring at us both. That was why not.

TEN

It was close to midnight when Tiffin and I stumbled through the front door of my cottage. The police and the medical examiner and his team had gone, taking Vianna's body with them. I closed the cottage door behind me and leaned against it, afraid of what tomorrow would bring. I knew Henry from the Cherry Foundation would not welcome this news.

There was also the issue of keeping the Farm open tomorrow. I was hoping the police would only cordon off the church and let the rest of the village remain accessible, but as of yet, no decision had been made. The chief said he would let me know in the morning. And morning was just a few short hours away for me. I awoke at five every day during the high season to check and recheck that the Farm was ready for the onslaught of visitors.

Tiffin sniffed around the room. Maybe he was making sure the place was secure after the last few hours we'd had. Jason and Hayden weren't on the main floor. Tiffin ran to the foot of the stairs and looked up.

"Okay, boy," I said. "You can come with me to check on them." Usually Tiffin was relegated to the main floor because upstairs was Frankie's domain, but I knew the dog wouldn't be able to rest until he saw with his own eyes that his boy was all right.

Tiffin and I crept up the stairs. The door to Hayden's room was open just a crack. I pushed lightly on it and it swung inward. When I peeked inside, we found Hayden asleep in his bed with his right arm flung over his face. Frankie was on his pillow and opened his one good eye, appraising us.

Jason lay on a blanket on the floor, also asleep. He was using Hayden's dinosaur stuffed animal as a pillow for his head. He faced the doorway, as if he'd positioned himself to be ready to protect Hayden if the need arose.

I felt my face soften as I watched the two boys sleep. Brandon had agreed to talk to Jason tomorrow. She'd wanted to question him tonight, but I'd been able to convince Chief Duffy that tomorrow would be better, and he'd told his detective to wait. That gave me the time I needed to warn Jason about the oncoming interrogation. I saw no sense in waking him now, though. That could wait until tomorrow too.

I tiptoed into the room and around Jason's sleeping form. Under Frankie's close observation, I gently lifted Hayden's arm from over his face and tucked it under his superhero sheets. He sighed in his sleep and his pink lips curved into a smile. I wished I knew what he was dreaming about to put such a peaceful expression on his face. I knew my dreams that night would be far less pleasant. I kissed his forehead and tiptoed back out of the room.

Tiffin whimpered in the hallway. I left the door open a crack, as it had been before, and went back downstairs.

I'd just reached the main floor when there was a light knock on the cottage's front door. Tiffin ran to the door with his tail-less rump wiggling happily. I figured it must be Chase.

When I opened the door, Chase stepped inside and wrapped his arms around me in a hug without saying a word. Then he kissed me.

"Hayden and Jason are upstairs," I said as I pushed him away.

"Are they asleep?" There was mischief in his eyes. There was always mischief in Chase's eyes. Why he was attracted to me and my serious workaholic ways remained a mystery.

I pushed him away, and he let me. "Yes, they're asleep. I'll make some coffee."

"Make it decaf unless you're not planning to sleep tonight." The teasing sound was back in his voice.

I ignored him and went into the kitchen to remove the bag of decaf coffee from the refrigerator.

Chase sat on one of the two bar stools at the kitchen's island and watched me work in silence for a moment. "I'm staying here tonight," he said finally.

"You can't. Hayden's here." I turned the coffeemaker on and the water began to boil. I did this to protect Hayden and maybe, I'd admit, if only to myself, to protect myself as well. "We'll be fine. Jason's here."

"Kelsey, someone was murdered less than a quarter of a mile from where we are right now." He leaned over the counter with a serious expression on his face for once. "And if a killer stormed in here, Jason would be completely worthless when it came to defending you and Hayden."

That might be true. "I'm perfectly capable of defending myself and my son." I frowned.

"I know you are." He leaned back on the stool as if he realized he'd taken his argument a step too far.

"Besides, whoever killed Vianna wanted to kill Vianna. That doesn't have anything to do with Hayden and me."

Chase didn't look convinced. "Please. Let me stay. For me. It would make me feel better if I knew you and Hayden were safe."

I sighed. It would be nice to have him there. I knew I might actually get some sleep knowing Chase was nearby, not that I'd ever let him know that.

"I'll sleep on the couch and be a perfect gentleman," he said.

I arched my brow.

"I will!" he said, as if aghast. "Your virtue is safe with me, dear lady."

Despite myself, I laughed. "Okay. Fine, but just for tonight."

His face broke into a grin. I felt like I'd just given Chase an inch that he would interpret as a mile or two.

Twenty minutes later, I was smoothing a clean sheet over the sofa for Chase to keep him cool while he slept and to keep as much cat and dog fur off of him as possible. Chase stood behind me, holding the bed pillow I'd given him. "I feel spoiled. What service."

"Just go to sleep," I muttered.

His brows went up. "No good night kiss?"

This was going to be trouble. A knock on the cottage door saved me from answering.

"Who could that be?" I asked, moving toward the door.

"My guess is Candy. She doesn't sleep when she's on a big case," he said, following me.

I frowned, trying not to imagine what else he might know about the police detective's sleeping habits.

Tiffin stood at the door. His rump wasn't wagging to tell me it was a friend on the other side, but he wasn't on high alert, so I realized it was someone he knew. I opened the door to find Eddie. My typically pristine ex-husband appeared disheveled. His dark hair, which was always combed perfectly in place, stood on end, the collar to his polo shirt was askew, and there were dark circles under his bright blue eyes.

I stepped back. "Eddie! What are you doing here?"

"I need your help." He pulled up short when he saw Chase, who still was holding the bed pillow, standing behind me. "What's *he* doing here?"

"What does it look like?" Chase snapped back. There was no love lost between those two.

"Is he here when my son is here?" Eddie wanted to know.

I stepped in between the two of them. "Eddie, back off," I ordered. "Chase is staying the night because of what happened in the village this evening. I assume you heard about it, which is why you're here."

Eddie looked as if he wanted to argue.

"And," I went on, "he's sleeping on the couch—not that it's any of your business."

Eddie looked around us at the couch and seemed to be satisfied when he saw the sofa made up like a bed. "I heard about what happened."

I knew what was coming next. I would hear a long argument as to why Hayden wasn't safe living with me on the Farm because of yet another murder on the grounds. I wasn't in total disagreement with him when it came to that argument, but I still had no intention of giving him and Krissie shared custody of my son. "Hayden is fine.

He's sleeping upstairs. He doesn't know what happened, and I plan to keep it that way."

Eddie ran his hand through his hair. "I'm not here about Hayden."

"Then why are you here?" I asked.

"It's Krissie," he said, and his face fell. "She's been taken to the police station for questioning. They think she killed Vianna. You have to help her."

"You've got to be kidding me," I muttered under my breath.

Eddie sat down in the middle of the sofa, on the clean sheets I'd just placed there for Chase, with his head in his hands. "What am I going to do?"

Chase leaned against the kitchen counter with his arms folded across his chest while I perched on the edge of the coffee table, ready to spring away from both of them. I was both figuratively and literally between the two men. The irony of the situation wasn't lost on me.

"Have you spoken to your brother?" I asked Eddie.

Eddie's younger brother, Justin, was an environmental law attorney. He wouldn't be much help with criminal defense for Krissie, but at the very least he could put Eddie in contact with an attorney who might be able to help him.

He nodded. "Yes, and the criminal lawyer he suggested is down at the station with Krissie right now. Justin is there too."

I slid back onto the coffee table, since I was close to falling off of the edge. "Again, Eddie, why are you here? You have a defense attorney for Krissie. I don't know what I can do."

"You can help me." His eyes flicked in the direction of Chase. "You have connections with the police. You can help protect Krissie from whatever they plan to do to her."

Even though Chase was behind me, so I couldn't see him, I felt the hostility he threw in Eddie's direction.

I shook my head. "Eddie, I can't do anything. I don't have an in with the police."

He dropped his hands from his face. "Of course you do. Three, now four, people have died on Barton Farm and the museum remains open. You have to have some clout, keeping this place in operation when it should so clearly be condemned. You must have something over the police to make that possible."

I glared at him. "If you're trying to talk me into helping Krissie, I suggest that you use another argument, because that one isn't going to work. Ever."

"What she said," Chase added.

I glanced over my shoulder and gave him a look. He flashed a smile in return.

"Kelsey," Eddie said. "I'm telling you Krissie didn't do this. She wouldn't hurt a fly." He stared into my eyes with so much earnestness that it took me back to that time we'd loved each other and I'd trusted that face with my whole heart.

Then I remembered that he'd had the same expression when he'd denied his affair, even after I saw him with the other woman. Twice. How could I believe anything he said? He'd lied to me for months with the worst possible lie, telling me he loved me when he didn't, telling me he was faithful to me when he wasn't.

I shook my head. "I'm sorry, Eddie. I can't help you in this case. Krissie's family has money. They can hire the best lawyer that money can buy. That will have to be enough." I stood up, walked to my cottage door, and opened it. The warm night air floated into the cottage and carried the faint scent of campfire. "I think it's time for you to go."

Eddie joined me at the open door, but he made no move to walk through it. "What about Hayden?"

His question stopped my heart. "Hayden? What does any of this have to do with Hayden?"

"Do you really want our child to look on as his stepmother is accused of murder and possibly put on trial? Think of how it would affect him." The sad expression was gone from his blue eyes. All I saw now was determination, determination to achieve what he wanted at any cost, even using his only child as a pawn to do it.

"She's not his stepmother yet," I snapped. "The two of you aren't married. You shouldn't be bringing Hayden into this conversation at all."

He ignored my reprimand and said, "Maybe you killed the wedding planner and framed Krissie to stop the wedding, then? Is that it?"

I stared at him open-mouthed. I couldn't believe that just moments ago I was feeling sorry for this jerk.

Chase was there in an instant, next to Eddie. "Just get out."

I placed my hand on Chase's chest and gently pushed him back. This was my battle.

Chase looked at me. After a beat, he stepped back, and I dropped my hand. I returned my focus to Eddie. "Listen to me, Eddie, and listen closely. I had nothing to do with Vianna Pine's murder, nor do I want anything to do with Krissie's involvement with it."

"Krissie had nothing—"

I held up my hand to cut him off. "I don't care. The reason why I care about what happened is because it happened here on my Farm and because a woman was murdered. Yes, she was an annoying woman and, as far as I know, she only cared about making everything perfect for Krissie's wedding day, but she was someone to another person out there. She was someone's daughter. That should be more important than any inconvenience that Krissie is going through right now. If Krissie is as innocent as you say she is, the police will know that. Detective Brandon and Chief Duffy are both very good cops. They won't arrest the wrong person."

Chase stepped forward and opened the cottage door a little more widely. "I think we're done here."

Eddie looked from me to Chase and back again. He walked through the door and turned to face Chase and me. His eyes narrowed as he stood on the top step of my tiny front porch. "I will remember this, Kelsey. When it comes time to present my case for Hayden's custody in court, I will remember this conversation."

My chest tightened. "Stop using your son as a weapon."

Before he could respond, Chase slammed the door in his face.

ELEVEN

THE NEXT MORNING, ON the walk between my cottage and the visitor center, Hayden and Tiffin ran a little bit ahead of me. I kept them in my line of sight. The sun was bright, but I knew danger lurked somewhere on the Farm grounds. I needed no more proof of that than the body I'd found at the foot of the church steps the night before.

Chase had left the cottage around six. He was out the door before either Jason or Hayden came down the stairs. I was grateful he left without complaint. I didn't want anything else to upset Hayden's life. But I had a feeling Krissie and Eddie weren't going to make as much of an effort to shield Hayden from what was going on with Vianna's murder.

Then again, we didn't know for certain that Vianna was murdered. Yet. She might have just fallen to her death accidentally. The only indication that foul play was at work was the shadow I'd seen fleeing the scene. That said, I didn't know how she could have simply fallen through the window. It seemed to me that there must have been a force of some kind to send her flying through the wooden slats. Like being thrown or pushed.

I opened the side door that led into the administrative wing of the visitor center. Hayden and Tiffin raced inside. "I'm going to visit Judy!" Hayden shouted as he ran down the hallway. Laura, who stood just on the other side of the door with two extra-extra large coffees from the local coffee shop in either hand, flattened her body against the wall as Hayden and Tiffin flew by.

When they disappeared around the corner that led into the main part of the visitor center, she held one out to me, and I took it with a grateful smile.

"It's black with no sugar, sweetener, cream, or milk. Boring. Just how you like it." She sipped from her cup and sighed. "Mine, on the other hand, is fully loaded."

I held the cup under my nose and inhaled, enjoying the aroma. I was feeling better already.

She shook her head. "I don't know how you can drink that stuff without something in it. If that's what it takes to weigh as much as a Popsicle stick, I'm not interested."

Laura was a big woman, tall and thick, with the most beautiful mane of red hair I'd ever seen. She also had perfectly symmetrical features. She was stunning. Conversely, I was petite, with brown eyes and my hair tied back in an ever-present French braid. There was nothing stunning about me except my stubborn streak, which was legendary.

"Thank you for the coffee," I said. "Boring is my style. I could really go for boring right about now."

Laura nodded and walked toward my office. "Considering you found another dead body . . . I need details."

"I knew the coffee would have a price." Following her, I removed my keys from my pocket, unlocked the door, and let us inside the cramped space. I moved a stack of catalogs from one of the two chairs in front of my desk and set them on top of a low bookshelf so Laura had a place to sit. Then I sat on my aged wooden desk chair and leaned back with my coffee under my nose. The heavenly aroma soothed my nerves. Laura closed the door after us and took her seat.

"How did you hear about it?" I asked.

"Chase called me very early this morning," she said. "It must have been about six. He's lucky I answered, as I was in a deep sleep dreaming about Colin Firth—the *Pride and Prejudice* version, of course. I watched it last night from beginning to end, starting the moment I got home from the Farm yesterday afternoon."

"That's dedication," I said. The miniseries had to be six hours long.

She sighed. "What else is a single girl teacher to do in the summer?"

I rolled my eyes. I didn't want us to stumble down the road of Laura's single status again. She was lovely, funny, and whip-smart. She didn't need a guy, in my opinion, nor did any deserve her. It wouldn't do any good for me to repeat this sentiment to her, though. She'd heard it many times before.

She sipped again from her cup and sighed. "What I want to know is, why did I have to hear about it from Chase?" She arched her brow. "I'd have thought my best friend would text me to let me know. Something like, 'Hey, found a dead body. Hope you and Mr. Firth have a great night.'"

"I was going to call you as soon as I got here this morning. I was just too tired last night, especially after Eddie left."

She held up her hand in the universal sign for stop. "Hold up. What? Eddie was there?"

I sipped my coffee. It was perfect. Strong and bitter. "Chase didn't tell you that part?"

She jerked forward and sloshed coffee on her shirt. "No, he never mentioned Eddie. I would have remembered if he mentioned Eddie!"

I gave her a level stare. "You're more freaked out that I saw Eddie last night than you are about me finding a dead body. You might want to reexamine your priorities."

"Would it be wrong to say I am? Because it's the truth. Why was he there?" She leaned back into her chair.

"Apparently the police took Krissie in for questioning, and Eddie stopped by because he wanted me to help her. He thinks I have some kind of pull with the police."

"What? Of all the nerve. I swear, the next time I see him I'm going to kick him. I've wanted to kick him for years, but I've held back for your sake. But no more. Oh no, he's crossed the line now, and as your best friend, I have the right and privilege to kick."

I rubbed the corner of my eye in the preemptive strike against the eye twitch that I suspected this conversation would bring on. "No kicking."

She ignored me and went on. "I can't believe he came to your cottage in the dead of night to ask you to help Krissie. Like you would do anything for that—"

"She'll be Hayden's stepmother, for better or worse."

"For worse," Laura grumbled. "Definitely for worse."

"I can't believe she's capable of murder, especially murder that had the potential to ruin her own wedding or put her in prison on her wedding day. She's too selfish to do anything that would have such an impact on her own plans."

Laura frowned. "We'll agree to disagree on this. I think she's positively horrible. And I don't doubt she's capable of murder. Tell me everything."

I sighed and shared what had happened the night before, from beginning to end. It was much easier to tell my best friend, who interjected the occasional snarky remark, than it was to tell Detective Brandon.

When I was done, Laura shook her head. "What are you going to do? Are you going to try to help Krissie?" Her tone told me she still thought it was a terrible idea.

"I don't know." I was beginning to waffle on the issue. I could feel it.

"But then again, maybe helping her will help you." Laura tapped her index finger on her chin.

I gave her a look. "How?"

"It just occurred to me that maybe if you *did* help them, like get her off the murder rap, then you could use it as a bargaining chip to tell them to stop moving forward with the custody case."

I stared at her over my coffee cup. "We don't know if Krissie's been charged for murder. We don't even know if it *was* a murder. She was just called in for questioning and Eddie flipped out."

"But I still think you could use it to your advantage."

I shook my head. "That's a terrible idea. Probably the worst idea you've ever had."

Laura didn't have children. She couldn't understand what a dangerous idea that was, and, worse, how it could hurt Hayden. Above all else, I had to protect my son. Thankfully, she didn't appear to be offended when I nixed her suggestion. I knew she just wanted to get Eddie and Krissie off my back, but using Hayden wasn't the answer.

I wished that my ex-husband knew that too. I figured we would all be a lot happier if Eddie learned that lesson.

Laura shrugged. "I'm only trying to help. It's my job as your best friend, remember?"

"That reminds me, best friend. Shepley said something odd yesterday."

She raised one of her eyebrows. "Odder than normal for Shepley?"

I nodded. "He said that because of the wedding I was letting other things around the Farm fall through the cracks, and that people are talking about it."

She stared at me over her coffee cup. "You were talking to Shepley? No one talks to Shepley if they can avoid it."

"Maybe he's right." I thought of the missing artifacts. The artifacts had certainly fallen through the cracks.

Laura waved away my comment. "That's just Shepley trying to stir up trouble and make you worry. Everyone knows this wedding wasn't your idea, and you're doing a wonderful job managing the Farm *and* the wedding." She paused. "At least you were until the wedding planner fell out of the window."

"Gee, thanks. You really know how to make me feel better, Laura."

She smiled. "It's what I'm here for."

There was a knock on the door, and without waiting for an answer, the door opened. Benji stuck her head inside. "Kelsey, the police are here."

I swallowed. "Here we go again." I stood up, leaving my coffee on the desk.

Laura stood too. "At least dealing with dead people is become second nature to you. You're a pro. You got this."

For some reason, I didn't find that all that encouraging.

We followed Benji through the visitor center to the main room, which was where we greeted our guests when they first arrived on Farm grounds. Detective Brandon stood in front of the large mural we'd commissioned over the winter, which depicted the six generations of the Barton family who'd lived on the land—from the first arrival of Jebidiah Barton in 1805 to the final descendants who'd donated the land to be turned into a museum. That museum idea didn't happen overnight, however. Many years went by and many dollars were spent to make Barton Farm, the living history museum, a reality. It wouldn't have happened at all if it weren't for Cynthia Cherry and her foundation.

The detective turned to Laura and me, and I noticed that Benji was standing a little off to the side, fiddling with her radio again. The only reason I continued to notice this was because Benji wasn't one to fiddle. My confident assistant usually gave off the air that she was in control. That's what made her so great at her job.

"Detective?" I asked. "Are you here to tell me if we can open this morning?"

She scowled. "Yes, and you can." She didn't even attempt to hide the fact that she wasn't happy about it.

I felt a smile forming on my lips until I heard her say "but."

"But," she said, "the church is off limits, as you know, and also the area where the deceased hit the ground."

I winced when she said this. The memory of Vianna's broken body was still too fresh in my mind.

"It will be roped off with crime scene tape."

"For how long?"

"That's yet to be determined," the detective replied.

My wince grew stronger. I didn't like the idea of Farm visitors seeing crime scene tape and asking questions, but I supposed it couldn't be helped unless I decided to close the village side of the Farm. And I didn't want to do that. The Farm was always in need of money, so I couldn't afford to do anything that might drive guests away.

"I understand," I said. "Thank you for allowing us to open."

She raised one of her perfectly formed auburn eyebrows at me. "It wasn't my decision."

I was sure that it wasn't. Despite my plans not to get involved, I found myself asking, "I heard that Krissie Pumpernickle was taken to the station last night for questioning."

She frowned. "Who told you that? Chase?"

I swallowed. Did every conversation have to be so prickly with this police detective? I was guessing that the answer to that was yes, especially where Chase Wyatt was concerned. "No, I didn't hear it from Chase." I made a point not to tell her that Chase was with me when I heard that news. "Eddie told me."

"Interesting," she mused. "Yes, we brought Krissie in for questioning."

"Why didn't you question her at her home? I didn't have to go to the station, and I'm the one who found the body."

Her eyebrow shot up again. "Would you have preferred to have been questioned at the station? I can arrange that in the future."

Now it was my turn to frown.

Brandon pulled a tiny notebook out from the inside pocket of her jacket. "Krissie wasn't cooperating. I thought if I took her to the station, she'd be more forthcoming."

"And how did that go?"

She glanced up from her notebook and stared at me. "How do you think?"

I smiled. I could imagine. I would have given up a month's salary to see Krissie being taken to the police station.

Brandon snapped her notebook closed. "As far as we know, she was the last person to see Vianna alive, and according to reports, they had quite a row at the dress shop while Krissie was having her final fitting. Krissie threatened Vianna a number of times during the argument."

That would have been after Krissie met the drunk Abe Lincoln. I grimaced. I'd forgotten about the inebriated reenactor up to that point. He was something else I would have to deal with.

"According to what reports?" I asked. "Who told you there were threats?"

"That's confidential police information."

I arched my brow at her. "Oh really." I was helping with Krissie's wedding, so I knew who her dress tailor was. It would be easy enough to find out who might have overheard the argument. I mentally added that to my To Do list.

Brandon glared at me as if she knew that I wouldn't give up that easily.

"Krissie has been awful to everyone since the moment we started planning the wedding," I said. "I don't really think an argument with Vianna qualifies her as a murder suspect."

"You don't think she did it?" Brandon asked.

"I don't," I said with reluctance. "Look how Vianna's death has impacted her wedding. Krissie is selfish. Bottom line, she wouldn't do anything that could potentially damage her dream wedding. There's just no way."

Brandon wasn't convinced. "People do many stupid things in the heat of the moment. Trust me. As a cop, I've seen it too many times before."

"Was a crime even committed?" I asked. "Maybe Vianna fell from the window."

Brandon shook her head. "It seems very unlikely. It would take a lot of force to bust through the wooden slats like that, even though the wood was old and brittle. My working theory is that she was pushed or thrown through the window. Since you saw someone running away from the scene of the crime, that theory works."

I shivered as I thought of someone tossing Vianna out the bell tower window. She was a tiny woman—just like I was. She could be picked up and thrown. Even so, the person would have had to be extremely strong or lucky (or unlucky, depending on his or her intentions) to make her break through the window like that.

"Is Krissie under arrest?" I asked.

"No," Brandon said, as if she wasn't happy about this either. "I let her go. I didn't have enough to hold her, and she's not the only suspect."

"Oh?" My ears perked up at the news.

"It's early in the case. Of course, there's more than one suspect. We have to keep our minds opened to other possibilities until the evidence leads us to the right conclusion."

I wanted to say that when Cynthia Cherry's nephew, Maxwell, was murdered on Farm grounds last summer, Brandon hadn't been too open to other suspects when it looked like I was the killer. Maybe she'd changed her tactics in the last year. Or maybe she just didn't like me.

"So, like who?" I asked. "Who are the other suspects?" I couldn't stop myself from asking the question. It was like a compulsion on my part to always know the who, when, where, and why. Not to mention that the murder—if it was murder—had taken place on my Farm.

Detective Brandon frowned, but to my great surprise, she said, "Life in Vianna's company wasn't all happy vows and wedding cake tasting. There are real signs of relationships beginning to unravel there."

I was about to ask the detective what she meant by that when there was a crash behind us and I found Benji staring at the ground. Her radio lay on the hardwood floor in half a dozen pieces.

TWELVE

THE RADIO'S INTERNAL WIRES were exposed, and pieces of black plastic were scattered every which way. As with the fate of Humpty Dumpty, no amount of Super Glue was going to put that radio back together again.

Benji dropped to her knees, and her hands trembled as she gathered up the pieces of her broken radio.

I squatted beside her and handed her one of the tiny pieces closest to me.

"I'm such a klutz," she mumbled.

I studied her. Most of her face was hidden from my view by her braids, which fell over her cheeks while she worked. Benji wasn't a mumbler. Benji wasn't one to get rattled from a broken radio. There was something more to this than the radio.

Her hands continued to shake. "I'm so sorry. Think this radio is a goner."

The radio was, in fact, a goner, but I didn't much care about that.

"It's no big deal, Benji," I reassured her. "There's an extra radio in my office. Go get that one."

She met my gaze and looked as if she might cry. I would have known then that something more was definitely going on with her even if I hadn't already suspected it before. In the years that I'd known her, I'd never seen Benji cry. Not once. Not even the time that Mags, the oxen, stepped on her foot and broke it. Benji had sworn a blue streak, but she hadn't cried. And that would have been a time to cry. I knew I would have.

Detective Brandon cleared her throat and I looked up. The detective loomed over us, so I hopped to my feet. I was still at a height disadvantage by a good eight inches, but at least I didn't feel like a bug under a microscope any longer.

"I'm heading over to the village to see about the crime scene," Brandon announced. "I have some officers over there securing the area so you can open the Farm at the normal time. I'll also be questioning Jason, your farmhand."

"I need to be there for that," I said.

"I have to check in with my officers, and then I'll interview him after that. You can come over and observe, if you like," she said unconcernedly.

"I do like," I said.

The detective nodded and turned toward the sliding glass doors that led out onto the Farm grounds. Benji stood up with the broken pieces of the radio in her hands.

I gave the detective the brightest smile that I could muster, which was just at half wattage. "Thanks. That's much appreciated."

She merely grunted and marched out of the visitor center.

When she'd gone, I turned to Benji. "What's going on?"

Her dark brown eyes were huge, and she paled. "I have to tell you something," she said in a low voice.

"Clearly," I said. "What's gotten into you?"

She scanned the visitor center. The only other people in the room were Laura, Judy, and Hayden. Hayden was telling the two women a story that featured Frankie burying my reading glasses in his litter box. I knew the story might take a while with Hayden as narrator, so I said, "Tell me."

She took a deep breath. "You see, I've been—"

"Kelsey Cambridge." A stern voice interrupted our conversation. "We need to talk to you."

I turned to see Henry Ratcliffe and a late-middle-aged couple come through the doors into the visitor center. How many times had I told Judy that we needed to keep all doors locked until the Farm opened? We needed to keep out both visitors who arrived too early and people like Henry.

I forced a smile onto my face. "Henry, it's so good to see you," I lied through my teeth. "I was just about to call you." More lies.

By the way Henry's eyes narrowed, I suspected he knew it.

Benji adjusted the broken pieces of her radio in her arms. "I'll grab that new radio and run over to the village to make sure everything's secure before the guests arrive."

I grabbed her arm. "Can you go be with Jason when the detective questions him, in case I can't get there in time? I want to be there, but"—I glanced at Henry—"this could take a while. Jason will need the support."

She nodded. "Sure. I won't let the detective eat him alive."

"Thanks," I said, relieved. Benji wasn't one to go out of her way to help Jason. She insisted on calling him "Barn Boy." It's not that she ever said it directly to him—that would be bullying, and I'd never stand for it—but she was fond of using the nickname when it was just the two of us despite the many times I'd told her to stop.

Whatever Benji had needed to tell me would have to wait. I watched her disappear in the direction of the administrative offices to get the new walkie-talkie. As much as I wanted to go with her and be there for Jason, I knew it was better if I stayed back and dealt with Henry head-on. I hoped I'd still have enough time to check the grounds before we opened. I trusted Benji, but I wouldn't be completely satisfied that the Farm was ready for business if I didn't give it a once-over myself.

I turned my attention back to Henry Ratcliffe. Some would describe the man as a silver fox. He had lush silver hair brushed back from his perfectly tanned forehead. In his heyday, I supposed, he'd been a catch in the yacht club scene. Not that there were any yacht clubs in New Hartford, but had there been, Henry would have been their king in the 1980s. Now he was a retired attorney who was doing his very best to stay in control by taking on the leadership of the Cherry Foundation's board of trustees.

I knew the couple he was with, too, and I can't say I was thrilled to see them that early in the morning. Krissie's mother, Teresa Pumpernickle, was an older version of her beautiful daughter, but with her hair cut short and larger jewelry choices that even I could identify as expensive. The diamond on her ring finger alone must have been worth the Farm's entire annual budget, including salaries and benefits for the employees. The man, who was the same height and width as his wife, was Krissie's father, Heath Pumpernickle. Although I'd met Krissie's mother before, this was the first time I'd ever seen her father outside of photos.

I didn't know where Mr. Pumpernickle stood on the wedding, but Teresa, the mother of the bride, was a huge fan of it and had wanted to be involved from the moment Eddie and Krissie announced their engagement. Unfortunately, her daughter had told her to butt out. Krissie believed that this was her wedding, which of course it was, but she wanted no input on the planning from her mother. As Vianna had discovered, it was Krissie's way or no way. Still, she gladly accepted money from her parents to pay for the wedding of her dreams; it was only their opinions that were not welcome.

"Kelsey," Henry began, in the dour voice I assumed he'd mastered in the courtroom. Outside of a court, it sounded both pretentious and overplayed, but then again, maybe that was the persona that Henry was going for. I wouldn't put it past him. "Kelsey," he repeated, "I assume that you know Mr. and Mrs. Pumpernickle."

I held my hand out to them. "I've met Teresa, yes. Nice to see you again. I'm sorry about what has happened." I found myself apologizing even though Vianna's death wasn't my fault; it was an automatic reaction from years of dealing with the public. Take the blame and they'd get over it faster. Blame them and it would never end.

Teresa took my hand in both of hers. "Isn't it just awful? We so hope that you can help us. If anyone can clean up this mess, it's you."

"This mess? Are you referring to the wedding?" I tried to remove my hand from her grasp, but she held it fast.

"Not just the wedding, although we have every intention of going forward with it despite this complication," Heath Pumpernickle said.

Complication? Was that how Krissie's parents viewed Vianna's death, as a mere complication?

His wife nodded. "Every intention in the world. Eddie is such a wonderful man and a perfect match for our daughter. We want to see them together in wedded bliss."

I wondered if the elder Pumpernickles remembered that Eddie was my husband once upon a time and the father of my only child. Either they'd forgotten or were oblivious to how a comment like that would make me or any reasonable person uncomfortable. Krissie's mother still held tightly to my hands, and I gently yanked them free.

This wasn't a conversation to have in a public place. I glanced around the visitor center. Even though Laura, Judy, and Hayden were the only ones nearby, I thought it would be best to find a more secluded place to talk this over. "Why don't we go somewhere a little more comfortable to discuss this?" I suggested.

I didn't bother waiting for them to agree or disagree as I led them through the glass doors onto the Farm grounds. To the left of the visitor center, there were a number of picnic tables. We usually used them for school groups eating their lunches. I stopped at the first picnic table and gestured for them to take a seat.

Henry arched his brow. "Is this supposed to be more comfortable?"

"It's better than standing," I said. "But if you prefer to stand, that's up to you."

"It's fine," Teresa insisted as she perched on the edge of the picnic bench. Her husband took the seat next to her and looked as if he was about as thrilled with the accommodations as Henry was.

"We may not be able to have the wedding in the church, considering what happened," I began, deciding just to get to the point. "The police don't know when the church will be released."

Teresa covered her mouth with her hand, and her husband shook his head. "Surely, the police will be done cleaning everything up by Friday evening," she said. "It's only Wednesday. I'm certain that by then it will be like nothing ever happened."

Like Vianna never happened.

I swallowed. How terribly sad that this family, who'd been working with Vianna for months, could so easily dismiss the wedding planner now that she was dead and no longer of any use to them.

"There has to be a way the wedding can be in the church." Teresa went on. "People are flying in from all over the country for this wedding, and the church was on the wedding invitation. The wedding has to be at the church."

I winced. "As I said, I don't know if that's possible."

Teresa flattened her hands on the picnic table. "You have to make it possible. There is no other option."

I shifted back in my seat, creating as much distance between Teresa Pumpernickle and myself as was possible, which wasn't much considering we were seated at a picnic table. The picnic table had been a bad idea. "I'm so sorry about this. I'm really am. But I don't know how I can help."

"You can make the police release the church," she said.

I raised my eyebrows at her. "What makes you think I have that kind of power? I can't make the police do anything. They have to follow their procedures and protocols."

She wasn't convinced. "Eddie said you were friends with the police."

I thought of Detective Brandon. I wouldn't call us friends. Then there was Chief Duffy, but he wasn't a friend either—he was Chase's uncle. Eddie had misled her with that statement. The question was, had he misled her accidentally or on purpose?

"I know many of the people on the police force," I said, "but I wouldn't say we're friends. More like tolerable acquaintances. I can't make them do anything."

"Isn't your boyfriend a cop?" Henry jumped into the conversation. His elbows were on the table, and the tips of his fingers were pressed together in a steeple pose. I wasn't sure I'd have seen a steeple in the shape of his hands if it hadn't been for Vianna's fall from the bell tower.

Surprised he knew I was dating anyone at all, I turned to him. I'd certainly never told him about Chase. I reminded myself that New Hartford was small, but still, the thought that Henry was keeping tabs on me—even if his information wasn't accurate—was unsettling. He could have heard this news from any number of sources, of course. The question was whether or not he'd stumbled on the information about me or if he'd been spying.

"Chase is an EMT, not a police officer," I said coldly.

Teresa's face fell so much I almost lost my resolve and offered my help.

"I know the wedding is important, but I think we should all remember that a young woman lost her life last night," I said. "I'm sure she has family that's mourning her."

"Vianna was an only child and both of her parents are dead. She doesn't have any real family to speak of," Henry said, with such certainty that I blinked at him. How would he know this much about the wedding planner?

"And what about our daughter?" Teresa riffled through her tiny purse, came up with a tissue, and dabbed it in the corner of her eye where a tear was threatening to spill over onto her cheek. "She's our only child. You must understand how upset we are, and how we don't want anything to ruin her big day. You have a son."

What was with the Pumpernickle family and laying the mother guilt on me? I stood up. "I'm so sorry. I wish I could help you, but I can't. Chief Duffy is a good man, and Detective Brandon … " I paused, searching for the right word. "Well, she's a smart cop. They'll find out who did this. I have no doubt."

Mr. Pumpernickle slammed his hand on the picnic table top, and the rest of us jumped. "But our daughter has to worry and wait while the bumbling police stumble onto the right conclusion? This is her wedding week. Our blameless princess has to suffer until this detective of yours has it all figured out."

I wouldn't call Krissie a blameless princess, but then again, I wasn't her parent. However much I loved Hayden, I would never call him a blameless prince. I knew what my child was capable of.

I was starting to see why Krissie was the way she was. Spoiled to the tenth degree. If the wedding ever did come to pass, Eddie would be in for a treat farther down the line. I can't say I felt sorry for him.

Krissie's mother had covered her mouth as if I'd sworn in her presence. Her husband took her hand in his and glared at me. "The wedding must go on," he said. "Our princess needs this. She has to have something to look forward to. She's been planning for this wedding for years."

Years? I bit back a smart retort.

"And it has to be here at Barton Farm," his wife added as she touched a tissue to the corner of her eye. "It's Krissie's dream."

"If you insist on going forward with the wedding on Friday, I can agree to that. When Krissie is ready, she can meet with me and I'll show her alternative places on the Farm grounds where we could host the ceremony, just in case we need them. We could even have it here in the visitor center. There's plenty of space."

"No," Mr. Pumpernickle yelled. "It must be in the church, just as the princess wanted it to be."

"I understand that's what Krissie wanted," I said more slowly, hoping that my message would sink in this time. "But unfortunately, that's not my decision. The police closed off the church. It's up to them to reopen it. As much as I want to, I have no authority over the church at the moment. I'm happy to tell Krissie that directly."

"She's not up to it today. She's just devastated by her ordeal last night. Eddie is with her. He's such a thoughtful and loving man," Mrs. Pumpernickle said.

He was a good father. I had to remind myself of that fact often, and much more regularly since I'd been roped in with helping plan his second wedding. Hayden loved Eddie. That was the most important thing. That was the thing that I had to keep telling myself in the midst of this crazy situation, which was becoming crazier by the minute.

Henry folded his hands on the top of the picnic table. "Mr. and Mrs. Pumpernickle," he began. "I can assure you Kelsey will do everything within her power to make your daughter's wedding as beautiful and memorable as she dreamed it would be, because Kelsey knows how important this wedding is to the future of the Cherry Foundation and Barton Farm. I personally will talk to the police chief to find out if we can get this business with the church sorted out."

I opened my mouth, but Henry was faster. "In the meantime, she might just find the person behind this terrible incident." He eyed me. "Finding killers is something she excels at."

THIRTEEN

THE PUMPERNICKLES AND HENRY left soon after that. I sat at the picnic table for a few minutes after they'd gone, gathering my bearings. Henry had trapped me. Game, set, match. If anything, I hated the feeling of being trapped. Whenever I felt trapped, like for example in my marriage, I bolted as fast as I could in the opposite direction. I didn't know how to escape this snare Henry had set and in which I was so deeply entangled, but I would, given time. He couldn't continually threaten the Farm when I balked at doing something. I had to find a way to stop him from using it as a weapon. With the Pumpernickle wedding apparently still just a few days away, time wasn't a commodity I had.

I needed my assistant to back me up on this. I radioed Benji. "Benji, Benji, come in."

There was just enough static on the other end of the radio to make me believe her radio was on. I frowned at the device. Then I remembered Benji's love of the word "over." "Benji, Benji, come in. *Over.*"

Still nothing. I repeated my request, and the radio crackled.

"Kelsey?" It was Jason's voice to come over the radio. His was the last voice I'd expected to respond, considering his aversion to using his own radio. "This is Jason." His voice was tentative, as if he was uncertain even of his own name.

"Jason, is Benji around? She was coming over to the village."

"Yeah," he said. "She's in my trailer now."

This was an unexpected announcement. "In your trailer? Why on earth would she be there?"

Nothing but static came over the radio.

"Jason?" I asked.

He still didn't answer.

"Are you in your trailer?"

"No," he said finally. "Benji is in there."

I felt my forehead wrinkle. I couldn't think of any reason why Benji would go into Jason's trailer. She barely tolerated Jason.

"Can you come here? I think you'll want to." His voice was shaking, but I didn't know if it was his normal nervousness, the police interview, or heightened for some other reason. I knew Jason liked his routine and his privacy—he wouldn't like Benji being in his trailer, but he wouldn't have tried to stop her if she was determined to get inside of it. Not many were about to stop Benji when she made up her mind, myself included.

"I'm on my way." I hooked the radio back onto my belt and jogged in the direction of the village. My head felt the jarring of my footsteps every time my sneaker hit the pebbled path. If any day was destined to give me a migraine, it was today. We still had time before opening; hopefully, I could discover what was going on with my assistant before the visitors arrived.

As callus as it felt, considering Vianna's death, I had to get a jump on Krissie's wedding, which now lay more heavily on my shoulders than ever. I needed to find out if Piper knew all the arrangements for the wedding.

I reached the village in time to see Detective Brandon on the green, crossing the crime scene tape with several other cops and entering the church. I was dying to see the interior of the church myself. I hoped there wasn't damage to the historic building beyond the broken window in the bell tower.

Assessing the damage would have to wait, though. I needed to know what was going on with Benji at Jason's trailer.

I followed the path behind the large barn and through the trees to where the trailer was located. The mobile structure was set far enough back that unsuspecting Farm visitors could never guess that there was a twenty-first-century trailer by this nineteenth-century village. It had been a battle to convince the Cherry Foundation board to allow the trailer to be placed near the village. But Jason had been living on the Farm grounds long before I knew about it. Homeless, he secretly slept in the barn with the oxen and sheep every night. When I discovered this and learned his story, I did what I could to give him a home on the Farm. Henry Ratcliffe had not been amused. Despite working for a nonprofit, Henry wasn't much for charity.

Jason was pacing back and forth in front of his trailer, giving it furtive glances. His long thin limbs swung back and forth with every stride. When he saw me, his shoulders slumped in relief.

"Where's Benji?" I asked, without a greeting.

He pointed at the trailer.

Remembering my manners, I asked, "Are you okay? Sorry about the police interview. You look a little wired."

"A little wired" was putting it mildly. The skin across Jason's thin face was tight, and he looked like he wanted to bolt. I knew that he didn't like people in his personal space, but his visceral reaction to Benji in the trailer seemed a tad extreme even to me, and I was accustomed to his antics.

Jason licked his lips. "It's fine. But Benji won't let me in."

I frowned at the trailer. "Did she say why not? Did she say why she went in there in the first place?"

He shook his head. "She's not alone," he whispered.

"How do you know that?" I studied his narrow face.

"I heard a voice, and it wasn't hers. Someone else is in there." He dropped his gaze to the ground.

My brows shot up in surprise, and I realized that this was what was making him so visibly nervous. "Who's in there with her?"

Jason shook his head. I didn't know if that meant he didn't know the answer or just refused to tell me. I reminded myself I needed to be patient with my farmhand, and the fact that he'd told me on the radio that Benji was there was a big step in the right direction. Little by little, I was earning his trust. It wasn't a good idea to throw it away now just for a little information.

I tried a different question. "Have you been inside?"

He shrugged.

I sighed, knowing I'd gotten just about all I could out of him. "Thanks for answering the radio."

There was only one way to find out who was inside the trailer with Benji, and that was to go inside myself. I didn't have time to waste asking Jason what was going on when he clearly didn't know or wouldn't say.

I knocked on the trailer door. There was no answer. The door was cracked ever so slightly. I pushed lightly on it, and it opened inward. I stepped inside. The room smelled like clean hay and soap.

As usual, Jason's trailer was as neat as a pin. He was fanatical about keeping everything in its place. I'd known him to straighten books that sat askew on the counter at the visitor center, on the rare occasions that he was inside that building, which never happened when there were actual guests on the farm. Jason disliked the visitors to the Farm as much as Shepley did. However, while Shepley's dislike stemmed from disgust, Jason's stemmed from fear and uncertainty.

Benji was sitting on the edge of Jason's neatly made bed, next to a girl with blond hair highlighted with blue streaks. I immediately recognized Piper, Vianna's intern. A thought hit me while looking at the girl—would Vianna still be alive if I'd said yes to her putting lights on the church steeple? If I had, she wouldn't have been up there in the middle of the night. I swallowed and pushed the thought aside. I didn't kill Vianna. It wasn't my fault. At least, that was what I tried to tell myself.

Piper wore a yellow dress with white birds printed all over it. She held onto Benji's hand as if her life depended on it. Large tears slid down her pale cheeks.

I looked from Benji to Piper and back again. Throughout the four months I'd worked on Krissie and Eddie's wedding, Vianna, Piper, and Benji had been together many times in the planning process. In all that time, I'd never seen Piper and Benji so much as nod at each other, and here they were sitting on Jason's bed holding hands.

"What are you doing in here?" The question was more direct that I intended it to be.

"Kelsey, we need your help," Benji said. She leaned forward but didn't release Piper's hand.

It seemed that a lot of people needed my help as of late.

I raised my eyebrows. "We?" I tried not to stare at their intertwined fingers as I asked this.

Benji stared at me with her big brown eyes. "The police think Piper killed Vianna. You have to prove to them that she didn't kill her boss." The words came out in a breathless rush.

My eyes fell to their hands. I couldn't help it. "Do you two know each other? I mean, I know that you know each other, but ..." I trailed off.

Piper removed her hand from Benji and folded it with her other hand on her lap.

Benji glanced at her with such concern and tenderness I immediately understood their relationship before Benji spoke.

"Piper and I are together."

My mouth fell open, even though what she said only confirmed what I knew to be true. I wasn't so much surprised that Benji had a girlfriend; I knew she was gay. Everyone on the Farm knew. It wasn't a secret, and I wouldn't want it to be. What made Benji's pronouncement so shocking was that *Piper* was her girlfriend.

"How long have you been dating?" I asked. Again, the question popped out of my mouth sounding blunter than I wanted it to.

Benji met my eyes. "Six months."

I stared at her. I was her boss, but I also thought I was her friend, a close friend. I thought she would have told me about her girlfriend. She'd always told me about her past relationships.

Piper smoothed the skirt of her yellow dress. "You're probably wondering why you didn't know about us. I know you and B are close."

B? I'd never heard Benji called anything other than her given name. "We are," I said.

Piper tucked a blue strand of hair behind her ear. "I asked her not to tell you."

I raised my eyebrows. "I don't have anything against Benji being in a relationship with whoever she wants."

"She knows that," Benji interjected. "I told her that."

"Then ..." I trailed off. I couldn't think of any reason Benji would want or need to keep this relationship from me.

"It all had to do with me," Piper said, sitting up a little straighter. "I asked her to keep it quiet in general until this wedding was over. I was afraid of how Vianna would react. She was very strict about not mixing work with pleasure. She wouldn't do it, and she wouldn't want anyone who worked for her to do it. My internship isn't paid, but Vianna was the best-known wedding planner in the area. If I interned for her for a year, I could take my pick of wedding planning jobs in the state. She was that good. Everyone wanted her to plan their wedding because she was so fully committed. Everything was about the weddings that she was working on." She gave me a half smile. "You might have noticed that."

"I noticed," I said, thinking of how obsessed Vianna had been with Krissie's wedding. "But if you two have been dating for six months, that would go all the way back to January. I didn't start working on the wedding with Vianna until the end of March."

Benji stood up and began to pace the trailer. There wasn't much room for it. Piper pulled her legs up onto Jason's bed so that Benji could pass, and I pressed my body back against the tiny kitchen counter.

Benji marched past me and said, "It wasn't until Piper started coming to the Farm on a regular basis that we got serious. Up until then it was more just hanging out."

"Okay, fine," I said. "The two of you are together, and now I know why I didn't know before. It's fine." I turned to Benji, who'd reached the end of the trailer and did an about-face coming back the other way. I stepped in her path. "I just want you to be happy."

Benji stopped midstride. "I know that, and one way you can make sure I'm happy is to help keep Piper from going to prison."

I turned my attention back to Piper, who remained crossed-legged in the middle of the single bed with her skirt spread over her legs like she was at a Sunday afternoon picnic, not sitting in my farm-hand's trailer talking about secret relationships and murder. "Okay, tell me why the police suspect you."

"I'm her intern," Piper said. "I know everything about her business. Of course they would look at me."

I shook my head. "There has to be more to it than that. Vianna had a lot of people working for her. They might all be a suspect to some extent, but something tells me the two of you are worried about this for more than one reason."

Neither of them said a word, so I tried to change my line of questioning. "How did you end up here in Jason's trailer in the first place? Seems an odd place for a meeting."

Piper took a deep breath. "The police questioned me at my apartment first thing this morning, and I knew that I needed to see Benji. I know I shouldn't have come here. I tried to stay away, but I needed to see her…" She trailed off.

"She texted me while I was keeping an eye on Barn Boy during the police interview." Benji perched on the edge of Jason's bed again and Piper patted her back.

I gave her a look.

Benji rolled her eyes. "Okay, keeping an eye on *Jason*. The detective interviewed him near the barn. It didn't take long. I asked Piper to meet me at Barn Boy—*Jason's*—trailer because it's out of the line of sight."

"The police questioned you this morning?" I asked Piper.

She nodded. "By the time they left, I was half convinced I'd killed Vianna."

"Who was the officer who interviewed you?" I asked, even though I knew very well who it was, having been interviewed by Brandon many times myself—and every time, she'd tried to convince me I was guilty even when I knew perfectly well that I wasn't.

"Detective Brandon," Piper answered, as I expected her to.

"Do you have an alibi for the night of the murder? A roommate or someone who can vouch for your whereabouts?" I glanced at Benji. "Were you together?"

Both shook their heads.

"I was at my parents' house last night. I went straight there after I left work," Benji said. "My brother was home and Mom wanted us to have some family time."

Piper looked down at her hands clasped on top of her skirt.

Benji touched her shoulder. "Tell her."

Piper looked at Benji with her big brown eyes, and then at me. "I was here last night. That person who you chased into the woods—that was me."

FOURTEEN

I BLINKED AT HER. "You? You were the person inside the church? The person who ran away from the scene of the crime?"

She nodded, and a tear rolled down her cheek. "I was, but I didn't kill her. I swear."

I pushed off of the counter. "And the police know this? You told them?"

"I didn't tell them." She wrung her hands. "That's the worst part."

"Why does it make it worse?"

"Because the detective knew." She sniffled, and Benji wrapped an arm around her shoulders.

"How?" I began to pace.

She gripped her hands together so tightly that the knuckles turned white. "They found the tracks I made and matched them to the boots I was wearing last night. When the police came to my apartment, those same boots were sitting just inside of the door covered in mud. I never thought I would have to hide them. I wasn't thinking of that at all when I ran away from the Farm. I just knew that I wanted to get away from there as fast as possible."

I winced. Physical evidence putting Piper at the scene of the crime and proving that she fled the scene wasn't good news for her, not in the least little bit. "You saw Vianna fall?"

She blinked tears away. "No. I didn't see anything because I was late getting to the church. By the time I got there, Vianna was already in the bell tower. I was debating whether I should go up and help her when I heard her fall."

"Debating?" I asked.

Piper nodded. "I knew she would be furious at me for being so late. Vianna was very punctual. If she said that she was going to be somewhere at a certain time, she was going to be there no matter what. She expected it from her staff too."

I considered this. I suspected that Piper was probably right about Vianna being angry with her, but still, that wasn't a motive for murder. "Why would the police think you'd want to hurt Vianna?" I asked.

"I didn't do it." Piper shook her head for emphasis.

I held up a hand. "I know that, but there has to be a motive the police are going to use to argue you're the killer."

She shook her head.

"There must be a motive," I repeated quietly.

She licked her lips. "It might be the fact that I've gone to jail before."

I stared at her a second time, completely caught off guard by this answer. Here was this beautiful girl, whom Benji obviously adored, and she was telling me she was a murder suspect with a record. It did not compute. "Come again?" I asked, with the hope that I'd misheard her.

"I've been to jail before." Her voice was low.

"For what?" I asked.

She shook her head. "That isn't important."

I folded my arms and stared at the two girls. "I think it's very important. What sent you to jail?"

She winced.

"That's in the past," Benji said. "It has nothing to do with what's going on now."

I disagreed, but I let it slide for the moment. "Okay, say you went to jail for *something*. Why would you kill Vianna? Did she know what it was?"

Piper squirmed on the bed, mussing the bedspread. Jason was going to have a fit when he saw that his bed was disturbed. She nodded and looked at her hands.

Benji looked at her girlfriend and seemed to come to a decision to take over the talking for her. "The police believe that Piper killed Vianna because Vianna knew about her past crime and used it as a weapon against her, to keep her in line and loyal."

"It isn't completely untrue," Piper said, not looking up from her hands. "I didn't kill Vianna, but she wasn't above throwing my arrest in my face whenever it suited her. I told myself that it didn't bother me. I just needed to make it through this year, and then I would be rid of her forever."

"The police believe," Benji continued, "that Piper couldn't take Vianna's threats to expose her anymore and snapped while they were hanging those lights in the steeple. They believe that she pushed Vianna through the window in a fit of rage."

I nodded. "So you have motive, means, and the opportunity to commit the murder, but that doesn't explain why you're here right now. Why haven't the police arrested you already?"

"The detective said I wasn't allowed to leave the area." Piper brushed a tear away from her cheek. "I don't even know why she bothered to tell me that. I don't have anywhere else to go. Everyone I know lives in New Hartford, and Benji is here."

I thought of something for the first time. "Do the police know about the two of you?" I waved my hand back and forth to include both of them in my question.

Piper shook her head. "I didn't say anything about Benji."

"I never talk to the police if I can avoid it," Benji said. This much I knew. Benji didn't care for Detective Brandon, although I suspected that was out of loyalty to me more than due to any other factor.

I frowned, thinking there had to be a piece missing to the puzzle. What would stop Brandon from arresting Piper? I'd known her to arrest people on far less. I wondered if after those past mistakes, she was being very cautious about this case, but that was hard to believe. Being cautious wasn't part of Brandon's style.

Bang bang bang! There was a harsh knock on the trailer door. "Kelsey!" Detective Brandon called. "I need to talk to you."

Piper's mouth fell open.

"What are we going to do?" Benji asked as her eyes traveled around the trailer. She was looking for a place to hide. The only option was the tiny bathroom, but I knew Brandon would look there if she was the least bit suspicious that someone else was in the trailer with me.

I pushed off of the counter. "I'll talk to her. You two stay here and leave when the coast is clear."

"Are you going to help us?" Benji asked. Her dark eyes were huge and pleaded with me. "Can you help us?"

Another plea for help to solve this case, but unlike the pleas that Eddie and the Pumpernickles made, my son was not a bargaining chip in this one. Benji was asking as my friend. It was a plea I couldn't refuse. "Okay," I whispered.

Tears gathered in the corners of Benji's eyes. She looked as if she wanted to say something, but there was no time. We would have plenty of time later, and I would talk to the girls again. I needed more details about Piper's past crime.

"Cambridge, come out here or I'm coming in," Brandon shouted at top voice.

I heard her hand on the door handle. The trailer wasn't locked. All the detective needed to do was step inside the trailer and she'd see Piper there with Benji and me. Until I sorted out Piper's involvement with the murder, I couldn't let that happen.

"I'll do what I can," I said.

Benji hopped off the bed and hugged me. "Thank you, Kelsey. I'm so glad you're my boss." She met my eyes. "And my friend. I'm more grateful that you're my friend."

"I'm glad you're my friend too." I hugged her back.

I shooed the girls back to the far end of the trailer, so that they wouldn't be seen when I opened the door. When I thought they were far enough back, I opened the door and found Brandon on the top step. I blocked the doorway with my body, even though it was extremely uncomfortable to be that close to the police detective.

"Are you going to let me out of the trailer, Detective? I thought you wanted to talk to me."

Behind her, I saw Jason standing on the path halfway between the trailer and the barn. It was as if he wasn't sure whether he should run to help me or run away. The fact that he was torn by the choice showed how much progress he'd made in the last year. A year ago, he would have fled without a backward glance at me.

"What are you doing in there?" Brandon's tone was sharp.

It was a fair question, but I knew, since it was coming from the detective, I needed to come up with a satisfactory answer and quick.

"I'm happy to tell you if you'll let me out of the trailer." I stared down at her. For once I had the height advantage on her.

She stared at me for a moment, but finally backed up and let me step out. I hopped down the two steps to the ground, and again I was significantly shorter than the detective. I missed the height the trailer had given me.

The door slammed closed after me. I glanced at Jason, who remained frozen on the path leading to the barn. "I was just doing an inspection of Jason's trailer," I said. "I do periodical inspections, and he knows they're a stipulation for him to live on Farm land."

She raised her brow at me. "And you had to do that today, the day after someone was murdered at Barton Farm?" She folded her arms across her ample chest, which her oversized clothes were unable to hide, and rocked back on the heels of her plain black cop shoes. "Or are you getting so used to people dying at the Farm that it's just business as usual?"

I ground my teeth. I would never get used anyone dying, and certainly not anyone dying on my Farm. "I saw that the officers around the church were occupied, so I came over here to check on

Jason after his interview and pass the time until the church is secure." I eyed her. "I thought it was best to stay out of the way of the investigation."

She snorted at this. I can't say that I blamed her for that.

She pointed at the trailer "You were in there alone?"

"As you can see, Jason is out here." I gestured over her shoulder at my farmhand. "There isn't anyone else who would go inside his trailer."

"Is he the only one who goes in there?" she asked.

"Jason likes his privacy."

She looked like she wanted to continue this line of questioning. It was time to change the subject. "How is the investigation coming?" I asked.

She was quiet for a moment, and I thought that she wasn't going to answer me. Finally, she said, "We'll have this case wrapped up soon. I have a very strong suspect in my sights."

"Krissie?" I asked, sounding a little too hopeful. I didn't want Krissie to be a murderess, but I'd much rather it be her than Piper. Besides, Krissie would be ruling the inmates by the end of her sentence.

Brandon frowned. "Krissie Pumpernickle is, of course, a suspect, as I told you before."

"Are you ready to tell me who the other suspects are?" I waited for her to reveal Piper's name.

The detective simply smiled in return, letting me know that this line of questioning was a waste of time.

I stepped around her and started walking toward the village. "Why don't you show me the crime scene area around the church, so that I know for certain where the tourists are and are not allowed to go?"

"In a minute." Detective Brandon jumped up the trailer's two steps.

I realized it had been a miscalculation to move out of her way. The detective threw open the trailer door and shouted, "Ah ha!"

I winced, half expecting to hear Piper and Benji's surprised screams. No sound came, and Brandon disappeared inside of the trailer.

I ran into the trailer after her. It was empty. The girls were gone.

At the back end of the trailer, there was a small, open window. The plain white curtain that covered it fluttered in the breeze.

FIFTEEN

With much reluctance, Detective Brandon stepped out of the trailer. I waited for her with a bright smile on my face. I didn't know how the girls had fit through that window, but somehow they'd shimmied through it. Benji would tell me about their escape later whether she liked it or not. She owed me that much.

The detective grunted at me as we made our way down the path. I noticed that Jason had slipped away while Brandon searched his tiny home from top to bottom. Since she didn't know that Piper and Benji had been in there, I wasn't sure what she'd been looking for. I suspected that she'd insisted on searching it in order to annoy me more than for any other reason.

I broke the silence. "Is there any chance that the church will be reopened in time for the wedding ceremony on Friday?"

She scowled at me, and I took that as a no. At least now I could tell Henry and the Pumpernickles that I tried to use my influence on the police and failed.

We came out of the woods, and the church's signature white steeple stood out against the bright blue sky. From my vantage point north of the building, I couldn't see where Vianna had broken through the south-facing window and fallen to her death on the stone walkway below. From my spot, the church looked peaceful, perfect, and pristine. No one would ever think anyone could be killed there, but Vianna had been.

I wondered what it was like for her the night she died. Had she known that she was in danger? If so, why did she go to the church alone to hang the lights? But I corrected my thoughts; Vianna hadn't planned to be alone. Piper was supposed to meet her there.

But what had Vianna been thinking, anyway? Did she think I wouldn't notice dozens of twinkle lights hanging from the church steeple the next morning? Or that if I noticed, that I would let it go and not insist she take them down immediately? If she thought that, she didn't know me very well. Then again, I hadn't really known her either. She'd been a mild annoyance in my life, a messenger from Krissie, one of Krissie's minions. No more, no less, and now she was dead. There was no chance of knowing her anymore.

I followed the lines of the church upward from its foundation to the steeple. In my mind's eye, I watched Vianna hang lights inside. She would be nervous because she knew that she didn't have my permission to do it, but she was much more afraid of Krissie Pumpernickle—and what the outspoken bride could do to her and her reputation as a wedding planner—than she was of my silly rules.

Then I remembered another shadow—the one I'd seen in the window of the steeple. Piper said she'd never gone up into the bell tower … which meant that someone other than Piper must have been in the church that night. Again in my mind, I saw a dark shape move up the winding stairs to the balcony, where there was a ladder that led up into the bell tower. The inky shadow snuck up on Vianna and pushed her toward the window with such force that she broke through the wooden slats and fell to her death.

I shivered. I wasn't usually one who had visions or fantastical thoughts. However, the images in my head were so real, I could have sworn it was how it happened. But even if I said "yes, this is what happened to cause Vianna's death," it still didn't mean I knew who that shadow or killer was. The only candidate was Piper. She was the only one I *knew* was at the church. Had she seen the shadow in the tower? Or, even worse, had she been that shadow after all?

I followed Brandon around the side of the church with these troubling thoughts in my head. Yellow crime scene tape ran across the church's front door in a large X, and crime scene techs with lab kits and equipment ducked under the tape as they made their way in and out of the church.

Despite trying not to look, my eyes fell to the spot where I'd first seen Vianna's broken body. Vianna was gone. She'd been whisked away in the night by the medical examiner's office. The shards of wood from the window had also been picked up.

I stared up at the broken window. The police had removed the frame of the window itself. I guessed they planned to take it back to the lab and test it for fingerprints and other CSI-like tests. I would have to do something about the opening as soon as the police would allow it. If not, rain, wind, and critters could enter the church and damage it. I wouldn't allow the church—the over-two-hundred-year-old building—to come tumbling to the ground on my watch.

"Like I said," Brandon began, as if reading my thoughts, "the church is off-limits. The crime scene techs will be just about done inside." She checked the time on her cell phone. "You still have forty-five minutes before the Farm opens. They'll be long gone by then."

"Is the church the only place we can't access? What about in front, where…" I couldn't finish the statement. It seemed too callous to ask, but I did need to know if I had to block off a certain area of the pebbled path from tourists.

"We've gathered the evidence we need from the location where she landed," the detective said.

I nodded. "Was that all? Is there anything else I need to know?"

Brandon looked down at me, and not for the first time, I regretted being so much shorter than her. I wished just once I could look her in the eye and show her that she couldn't intimidate me.

"One more thing. You said that Eddie, and also Krissie's parents, came to the Farm to talk to you about Krissie's situation. Why? It seems strange to me they came to you when you're Eddie's ex-wife."

"They thought I had some pull with the police."

Detective Brandon bent over in laughter. She placed both hands on her knees for support.

I scowled at her. "I'm glad you find that so amusing."

Still bent at the waist, she waved at me with her right hand. She was unable to speak.

"Are you done?" I asked in a deadpanned voice.

She straightened up, but one final chuckle escaped her lips. "I—I think I'm done," she gasped.

"Don't worry, Detective," I said. "I told them that I don't have any pull with the police. In fact, I have no interest in helping Krissie Pumpernickle's cause. I don't care how many ways her parents or my ex-husband ask for my help."

She relaxed. "I'm glad to hear that, because I've lost all patience with your meddling in my investigations. Do you understand me?" All the humor had left her face.

I ground my teeth and took a step back. "Just focus on finding out who did this, Detective Brandon, and don't worry about me. I'm here to run the Farm. Nothing else."

"Make sure that it stays that way," she said. She spun on her heel and marched in the direction of the visitor center.

I could still see her stomping down the pebbled path when my cell phone rang. I pulled it from the back pocket of my jeans and was startled to see that it was Eddie. Eddie never called me. Ever. He was more comfortable with email or texts. In fact, he told me he was marrying Krissie in a mass email. Our communication was best in written form. If it wasn't for the advent of texting, I doubted I would ever know where or when he planned to pick up or drop off Hayden.

Then again, it was out of character for Eddie to drop by in the middle of the night asking for my help. I had a feeling this call was going to be in the same vein. I put the phone to my ear. "Eddie?"

"Kelsey! Thank God I caught you. I need a favor," Eddie said.

He was nothing if not predictable.

I held the phone away from my ear for a moment and stared at it. It seemed that I was the granter of favors for so many people as of late. I put the phone back up to my ear. "You mean, you need another favor, other than the keep-my-fiancé-out-of-prison favor?"

He sighed as if he knew I wasn't going to make this easy for him. And I wouldn't. I'd stopped making things easy for Eddie the moment I found out about his affair.

"It's the florist," he said.

I frowned. "What about the florist?"

"We need to make sure he gets the flower order correct. Vianna was supposed to do that."

"Then call him," I said.

There was a long pause, and I heard whispering. I was willing to bet Krissie was in the room with him, coaching him on what to say in order to convince me to do her bidding. She was a determined woman, I would give her that. The whispering continued.

"We'd like you to meet with the florist to go over the flowers. There's been some mistake, and last we heard, he'd included carnations in our order. Krissie hates carnations. You were working with Vianna, so you know Krissie's vision for the wedding."

I rolled my eyes. "I know this is hard for you to understand, Eddie, but I have a job. There are many things I do at Barton Farm that have nothing to do with your wedding. I can't just up and leave the Farm in the middle of the high season to talk to your florist, especially when I suspect that Krissie or *you* are more than capable of doing it."

"She really wants you to do it," he said in a voice that was one short step away from whining.

"I'm sorry to hear that, because it's not going to happen. If that's all," I said, "I have work to do."

"But—"

I interrupted him, "If she's not up to it, can't her parents do it? I think her mother is more than eager to help."

There was a squeal of rage on the other end of the line that I suspected came from Eddie's betrothed. It was either that or they'd recently adopted a cat with adjustment issues. Hayden would have told me if his father had gotten a pet, so my money was on Krissie.

"No!" Eddie shouted. "You know Krissie doesn't want her parents involved in any of the wedding planning."

She was happy to ask them to pay for everything, of course.

I was tempted to point out the ludicrous nature of Krissie's request. Um, hello, I was the ex-wife! But if I went that route, she and Eddie were likely to try some dysfunctional family card or, worse, to threaten me about Hayden. As much as I hated to admit it, when it came to those two, I was stuck. At least for the next twelve years, or possibly sixteen, when my son would graduate college. I reined in my racing thoughts.

I took a deep breath. "Eddie, this is your fiancé's big day." Gag. "Surely she wants to take control of the details. It's her wedding."

"Can you go over to the florist's shop and talk to him?" Eddie was talking right over me, sounding desperate with concern. "Please. I'm so worried about Krissie."

I frowned. If Eddie had shown half the concern for me when we were married as he did for Krissie, we might still have been together. But as this thought crossed my mind, I realized that it wasn't what I'd have wanted. There was a good chance that even if Eddie hadn't had an affair, we'd still have divorced. We were different people now than when we'd met as children, and we needed different things out of life. I wasn't going to hold it against him that he found Krissie, who he seemed to be happy with, but at the same time, I wasn't going to be talking to the florist. I had a Farm to run.

"I know you're worried about Krissie," I began, a little more gently this time. "But that doesn't change anything. I can't go. It's that simple."

"You're the only one we trust to do it."

"You've got to be kidding me. Your ex-wife is the only one you trust to plan your wedding with your next wife? Do you realize how ridiculous that sounds?"

"I'm not kidding you. Krissie just left the room," he added in a low voice. "You're the only one that I trust to handle things, Kel. We know you're the best person for the job. Please do this one last thing for me. I'll never ask for another favor."

I was fairly certain that anyone who says "I'll never ask for another favor" is a liar. If Eddie was the one who was saying it, I knew for sure he was lying.

I could feel myself beginning to give in, but I did my best to hold my ground. "Eddie, I can't go talk to your florist. The Farm is about to open, and we have a crisis on our hands. It's important that I be here to greet the guests and make sure that everything goes smoothly."

There was a scuffling sound on the other end of the line, and I guessed that Krissie had reentered the room.

"Kelsey," Krissie said in my ear. "It's of the utmost importance that you go. If the flowers fall apart, the wedding will be ruined. They have to be perfect."

I'd have thought the wedding was ruined when the wedding planner tumbled to her death from the steeple of the church where the ceremony was to take place, but that was just me.

"Oh, hello, Krissie. How are you holding up?" Maybe small talk would distract her.

Sniffle. "Not well. I can't tell you what a horrible experience this has been for me. The police don't care about my fragile state. I'm the bride and should be treated with respect and kindness. All they've managed to do is make accusations and threaten to cancel my wedding. They can't do that to me. It's my wedding week!" Her voice became shrill at the end.

I couldn't help but enjoy it just a little that Krissie was getting the Detective Brandon treatment. It was nice that someone other than me was on Brandon's receiving end for a change.

"I'm so sorry to hear that," I managed, without one iota of laughter in my voice. I was extremely proud of that. "But as I told Eddie, I can't go and see the florist. The Farm is going to open in a short while and I need to be here."

"Kelsey, he's using carnations. Carnations! The wedding is Friday. I cannot have carnations. There's no way I'll be able to find a new florist on such short notice or one who's willing to make the bouquets how I want them."

With my free hand, I rubbed the spot just between my eyes to hold off a headache. It was a futile attempt. The headache was there to stay. I decided that it might be Krissie's voice that triggered it, because I always seemed to have one whenever she was speaking.

While I was on the phone, I saw Benji and Piper dash out of the woods. I wanted to wave and call out to them that everything would be okay. I didn't, because even though the detective was gone, I didn't want to draw any of the crime scene techs' attention to them.

"If you don't go," Krissie was saying in a low voice, "you leave me no choice but to call Henry Ratcliffe and tell him you're not cooperating with planning the wedding as you promised you would."

I groaned inwardly. Sure, she'd hate doing that. Not. Krissie would love every last second of throwing me under the bus. In fact, I wouldn't be surprised if she volunteered to drive the bus so she could run it over me. Twice.

Idly, I wondered where Piper and Benji were headed now. Technically, Benji was still on the clock, but I would let it slide under the circumstances. Heaven knows she'd picked up my slack many times when I'd had emergencies of my own.

I had agreed to help the girls, and I knew the florist and Vianna had worked together quite often. I thought of Piper and Benji. I sighed. Who was I kidding? I was going to go.

I stifled yet another sigh and said, "There's no reason to go to Henry. I'll go see the florist. I just need to make sure everything is settled for the Farm today, and then I'll head out."

"Armin will be happy to see you," she said, relieved.

I didn't know about that. Armin Coates and I had worked together many times before, and I'd say that at best my working relationship with the volatile man was cordial, and that was pushing it. New Hartford was small, so I didn't have many options for florists for special Farm events, and Armin did nine out of every ten weddings held at the Farm. Armin and I had a long history of our own.

"And thank you, Kelsey," Krissie added breathlessly. "This means so much to me. You know, after the wedding we'll be sisters in way. One big happy family."

I stopped just short of gagging. We would not be sisters. The thought made me queasy.

Eddie was back on the line. "I'll email you the changes Krissie would like made to the flower arrangements, to replace the carnations. You'll have it on your phone before you reach the car."

Armin was going to love this. I wasn't looking forward to my conversation with the florist.

Somehow, I'd once again ended up doing Krissie's bidding even when I was determined not to. My backbone wasn't nearly as strong as I thought it was.

SIXTEEN

JUDY SHOOK HER HEAD as I unhooked my radio from my belt loop and handed it to her. "I think this a terrible idea, Kelsey. An absolutely terrible idea. You shouldn't become any more tied up in this mess than you already are." Her scowl deepened. There wasn't any love lost between Judy and Eddie, or between Eddie and any of the Farm staffers. It was nice to know that my employees had my back.

I held the radio out to her. "Here. Since Benji and I are both off-site, you'll be the main contact if anything happens at the Farm."

Her brow furrowed. "Where's Benji? Isn't she supposed to be here?"

"She had a family emergency," I said.

Judy put one hand on her ample hip. "A family emergency? I saw her mother this morning at the grocery store, and she said nothing about it."

"I think it came up rather suddenly." I hated to lie to Judy, but I thought the less talk about Piper around the Farm the better, until things became clearer.

"I wished Gavin was still around to help out."

I nodded. "Me too." Gavin had been Barton Farm's director of education. He'd resigned right before the season began this year, taking a job at a large museum in Michigan. I knew it was the best thing for him—he'd had a tough winter, caught up in a bad relationship and a murder. He needed to escape. However, his absence left me in a tight spot, as Judy was the only year-round employee onsite whenever Benji or I left the grounds. Everyone else on staff was seasonal.

"Why don't you radio Laura and ask her to come to the visitor center to help out," I said.

"She'll want to know why," Judy said with an arched brow.

"Tell her I'll fill her in with everything else as soon as I can," I replied.

Judy pursed her lips and finally took the radio from my outstretched hand.

I smiled at her. "It should be a quiet day. It's a weekday and we don't have any special programs going on."

"Except for the police crawling all over the village." Judy sniffed. "It should be quite a show for the tourists." She patted me on the arm. "Don't worry, Kelsey. I'll take care of everything. I still think me being in charge is a ridiculous idea, but do what you have to do."

She hooked the radio onto the waistband on her skirt—a khaki one, of course. I figured Judy must have stock in khaki. I'd never seen her in anything else. And nine times out of the ten, the khaki was a skirt that fell to the top of her shoes. In a way, she looked almost Amish, with her long skirt and hair in a bun. I knew she wasn't and never had been. Her look did add to the ambience in the visitor center.

"Thanks. I think." I smiled at her. "If anything comes up, call me. I'll just be in town. I doubt that this will take too long." I glanced inside the gift shop, where Hayden was helping one of the gift shop workers stock the shelves. I frowned.

Judy smoothed the front of her skirt. "Don't worry about Hayden. We'll keep him occupied until his grandfather gets here in a little while."

I nodded. "Dad should be back from his tour sometime this afternoon."

Judy smiled. "I'm sure he'll have many stories to tell."

"Without a doubt." I waved goodbye to her and went out the visitor center's front door.

The drive to downtown New Hartford took all of fifteen minutes. The town had been established in 1806, shortly after the Barton family arrived and started Barton Farm. Like many of the settlements in the northeastern region of Ohio, New Hartford was settled by people from Connecticut looking for new land and new opportunities in Ohio's Western Reserve. Because of that, it had been named after Hartford, Connecticut. Like other towns in the area, it had a central square that was actually shaped like a circle. The green space had shops and small businesses all around it.

I drove around the square and took the branch that led out onto Miller Street, where Coates Flowers was located in a flat-faced stone building with a bright blue front door. There was a diagonal parking space near the door, and I took it. I hesitated before getting out of the car. I was willing to bet that Armin would not be happy to see me.

I gave myself a little pep talk, got out of the car, and had just walked around it and stepped onto the curb when the blue door burst open and a young man in an apron came flying out of it. He stumbled on the walk.

Armin Coates's large form filled the doorway, and he glowered at the boy. At shoulder level, he held a large sunflower head the size of a football.

The young man turned, ran in place for a second as if he were winding up his legs, and fled down the street.

"And don't ever come back!" Armin yelled as he threw the sunflower in the boy's direction, which unfortunately was also my direction.

The large blossom bounced off the side of my car and exploded. My car had been sunflowered. The color of the yellow petals smeared across the door. I didn't think there was any way I could recover from this insult.

"You will be sorry!" Armin then let out a string of what I could only assume were German curse words. Whatever Armin was saying, it sounded bad, and if I were that kid who was now breaking the sound barrier to run up the street and escape the giant German florist, I would get the heck out of there too.

I watched as the young man turned the corner and disappeared.

"Don't come back!" Armin yelled in English.

I considered that an unnecessary parting shot. There was no way that kid was coming back.

I also knew this wasn't the best time to talk to the man about the wedding flowers. Maybe I'd make a quiet retreat and come back later in the afternoon when he'd had a chance to cool down.

"Kelsey Cambridge," Armin said with a curl to his lip. "What are you doing off that Farm of yours? Have you all learned to use electricity yet over there?"

I frowned at him. So much for making a quiet retreat. I straightened my shoulders and walked toward the building. "Can we talk for a minute?"

He scowled down at me. Armin Coates was a huge man in every sense of the word. He must have been at least six five, maybe even taller, and he weighed well over three hundred pounds. He had the booming voice and personality to match his physical size. Not many people messed with Armin, but I wasn't many people. I wasn't going to let my diminutive size allow me to be pushed around by a giant.

"Are you here about the wedding, Cambridge?" he snapped. "I'm a very busy man. I don't have time for your Farm's little problems." His form filled the doorway. I didn't think even Frankie could have slipped into the building around him.

I arched my brow and looked up at him, refusing to back down. "My Farm's little problems? The Pumpernickle wedding is your little problem too."

"Not interested." He stepped back into the building and made a move to slam the door shut.

I took a step closer. "Do you know about Vianna?"

He froze and looked over his shoulder with a surprisingly pained expression on his wide face. There had been a rumor in town that Armin had an unrequited crush on the wedding planner, and I realized that this rumor, unlike so many others that flew around New Hartford, might actually be true.

"I heard she died in an accident, but not the particulars," he said finally. He made no move to close the door.

I grimaced. So Armin didn't know the how, why, or where. I thought it best not to fill him in on the location until I got a little more information from him.

"I heard the same," I said vaguely. "And I need to talk to you."

He met my eyes. "About Vianna?"

"Among other things, yes."

He scowled down at me.

"Armin, come on. You sunflowered my car. Give me a few minutes of your time."

His steely gray eyes fell on my car and the sunflower bits and seeds that were scattered about the sidewalk. It wasn't a pretty scene. "You're lucky I didn't throw a planter. If I had, it would have left a dent in the side of your car."

I didn't feel lucky, so I would take his word for it on that one. "Are you going to let me inside?"

"Fine," he said, but it came out as a combination of a grunt and a growl. He walked through the door and left it open for me. As I stepped over the threshold, I had the sinking feeling that I was a fly who'd just stumbled upon a spider's web.

The blue door opened into a small showroom full to bursting with beautiful bouquets. Canna lilies, roses, azaleas, and verbena poured over the edges of vases. Behind the sales counter, the space opened right into Armin's large workroom. While I'd worked with Armin many times on Farm weddings, this was the first time I'd ever been inside his shop.

The stone building had once been a law office that was broken into many rooms, but it appeared that Armin had knocked out all the walls he could in order to have an open floor plan. Occasionally a random wall or post would break up the workroom, and I could only assume they were still there because they bore the weight of the structure. Also, the interior of the building was modern. All bright colors—yellow, green, red, and orange—and clean lines. Armin had made no attempt to keep the historical integrity of the building. I guessed that some of the members of the New Hartford Historical Society would swallow their tongues if they came inside this place of work and saw what the florist had done to the two-hundred-year-old building.

Armin was already in his workroom, at one of the high wooden tables. He had a large pair of scissors in his hand and cut the long stems of half a dozen sunflowers with one determined snip.

I swallowed. Perhaps I'd made a miscalculation by coming in here.

He set half of the sunflowers aside and did the same thing with a grouping of orange daylilies. Then he looked up from his work. "What do you have to say about Vianna? Other than that she's dead."

I stepped into the workroom but took care to keep the high table between us. Because the table appeared to be custom built for Armin's large frame, the tabletop came up to my chest. I felt like Alice after she ate the shrinking mushroom. "Sorry," I said. "It's just that's a really big pair of scissors, and I just saw what you can do with a sunflower. You might understand my hesitation."

He put his scissors down on the cutting board and laughed. It was a loud guffaw, and I wouldn't be the least bit surprised if they heard it all the way back at the Farm, five miles away.

I felt myself relax a bit. Surely the florist wouldn't take the scissors to me if he thought I was funny, right?

A plastic container of sunflower heads sat just down the counter from him. At least now I knew where he got his ammo.

He caught me staring at the sunflowers. "Those are for the Pumpernickle wedding. My assistant had just finished cutting them all to

134

the proper size when I tossed him out." He said this like he was talking about the weather, not throwing an employee out onto the street.

"I thought you were giving Krissie carnations," I said.

Armin grinned. "I might have said that to get a rise out of her. She's a particularly annoying bride."

I couldn't argue with that.

He laid the sunflowers and daylilies out on the table in front of him. "My other assistant will be here soon. I like to get an early start in the morning. I let the young ones work late into the night. I did that once. I don't need to do it again."

"What about the guy you threw out of the shop? Will he be coming back?" I asked.

"Oh, him? I just fired him. He used baby's breath in a bridal bouquet. It's an unforgivable sin." Armin picked up his giant scissors again and resumed cutting.

"I'm sorry about Vianna," I said, trying to steer the conversation back on track. "I know that the two of you worked together often."

Armin frowned and dropped his gaze onto the flowers in front of him. "Vianna was the best wedding planner I've ever worked with. She was always organized, always ready with the colors and wedding details, and she put herself between the bride and groom and me." He selected a yellow ranunculus from a large basket on the table and set it in front of him. "You might have noticed that I'm not good with people, but with Vianna it was different."

My brow knit together. This was the first complimentary comment I'd heard about the wedding planner since she'd died.

He studied me. "I just realized that the groom's last name is Cambridge, same as yours." His eyes brightened with curiosity. "Coincidence?"

"No," I said. "The groom is my ex-husband."

"What?" Armin held onto the table and laughed. "Here I am, thinking I have problems, and you have to host your ex-husband's wedding." He placed a hand on his ample stomach. "Oh, what a world we live in!"

I waited a beat to let him regain control over himself. "Finished?"

"I think so." He grinned from ear to ear.

I removed my phone from my pocket. "The bride and groom emailed me a revised list for the floral arrangement."

His grin disappeared. "The sunflowers and daylilies are final. Listen, I went over the list with Vianna a dozen times, and they've made changes at least that many times if not more. I will not change it again. All the flowers have been purchased, and we're starting preparations now. No more changes can be made."

I held up my hands. "Hey, I'm just the messenger. Don't take it out on me."

He shrugged, as if that was of no consequence.

Behind him, the back door slammed closed. A young African-American man ran into the kitchen with his apron in hand. "Armin! Did you hear? Vianna is dead."

Armin's head snapped in the younger man's direction. "I know that." His voice was harsh.

"But do you know how she died?" He didn't wait for Armin to respond. "She fell off of the top of the church at Barton Farm!"

Armin's eyes locked onto me, and they were narrowed into steel slits. Uh oh. The scissors in his hand might be a problem after all.

SEVENTEEN

THE YOUNGER MAN STARED at me as if noticing me for the first time. "Who are you?"

"Kelsey Cambridge, Director of Barton Farm." I wiggled my fingers at him in greeting.

His mouth made an "O" shape and he glanced back at Armin. One of the blood vessels on the florist's neck was about to burst.

I shuffled away from the table. It was best to put some distance between the florist and myself.

"Um," the young man said. "I can come back later, Armin."

"No," Armin said through gritted teeth. He cut the ranunculus stems in half. "Lucas, finish up here. I need to talk to Cambridge outside."

I winced.

Armin set his scissors down and backed away from the counter. Without any questions, Lucas jumped into his spot and began cutting. Armin walked around the counter and headed in my direction.

I'd be lying if I said my body didn't automatically tense up as he approached. He stopped a few feet away from me.

"What should I tell them about their flower list?" I asked, stalling.

"You can say you went over it with me. The Pumpernickle woman will get what she gets at this point. She should feel lucky I'm providing the flowers for her wedding at all."

I didn't argue and headed for the front door of the building. I wasn't going to get any farther with him about the wedding flowers. I might as well find out what I could about his relationship with Vianna or what he might know about her death, if anything. I had to admit that he'd looked honestly shocked when Lucas announced where and how Vianna had died. If he'd been the one to push her out of the window, it wouldn't have been a surprise to him.

Outside, a small flock of house sparrows were cleaning the sunflower seeds off of the sidewalk. At least the flower was being put to good use. When Armin stepped outside, the sparrows flew away. They must have sensed danger. I wished I could fly away like those birds, but I needed to know what he knew about Vianna, for Piper's—and more importantly for Benji's—sake.

The florist removed a pack of cigarettes and a lighter from the pocket of his chef's coat. He lit one up in a practiced motion and after a long drag, said, "I hate these things."

"Then why do you smoke them?" I felt like it was a logical question.

He arched his brow to me. "Don't you ever do anything you hate because you can't stop it?"

A few things came to mind, but I refrained from mentioning them.

He nodded as if my silence was acknowledgment enough. "I thought so. We all have our crutches, don't we? We all do except for Vianna. She was perfect."

Considering the countless arguments I'd had with Vianna over Krissie's wedding, I couldn't agree with that, but I didn't argue with him. As Armin stood there, smoking one cigarette than another, I realized that I was dealing with a man in the midst of grief. It didn't matter what I thought of Vianna or what I thought of Armin either. In front of me was someone who'd lost a woman he cared about, and I needed to treat him gently.

"I'm sorry I didn't tell you that Vianna died at the Farm," I said.

He dropped the cigarette butt on the sidewalk and stamped it out with the toe of his shoe. "I didn't want to know the details. At least I didn't want them just yet."

"Was that the reason you ejected that assistant from your building?"

He eyed me. "I might have gone a little too far there, but he needed to go. Might as well make it memorable for him. Perhaps I took my feelings out on him, some."

"Perhaps," I said, doing my best to sound noncommittal. "I don't think he'll forget that exit anytime soon."

"No, I suppose not." He cracked a half smile when he said that.

It was time to get to the issue at hand. "How long did you know Vianna?"

"Eight years, give or take. If it hadn't been for her, I wouldn't have gotten my start in this business."

I felt my eyebrows shoot up in surprise. Vianna had to be at least ten years younger than Armin.

He lit another cigarette. "I've worked with every wedding planner in this area, and Vianna was the best. She had an eye for what worked and what didn't. She could see what needed to be done and could make it happen. She could see potential in others and tell them what they should be doing. That's what she did for me. I'd just gotten hurt in the minor leagues." He touched his shoulder. "I injured my rotator cuff. There was no chance for me to play again, and my dream of making it to the majors was dashed. I didn't know where to go or what to do."

I tried to imagine this huge man playing baseball. It was a hard image to grasp.

"I'd always liked to garden, so I got a job with a garden center in Akron. It wasn't too long before I was doing all of their floral displays. I seemed to have a knack for it. That's how I met Vianna. She was planning a wedding for her very first client, and she and the client were there looking at the flowers and plants." He took a drag from his cigarette. "As soon as I met her, I knew she was going to make it. She had the drive, and that killer instinct to get the job done at any cost. She and I worked together a lot after that, and I watched in awe as her business just took off. Within two years, she was the most sought-after wedding planner in the area. She just didn't stop. There wasn't a request a bride made that was too hard for Vianna to achieve, and she did it all with a smile. I told her that I wished that I could build something like she'd created."

"What did she say?"

"She told me I could. She said I was much better at floral displays than anyone else in town and I should open my own flower shop. She would work with me to give me a jump start. So I took her advice and put all of my savings into getting this storefront." He gestured at the stone building. "It was the best decision I've ever made."

"Wow," I murmured.

After a beat he said, "Vianna's weddings were always perfect. She was so organized and on top of everything. But not this one. I should have known something was wrong."

"What do you mean when you say 'not this one'?'"

He put his pack of cigarettes and lighter back into his pocket. "The Pumpernickle-Cambridge wedding was different. Vianna gave me multiple flower lists. She's never done that before. She'd always been able to talk the bride out of that many changes, at least as far as I knew. But this was change after change. I knew something must be off. Something was going on with her. She'd never let anything impact her work." There was a bitter sound to his voice.

"What do you think was going on?" I leaned forward on the balls of my feet. I might be getting somewhere in learning about Vianna's life.

"First, I'm ready to know everything now," he said. "How did she fall from the church steeple?"

I gave him the short version, leaving out the details and any reference to Piper. "I thought the police would have been here by now to question you," I said when I finished.

Armin's bushy eyebrows drooped. "Question me? Why on earth would they do that?"

I took a step back. "You worked closely with Vianna, and you were working with her on the Pumpernickle wedding. You might know something that will lead them to whoever did this."

He scowled. "I don't have anything to say to the police."

I didn't know about that, and I planned to suggest to Detective Brandon that she or someone else from the department take the time to talk to him, but not until I learned what he had to say about Vianna first.

Armin slumped against the building. "I shouldn't be surprised that she died trying to please a bride. That's what she was always trying to do. It was her life's work, and she took pride in it."

"Would she usually go as far as disobeying a direct order from the venue owner—in this case, me—to make a bride happy?"

He scratched the back of his head as he considered my question. "Maybe not that far. Usually she would be able to come to a compromise between the venue and the bride."

"Krissie can be awfully demanding."

He nodded. "Even so, Vianna should never have done it. Even if there wasn't someone at the church with evil intentions, it was dangerous and foolhardy to try to hang those lights." He patted his pocket as if he were considering whether or not to smoke another cigarette. "My theory is, she tried to do it because she was making up for being distracted throughout the wedding planning." He let his hand fall to his side.

I wrinkled my nose. "Krissie wouldn't be a bride who'd be open to a distracted wedding planner."

"But Vianna *was* distracted. I knew, because I knew her well. Something was going on with her. I asked her once, and she wouldn't tell me." The florist's face fell and he put his hand on his pocket again. "As kind as she was to me, we were never as close as I wanted us to be."

I knew that this was as close as he was going to get to admitting he'd been in love with the petite wedding planner.

"No matter what her distraction might have been, my money is on the bride as the killer," he went on. His mouth curved into a sneer. "I wouldn't put it past her to push Vianna out of that window."

Before I could say anything, he added, "Vianna had worked with every kind of bride that you can imagine. The indecisive bride, the loud bride, the timid bride, the weepy bride, the reluctant bride, and the runaway bride, but this bride, this bridezilla, seemed different. Even with all of her experience, Krissie Pumpernickle made her feel like she couldn't do anything right. Even if she did everything Krissie asked for, down to the most minute detail. She was so critical it was painful to watch. Normally I'd refuse to work for such a horrible client, but Vianna begged me to take this job. I'm their florist because Vianna wanted the best, and because I owe her for my career. I couldn't say no. Not even to a devil bride."

Devil bride. In the last four months dealing with Krissie's wedding, I'd heard Krissie called a lot of names by so many vendors, but "devil bride" was a new one. Krissie was spoiled and difficult, but I didn't think her faults went as far as to be devilish, most of the time, at least.

"Now that Vianna is gone, you could quit this wedding if it's so horrible," I said, then wished that I'd kept my mouth shut. If Armin quit, I didn't know what I would do about the ceremony and reception flowers.

He looked up the street in the direction his assistant had fled earlier. "I don't have much choice in the matter. I have a contract with the family to provide the flowers for the wedding. It's binding. I can't break that, as much as I want to."

That made sense. The Pumpernickles also had a contract with me to host the wedding at Barton Farm. They could break it, but they would lose their deposit. I wished they would, although after the visit from the elder Pumpernickles that morning, I knew that was never going to happen.

Armin cleared his throat. "And I'm doing it for Vianna. Her last wedding needs to be a great success, in her memory. I don't much care about the bride and groom, but I do care about Vianna's reputation. I want her business to flourish."

As he said this, another thought struck me. "Who will own the business now? Who will run it now that she's gone? Did she have a business partner?" I was surprised I hadn't thought to ask this question before.

The florist shook his head. "The wedding planning business was Vianna's whole life. I can't imagine who she would have left it to."

Maybe if I answered that question, I would also find the answer to the more pressing question of who killed her.

"If I was going to guess who might get it, it would be Piper," Armin said. "Vianna was molding her into the next big wedding planner."

I bit the inside of my lip. Benji had insisted that Piper was innocent, but if Piper got to take over Vianna's very profitable business if Vianna were to die, would she kill for that? And there was the issue as to why Vianna would choose an intern to leave everything to. She had other employees; I'd met many of them over the course of planning the wedding.

"Vianna didn't have friends," Armin went on. "I doubt she even considered me one. Her whole life was her work. She was a workaholic. It served her well. Look where it got her. She had a flourishing business, but now she's gone. She can't take the business with her." He sighed. "I might have loved her, if she'd have let me, but she always made it very clear that our relationship was never going to go there. Vianna wanted business partners. That was all. She didn't have time for anything else and didn't seem to miss it. Her job was her life. For her, success seemed to be enough."

I shivered. If I was honest with myself, Vianna sounded a little like me in that way. I could be a workaholic. My friends and family kept me sane, though, and I had Chase.

"Do you think she was happy?" I heard myself ask.

Armin looked me in the eye. "Yes, I would say Vianna was happy. She created her own life and didn't let anyone stand in her way. She was young, ambitious, and driven. If she'd lived, who knows how far she could have gone?"

"Do you wish Vianna had given you a chance?" I knew it wasn't a fair question, and one I had no right to ask.

His wide-open face closed off. "What I wish doesn't have any bearing on reality now, does it?" He removed another cigarette from his pocket and lit up. He blew a puff of smoke out of the side of his mouth and squinted at me. "What I don't understand is your interest in all of this. You didn't know Vianna, not like I did. Why do you care?"

I straightened my shoulders. "She was young and she died too soon, and she died on my Farm. I can't help but want to know what happened to her."

He nodded as if I'd passed some sort of test. "If you find out who did this, let me know, will you?"

I didn't reply, because by the stern expression on his face, I had a very bad feeling that if I told him who'd killed the woman he loved, I would become an accessory to another murder.

145

Without saying goodbye, Armin turned and walked back into his building. When he was gone, the flock of sparrows returned and resumed pecking at sunflower seeds on the sidewalk. I stood there in front of the bright blue door, and I couldn't help but wonder if I'd judged Vianna unfairly.

After visiting the florist, I had more questions about Vianna and the people in her life, not less. I pulled my ever-present notebook out of the back pocket of my jeans and made a note of what I'd learned. It didn't seem like much because the more I discovered about the wedding planner, the more I realized I'd known absolutely nothing about her while she was alive. I wished I could have known her better in life because in death she was revealing herself to be a person I might have liked.

I sighed and headed to my car. As I moved, the sparrows took flight again.

EIGHTEEN

AFTER LEAVING COATES FLOWERS, I had one more stop that I wanted to make before returning to the Farm. Krissie's dress tailor was located in a fancy shopping plaza about ten minutes from the center of town. It was the kind of place that I didn't go to often because I couldn't afford the clothing in the nice boutiques, nor in my daily life did I have any reason to wear them.

The shopping district was pedestrian-only. I parked in the lot to the right of it, and then walked along the faux-cobblestone sidewalk toward Tuxie Tailors. The bell over the door rang as I entered. There wasn't anyone in the front room, but I could hear the whirl of a sewing machine deep in the recesses of the building.

I glanced around and marveled at the stitching and workmanship on a dress draped over the dress form closest to me. I wished I could have Tuxie Tailors revamp our historical interpreters' uniforms at the Farm, but I would never be able to afford it on my costume budget.

The whir of the sewing machine stopped, and I stepped back from the dress form. A moment later, a rail-thin woman with frizzy hot pink hair stepped out from behind a curtain. She blinked at me from behind thick glasses. The frames were the same color as her hair. I assumed that had been planned. That color of pink didn't happen by accident.

She opened her arms. "Welcome to Tuxie's. How can I help you?" Her voice came out airy, like she was speaking from a great height, or perhaps from another plane.

"I'm Kelsey Cambridge. I just stopped by because I've been assisting with the Pumpernickle wedding, and—"

"The Pumpernickle wedding," the woman squealed. "You mean Krissie Pumpernickle's wedding?"

What else could it be? I wondered. If there was another New Hartford family with the surname Pumpernickle, that was most unfortunate. I nodded.

She waved her hands as if she were shooing away a stray cat. "Then leave. I have nothing else to say to her. She has her dress now. What else can she want from me?"

"I—I know that," I said, deciding to play it straight with her since saying I was associated with Krissie had completely backfired. I should have expected that. "I just wanted to talk to you about the argument Krissie and Vianna Pine had in your shop yesterday."

The woman placed the back of her hand to her forehead as if she was afraid that she might faint.

"Are you okay?" I asked.

"Oh, it was so horrible." She sniffled. "It gives me the chills just remembering how it was."

"The argument, you mean?" I asked.

"Argument," she scoffed. "It was a full-on shouting match. Let me tell you…" She made a sign of the cross. "That bride. She's one of the worst, and I've been in this business for over thirty years."

"I agree," I said.

She blinked at me. "You agree?"

I nodded. "Oh yeah. I'm the director of Barton Farm, and the wedding is to be on my Farm. I've been working with Krissie for months in preparation." I didn't add that Krissie was marrying my ex-husband. The woman didn't need to know that.

Her eyes brightened. "Oh, so you *do* know."

I nodded. I most certainly did. "You may have heard that Vianna has died."

She adjusted her pink glasses. "Of course. She dove from the steeple of Barton Farm's church. If I were her and had to listen to Krissie yip in my ear day after day like a deranged Chihuahua, I might have considered a swan dive too."

I winced at the image. "She didn't commit suicide. The police believe she was pushed."

The woman covered her mouth. "Oh my."

"And since it happened on Barton Farm, and I'm the director, I want to know what really happened and who is responsible for it. I'm sort of helping the police in their inquiry into Vianna's death."

Lies, all lies, my conscience whispered to me. I pushed the good voice away.

"I can understand that, honey," the woman said with a nod. "I'm happy to help you then. People in the wedding business have to look out for each other, but before I'll answer any questions, take off your shirt."

"What's that?" I asked, thinking that I must have misheard her.

"I said take off your shirt," she said, as plain as could be.

I gaped at her.

She put her hands on her hips. "You have a hole in your shirt. If you think that I'm going to talk to someone in my tailor shop with a hole in their shirt, you have another thing coming."

I looked down at my Barton Farm polo. "I do?"

She walked over to me and pointed to the tiniest of tiny holes on the seam on the left side. It had to be the size of a pinhead.

"Oh, that's nothing," I said, thinking of the many Farm polos I had back at the cottage that were in much, much worse condition than this one.

"Take it off," she ordered, leaving no room for argument, and she went as far as grabbing the hem and trying to yank the shirt from my body.

"Okay, okay," I said, jerking myself away. "I'll give you the shirt." I took another step back and pulled the polo up over my head. Thankfully I had a tank top on underneath, so I wasn't giving any pedestrians walking by a show.

She took the shirt from my hand and headed back behind the curtain. I stood there. A second later, she poked her head back out. "Are you coming or what?"

I followed her through the curtain. "Tuxie is your real name?"

"It is now. I changed it," she said, and sat at one of the four sewing machines in the room.

"What did you change it from?"

"No matter." She picked up a spool of thread.

Oh-kay. I glanced around the room, taking in my surroundings bit by bit. Tuxie's workspace was a cacophony of color and pattern.

A cluster of a half a dozen naked dress forms stood in one corner like a choir getting ready to perform. I found something about their pose unsettling and had to look away.

In the middle of the room were two long tables with sewing machines. Tuxie sat at one of those tables and removed a sparkly dress from the machine, which was what she must have been working on before I arrived. She put my shirt in its place.

She looked up at me with a needle bit between her lips. "What do you want to know?"

"What did Krissie and Vianna fight about when they were here?" I asked.

"Ahh," she said. "Well, I don't rightly know, but they were as mad as two wet hens when they were going at it, or I should say Krissie was. Vianna was calm as can be and had that sweet fake smile on her face that she always wore. I hated that smile."

I remembered that smile too, and I hadn't been a fan of it either. "Did you catch some of what they said to each other?" I asked hopefully. "Maybe I can make some sense of it."

"Maybe you can. I couldn't be sure." Tuxie moved the needle to the other side of her mouth and turned my shirt inside out. "Krissie said that Vianna had to come through with the lights that she wanted. Vianna said that it wasn't possible, that Barton Farm wouldn't allow it." She looked up at me. "I guess that means you."

I nodded.

She smiled as if pleased that she'd made this connection. "Then Krissie said it was non-negotiable, and that the Farm came through with Abraham Lincoln, so it should be no trouble at all to get the lights. She seemed to think getting Lincoln was harder." Her brow furrowed. "I'm pretty sure he's been dead a long while."

"He has," I said. It wasn't the place or time to start explaining historical reenacting to Tuxie. If she ever ventured out to Barton Farm, I would be happy to do it. And, ugh. I'd forgotten about drunk Lincoln. Again. I feared that I had something of a mental block when it came to him. "Then what happened?" I asked.

"Vianna again said it wasn't possible. She said it was a liability and safety issue. Krissie didn't much care for that, and that's when she started yelling." She took a breath. "She said she could ruin Vianna's career if she didn't get her the lights. Vianna didn't seem too concerned about it, though, until Krissie said she'd tell the world Vianna's secret."

My pulse quickened. "What secret?"

Tuxie shook her head. "Don't know. I had to kick them out at that point. Krissie was causing quite a scene. I had a couple of other customers in here at the time, and the arguing made them uncomfortable. I gave Krissie her dress and asked her and Vianna to leave."

Those other customers must have been the witnesses Detective Brandon alluded to.

"So, Krissie threatened the reputation of Vianna's business and then blackmailed her with some unknown secret," I mused.

"Looked like it to me." Tuxie changed the thread on the machine to one that was an identical match to my blue polo shirt. Her fingers moved so deftly that I almost missed it. She ran the polo through the machine and then inspected her work. "As good as new," she declared.

"Thank you," I said. I accepted the shirt from her outstretched hand and put it back on.

She nodded and peered at me over her glasses. "It's best to catch the holes and fix them before they become too big to handle. That's always been my motto."

I realize that Tuxie's motto could be applied to many things in life, including solving Vianna Pine's murder.

NINETEEN

When I got back to the Farm, I saw a news van parked in front the visitor center. A thin woman in a raspberry-red suit spoke into a microphone in front of a cameraman dressed in jeans and a polo shirt. A knot formed in my stomach. They had to be here about the murder, but I suspected there was something more to it than that. The wedding planner's death wasn't the first to occur on Farm grounds, and I'd never had a news van pull up to the front door of the visitor center before.

I parked my car in its usual spot, in the far corner of the parking lot, and walked over to the woman. As I got closer, I saw that she wasn't alone. My father, Roy Renard, was with her, recording a sound bite. His sandy but mostly gray hair was brushed back from his face, and he'd grown a beard, which was all but completely gray, for his Shakespearean acting gig. As usual, my father was dressed in jeans and a T-shirt, or at least he would have been if it hadn't been for the cape draped across his back, brushing the gravel parking lot.

My father had a fondness for wearing his costumes outside of the theater.

I groaned. Dad would do just about anything to be in front of a camera. And as much as I loved him, I didn't want him to be the one representing the Farm in this instance.

Laura, in her historical interpreter clothing and hair coiled at the nape of her neck, stood off to the side of the visitor center's main entrance. She waved me over.

I glanced at my father and felt like I was watching a train wreck in progress. After a moment of hesitation, I joined my best friend. "Tell me what's going on, and as quickly as possible."

"Well," she began slowly, drawing out the word for maximum effect.

"Laura," I said sharply. "There's a newscaster in the Farm's parking lot with a microphone in my father's face. I don't have time for the long version."

She took a deep breath, but before she could tell me what on earth was happening, I heard my father say, "My daughter, Kelsey Renard Cambridge, who is the director of Barton Farm, is right over there. You should talk to her about this."

At my side, Laura said, "Uh oh."

In my head, I thought of an exclamation that was a tad more severe.

The raspberry-suited reporter made a beeline for me. Her camera guy jogged in her wake. "Keep filming," she said to him over her shoulder.

Great. My deer in the headlights expression was recorded for posterity.

"Are you Kelsey Cambridge, the director of Barton Farm?" The reporter shoved the microphone into my face.

I stepped back. "Yes. What's this about?"

She tilted the microphone back toward her own face. "So you've been working on the Pumpernickle-Cambridge wedding with Krissie Pumpernickle."

"What—"

Before I could finish, she said, "It's seems odd that you have the same last name as the groom. Is he any relation to you?"

I wasn't going to answer that on camera. I repeated my question. "What's all this about? You're on private property. You have to have permission to film here, which I know that you don't, since I would be the one who'd grant such permission."

The reporter bristled. "I'm just doing my job, Ms. Cambridge. When a lost heiress is murdered, that's news and our viewers want to hear about it."

I blinked at her. "Wait, what? A lost heiress?"

She beamed as if I'd just given her a new puppy. "You don't know!" She waved to her camera guy, gesturing for him to zoom in on my face.

"Know?" I glanced back at Laura, who made a pained expression at me. "Know what?"

"Vianna Pine was the rightful heiress to the Cherry fortune and the Foundation."

I stared at the reporter for a second as what she said to me started to sink in. It took some time, because what she said didn't compute.

"There is no heir to the Cherry Foundation," I said finally, denying it. That was what I knew to be true. Maxwell Cherry, Cynthia's nephew, had died with no children. He was the only relative Cynthia had. There was no one left to make a claim on the estate, which was why Cynthia's massive home, all her money and possessions, and the Foundation itself had been left to the board, in a trust. Certainly if there was an heir, he or she would have presented him or herself before now. Cynthia had been gone for almost a year.

The reporter's grin grew even wider, as if she had a present for me and couldn't wait until I opened it. "Vianna was Maxwell Cherry's illegitimate and secret daughter."

That's when my mouth fell open. I was going to look extra attractive on television with flies zooming in and out of it, but I couldn't help it. What she'd said sent me reeling and took my breath away.

"But Cynthia left everything to the Cherry Foundation," I sputtered.

"Yes, she did," the reporter said, seemingly pleased with herself that she'd gotten such a shocked reaction out of me. I guessed that it was better for ratings. "But Miss Cherry's will clearly states that if she or Maxwell were found to have an heir, that person would inherit everything, including directorship of the Foundation."

Maxwell Cherry had a daughter? How was that possible? I, of course, knew how someone had a child, but how come no one knew about it—including Cynthia? When she was alive, she'd begged Maxwell to settle down, get married, and have a family. I knew she would have been happy to learn he'd had a child. She longed for another person in her life that she could take care of. I knew that was partly the reason why she took Hayden and me under her wing when I was freshly divorced and applying for the director job at the Farm. Cynthia had such a big heart. She just wanted to share it, especially with her nephew's children if he'd had any. And apparently he'd had one all this time and hidden it from his aunt. How could he keep that from her? How could he be so cruel?

"Can we get a quote from you about this latest development?" the reporter asked.

I shook my head and refocused my eyes on the camera and the woman in front of me. "No comment."

The reporter wouldn't give up that easily. "Do you know how Vianna's inheritance would have impacted Barton Farm? If Vianna was alive, it seems you would answer to her instead of the Cherry Foundation board?"

I stepped away from the reporter. "I know nothing of the kind."

"It could have changed everything for the Farm," the reporter said, still as happy as could be. "It could have changed everything for you personally too. Don't you live here on the Farm land?" she asked. "Does this make you a suspect in her murder?"

I stared at her.

Laura stepped between me and the camera. "Back off, lady." My best friend used her large size to her advantage and completely blocked me from view. "Kelsey, go inside of the visitor center. I'll take care of this."

The reporter stepped away. "I have a right to ask questions."

"No, you don't," Laura argued. "Kelsey already told you this is private land, so we're within our rights to call the police and have them escort you off Barton Farm. I hear Detective Brandon has been wanting to throw someone out of somewhere for a long time. This could finally be her chance."

The reporter dropped her microphone to her side. "Fine. Be that way. I think we have enough as it is." She waved to her camera guy.

"Come on, Sam, let's head back to the station and get this in the can."

I watched, still in a half daze, as they climbed into their TV van and drove away. After their tires spun up dust on the gravel lot, my father brushed off his cape and walked over to Laura and me.

He was beaming. "Kelsey, my girl, it's so nice to see you." He gave me a big hug. "I must say the theater troupe is doing beautifully. When will you be able to come out to one of my performances? I have the rest of the week off, but I'll be back at it come next week."

I closed my eyes for a moment. I couldn't believe he was talking about his acting troupe after what had just happened. Scratch that. I could believe it. I could believe it very well. I was his daughter, after all, and should have come to expect such a reaction.

"Dad," I said with a childish whine in my voice. "What were you doing talking to that reporter about Vianna Pine?"

He smoothed his velvet cape over his shoulders. "My dear, I knew nothing about it. I just arrived from my last showing, drove all night to be with you and Hayden. When I arrived, the reporter was just exiting her van and asked who I was and wanted a quote. Of course, I naturally assumed she'd heard about my great performance in Circleville, Ohio, as Hamlet's father's ghost. It wasn't until the camera was in my face that I realized she was actually wanting to ask about you and the Farm." He frowned. "If you'd texted me to say that yet another person had gotten killed on the grounds, I might have been better prepared for her questions."

He smoothed his cape over the opposite shoulder. I didn't know how he could wear that heavy thing—the temperature had to be in the eighties.

I glanced at Laura. "Why didn't you intervene?"

She held up her hands. "I was about to when you jumped out of your car like your tail was on fire. I knew I'd better tell you what was going on before you clocked one of the reporters."

"I don't hit," I said defensively.

Laura frowned. "I remember a couple of wallops you've given me over the years."

"Yeah." I folded my arms across my chest. "When we were kids. I haven't hit you since fifth grade."

"There was that one time in college …" She trailed off. "Besides, who scared them off at the end there?"

I sighed. "Thank you for that. Do we know if what she said was true? Has anyone called the Foundation to confirm this?"

"Don't know." Laura shook her head. "But there really is no reason to doubt the news. They check their facts. Someone must know for sure. The police, maybe …"

"And Henry Ratcliffe," I said. Even as I spoke his name, I wondered how long Henry had known. As the leader of the Foundation's board, he would have been the first to be notified that an heir had been discovered, and I knew he wouldn't be happy about it. This news would impact Henry just as much as it impacted me. If I was a murder suspect, then so was Henry Ratcliffe, times ten.

TWENTY

Two family vans pulled up, and kids and parents piled out. I was happy the news van had left before they arrived. The Farm didn't need any more bad publicity.

A little boy pointed at my father. "Look, Mommy, that old man has a cape. I want a cape!"

My father waved his cape back and forth, Batman style. The kids cheered and the parents smiled. I suppressed a smile of my own. Despite my father's misguided decisions about what to say to the press and his odd fashion sense, he was great with kids, which was why I was grateful to have him around in the summer to help out with Hayden.

I placed a hand on my father's arm. "Okay, Zorro, let's go inside and do some damage control."

My father bent at the waist and wrapped his cape around his body, cocoon style. The kids cheered again. Laura had to physically frog-march him through the sliding glass doors into the visitor center.

Judy met us at the door and handed me my radio back. "I'm glad to be rid of that. It's been wild since you left. It seems that you-know-what has hit the fan."

Laura raised her eyebrows and grinned. "I have no idea what you-know-what is, Judy. Maybe you should just come out and say it."

I hooked the radio back onto my jeans. I was happy to have it back. It was my security blanket. Right up there with the little note-book that I always carried in the back pocket of my jeans to jot down notes and ideas about how to improve the Farm. If Vianna had taken control of the Farm, would I have been able to do that anymore? Vianna's inheritance would have had a big impact on me, and it did give me a motive for murder.

I pushed the unpleasant thoughts from my head. "What's wrong, Judy? The reporter who was outside?"

She patted the bun on the back of her head as if to make sure that it was still there. "That's a start," she said. "I saw them, and I would have come out and told them to vamoose, but I was running interference inside here."

"What do you mean?" Laura asked.

"Mom!" Hayden called. He ran toward me full-tilt from the gift shop, but then he saw his grandfather. "Pop!" he cried, taking a sharp turn away from me to run into my father's waiting arms. Dad wrapped his cape around him and Hayden disappeared from sight. The only indication that my son was wrapped in the cape was his muffled giggles.

"Dad, can you take Hayden back to the cottage? You guys can hang out and have lunch. You haven't been able to spend as much time with each other this summer," I said.

My father looked up at me.

I gave him a pleading look, and he nodded. "Of course, of course. Hayden and I need to catch up. He can tell me all about Frankie's latest crimes and other goings-on at the Farm while I've been away."

"Grandpop," Hayden said. "We have attack chickens now!"

"You don't say," my father murmured, as if something like that was to be expected on Farm grounds. I was afraid that it might actually be the case.

And that reminded me—Krissie had requested that the chickens be removed for the wedding. I'd forgotten that little tidbit. I hoped she'd forgotten it too, but I severely doubted it.

Dad released Hayden from his cape. "Come along, young squire. After you tell me about the fearsome chickens, it's time that I taught you the ways of Shakespeare. We'll start with *The Tempest*, as it's your mother's favorite." He winked at me over Hayden's head.

Hayden cocked his head. "That's the one that starts with a shipwreck, right?"

Dad put a hand on his chest. "You know so much already. Let us be off!" With a flourish of his cape he ushered Hayden to the doors leading out onto the Farm grounds.

They had almost reached them when Hayden turned around and ran toward me. He wrapped his arms around my hips. "Love you!" Then he turned and skipped off to join his grandfather outside the visitor center. Tiffin was waiting at the door and met his two favorite guys, and then the trio made their way up the pebbled path.

At least one aspect of my life was in order, and it was the most important part.

After they'd gone, I ushered Laura and Judy to a corner of the visitor center. The families I'd seen in the parking lot were at the ticket booth purchasing tickets. I didn't want them to overhear our conversation.

When we were safely out of earshot, I turned to Judy. "Okay, what do you mean by 'running interference'?"

Judy shook her head. "That reporter outside—that won't be the last one by a long shot. It seems the news about Vianna being Cynthia's rightful heir broke a while ago, and I've been fielding phone calls asking for a quote since the moment you left." She eyed me. "Did you know that Vianna was supposed to inherit the Cherry Foundation?"

I rubbed my forehead. I could feel a headache forming just behind my temple. "I had no idea. The first I heard about it was from that reporter outside. Do you think there will be more calls about this?"

As if on cue, the phone rang.

"Reporters," Judy said, as if uttering some sort of curse.

"What did you say when you answered the phone?" I asked.

She sniffed. "'No comment,' of course. I know better than to talk to the press."

I wished that my father did too. "Why didn't you call me to give me a heads up?" I turned to Laura. "Or why didn't you?"

Laura raised her hands in surrender. "I didn't know anything until I went outside and heard what the reporter was saying. Then you drove up."

Judy smoothed a wrinkle out of her khaki skirt. "And I was too busy dealing with the onslaught of phone calls to call you."

I held up my hand. "I understand. I'm not blaming either of you. Detective Brandon and Henry Ratcliffe are another story. They both must have known. They could have at least warned me."

Laura cocked her head. "What are you going to do now?"

I removed my cell phone from my pocket. "Let me call Detective Brandon and get to the bottom of this. Please keep answering the phone in case it's a visitor with a legitimate question. If it's a reporter, just say 'no comment' and hang up, as you've been doing."

"You don't need to call her," Laura said. "She's over in the village. I saw her walking around there just before I found your dad with the reporter."

I frowned. I'd thought Brandon was done with the crime scene. Something must be up if she was back on Farm grounds and following up more leads.

"I'll go talk to her now," I said.

Laura grabbed my arm. "Have you eaten anything today?"

I tried to remember.

"Thought so," Laura said. "At least stop by the snack bar on your way out and grab some semblance of a lunch."

"I'll grab something after I speak to the detective." I was about to head out onto the grounds when Benji ran through the doors of the visitor center. She looked around and finally saw the three of us in the corner.

"Kelsey!" she gasped. "Did you hear?" She took a breath and then glanced behind her, at a family taking in some of the black and white photography of the Farm from years gone by.

"I have heard," I said. "I was just about to head to the village to talk to Brandon about it. Want to come with me?"

She grabbed her replacement radio from the sales counter and hooked it to her belt. "You bet. I'm with you."

I found myself smiling as we walked out onto the grounds.

We'd almost reached Maple Grove Lane before I asked, "How's Piper?"

Benji kicked a stone with the toe of her red Doc Marten. "She's better. Being interviewed by the police this morning really shook her up."

"Because she's been to jail before?" I asked as we reached the road.

Benji looked away from me, toward the north, as if she didn't want me to see her expression.

"Benji, why did she go to jail?" I had to know.

She scuffed the toe of her shoe on the road as we crossed. "I don't know."

I stopped in the middle of the street. "What do you mean you don't know?"

Benji grabbed my arm and pulled me to the other side. "You can't stop in the middle of the street like that."

"Hardly anyone drives down this road," I grumbled. "And you haven't answered my question."

Benji released my arm. "I don't know because I promised her that I wouldn't ask."

"When did you promise her that? Recently? Since Vianna died?" I asked my questions in rapid succession.

Benji scrunched up her face as if it pained her to answer. "No. Before."

"When?" I asked.

Benji shook her head. "I don't want to talk about it."

I frowned. "Benji, you asked me to help Piper. How am I supposed to do that when I don't have all the facts?"

The church came into view, and I could see Detective Brandon standing in front of it with her hands on her hips. Her head was tilted back as she stared up at the broken window in the steeple.

"Where's Piper now?" I asked before we reached the church.

Benji wrinkled her nose. "With Krissie."

I grimaced. "She is?"

"Yeah. Since Piper was working with Vianna on the wedding, it makes sense for her to take over from here. I know she's nervous about it, but if the wedding goes well, this could start her career. She may not have to intern any more. She can start a wedding planning business of her own, or find a job at one the big agencies in Cleveland. She can start paying back her student loans and maybe we could even go on a vacation."

I kicked a stone of my own. "I wouldn't mention anything about how Vianna's death could help Piper get ahead in her own career, to the police or to anyone else."

Benji stopped. "Why not? Oh!" she said as it dawned on her. "That might give her a reason to kill Vianna."

I nodded. Armin had perceived this motive just a few hours earlier.

"She didn't do it," Benji said defensively, flipping one of her braids over her shoulder.

"I know you care about her. I'll try to believe that, for your sake."

Benji's shoulders sagged in relief. "Thanks, Kel."

I folded my arms. "But to help her, I'm going to have to know what sent her to jail."

Benji sighed. "That's what I was afraid you'd say."

TWENTY-ONE

DETECTIVE BRANDON EYED US as Benji and I drew closer to the church. We were within a few feet when she said, "You win, Cambridge."

"I—I win?" I stammered. Of all the remarks the detective could have made when she saw me, I hadn't ever considered that one to be in the realm of possibility.

She shrugged. "Yep, you win."

I really would have doubted that I'd heard her correctly the first time if she hadn't repeated the remark.

"How did I win?" I asked.

She gestured toward the church. "You win access to the church. I got a call from the mayor just a little while ago, ordering me to release the church back into your care tomorrow morning."

"From the mayor?" Benji yelped. "Of New Hartford?"

I would have yelped it too if she hadn't beat me to it. "The mayor called you?" I still had trouble believing it. The mayor was an overweight, elderly man who'd been in office since the 1990s. As far as anyone in the village knew, he didn't do much more than play Solitaire on his city-paid-for laptop in his enormous office on the third floor of the town hall. Despite that, no one in the town had run against him in the last twenty years. The people of New Hartford like the status quo and a mayor who stayed out of their personal business.

Brandon nodded. "Apparently, he and your Henry Ratcliffe friend play poker together twice a week. Henry called the mayor and told him what happened. The mayor offered to take care of the 'little mix-up with the church,' so the mayor called me."

"Because Krissie insists on having her wedding inside the church even after what happened," I said. No wonder Brandon was upset. I certainly wouldn't want to receive a call from the town mayor like that.

The detective pointed her index finger at me and mocked pulling the trigger. "You got it."

I frowned. "Detective, you sound almost defeated."

She glanced at me before putting sunglasses over her eyes. "I don't like being called into the principal's office, as it were. The mayor doesn't care that this is an active crime scene, about the chain of evidence, or that a young woman was murdered. He just cares about winning at poker. Even more than that, I don't like an old boys club."

My frown deepened as it dawned on me how hard it must be for her to be the only female officer on the force. Yes, she was tough, and yes, she outranked most of the men there. However, the fact that she was a woman made her stand out, and stand out in a way that she didn't always want. I'd always suspected that she'd dressed plainly in order to be counted as one of the boys in the department. Now I was sure of it.

"In any case," I said, "I hope you were able to do whatever it is you needed to do in there in order to find out what happened to Vianna."

She frowned. "I'll find out who is behind this, and that's something I'm certain of."

Next to me, Benji winced. I knew that she must be thinking of Piper as a prime suspect in Vianna's murder. I realized that Brandon must know what Piper was guilty of.

"I'll let Krissie know what's going on," I said. "She'll be grateful that she'll be able to have the wedding ceremony in the church. It's her dream."

Brandon lifted her sunglasses and eyed me. "Was it her dream ever since she was a little girl, or just since she met you and wanted to make you miserable?"

I didn't even bother to answer.

The detective's lips curved in a smile. "Thought so." She seemed pleased with herself, and here I was a moment ago feeling sorry for her. There was no reason to feel sorry for Detective Candy Brandon, as far as I could tell.

I rocked back on my heels. "Did you know about Vianna's inheritance?"

Brandon smiled. "I was wondering when you would find out about that."

"It's hard not to when there's a reporter standing outside the visitor center asking what I knew about it." I scowled.

She dropped her sunglasses back down over her eyes. "I knew the press would get a whiff of it eventually. I just wish it had taken them a little more time."

"Why didn't you tell me? How long have you known?" I demanded.

She rolled her eyes. "I had no reason to tell you. And I've only known since we searched Vianna's apartment. We found paternity test results on her kitchen table that proved she was Maxwell's daughter."

"You just sat on that information." I threw up my hands. "It could be the reason why someone murdered her."

Brandon scowled, and deep lines appeared on either side of her mouth. "Of course I know that. And I didn't just sit on it. I was figuring out the number of people who knew who Vianna really was, thinking I could narrow down my suspect list." She eyed me. "You appear to be surprised by the news."

"I didn't know. Am I suspect?" I asked.

She chuckled. "Everyone is a suspect. Just some are more likely than others. And as far as I can tell, very few people knew. Only Henry Ratcliffe from the Cherry Foundation, and Vianna's assistant Piper."

Beside me, I heard Benji take in a sharp intake of breath.

I wasn't surprised to hear that Henry knew. Vianna would have gone to him first when she'd learned about it. Piper knowing about it was a surprise. I peeked at Benji out of the corner of my eye. She was playing with her new radio, flipping it over and over again in her slender hands. I had a feeling that the radio's days were numbered.

Another thought struck me. "How long did Vianna know that she was Maxwell's daughter? Why is this just coming to light now?"

The police detective studied me like she was trying to decide how much to tell me.

"If you don't tell me, I'll just go to Henry."

Brandon sighed. She knew this wasn't an idle threat on my part. "According to Henry, Vianna told him she found a letter and a handful of documents that her mother left her, telling her who her father was. Her mother passed away last year."

My heart constricted. "I knew she didn't have any family, but I didn't know she'd lost her mother so recently."

Brandon raised her eyebrows. "Did you have a reason to know? I wasn't under the impression the two of you were close."

"We weren't, but if I'd known, I would have . . . " I trailed off. I would have what?

"You would have what? Been kinder to her?" Her tone was ironic.

I clenched my jaw. "I might have been more understanding as to why she was being so difficult, if I'd known she was going through a hard time."

"Maybe you should just assume that everyone is going through something you don't know about and be kind to everyone," Brandon said.

The comment smarted because I knew she was right. And the fact that I had to hear it from her of all people, who was rude to just about everyone she met, made it that much worse.

"And you don't need to tell Krissie that the church will be available for the wedding," the detective added.

I frowned, surprised by her sudden change of topic. I'd expected her to continue to make me feel as terrible as possible. "I don't?"

"She already knows." Brandon nodded to spot behind me. I turned to see Krissie and Piper heading in our direction from Maple

Grove Lane. They weren't alone. Much to my surprise, they had Justin Cambridge, Eddie's young brother the environmental lawyer, in tow. What on earth was Eddie's brother doing there? I had a bad feeling about this in the pit of my stomach.

"Kelsey!" Krissie called across the wide expanse of lawn. "Thank goodness that you're here." She ran across the green toward me. Her stride was stilted because her pointy heels continually became snagged in the grass. Piper and Justin followed in her wake at a much more sedate pace.

Krissie wasn't the least bit out of breath when she reached me. She did teach people to exercise for a living, so she was in top physical shape herself. For the briefest moment, I wondered if that meant she'd be strong enough to throw Vianna through the window.

"Kelsey, did you hear the news?" she shouted when she was a mere three feet away from me.

"What news?" I asked, even though I assumed she meant the reopening of the church, not the reporters learning that Vianna was Maxwell Cherry's heir.

"The wedding will be in the church!" Krissie threw her arms around me. "Isn't it wonderful? I can have the wedding I always dreamed of." I grimaced as she hugged me. "You really came through for me, Kelsey!"

"I'm happy to help," I said. "But why is Justin here?"

Justin threw up his hands. "What, are you disappointed to see me, Kel?"

"Surprised is a better word." I frowned at my former brother-in-law.

He gave me his boyish grin in return. His dark hair was tousled as if he'd just woken up from a nap, which wasn't out of the question when Justin was concerned. I'd caught him snoozing mid-day more than once when I was married to his older brother.

Krissie gripped her small flower-printed handbag tighter. "Justin is here about the chickens."

"The chickens?" I asked. I didn't even bother to keep the surprise from my voice.

She nodded. "The attack chickens. They have got to go, you know."

I shot Benji a look. I knew that her calling Shepley's hens 'attack chickens' would come back to haunt me. Everything always did, when Krissie was concerned.

Benji must have thought the tops of her boots were the most interesting things in the world, because she stared at them intently. She and I would talk about the chickens later. She and I both knew it.

"They aren't attack chickens," I said. "They're just plain old free-range chickens. They're nothing to worry about."

"How can you even say that?" Krissie cried. "They charged me yesterday, before all this unpleasantness happened."

"Unpleasantness" was one way to describe Vianna's death.

"They were walking by," I said. "They didn't charge you."

Justin rubbed the back of his head, mussing his hair even more. Not that it made much difference in his appearance. Justin was boy-next-door cute, just like his older brother. And a long string of women had fallen for his charms. The problem with Justin was, he became bored easily and was always on the lookout for the next girl to charm. I noticed him give the detective a once-over. If I was kinder, I might have warned him that whatever he was thinking was a very, very bad idea, but as it turned out, I wasn't that kind. Justin was a big boy and would have to learn that lesson on his own.

Benji pushed her braids out of her eyes and spoke for the first time. "You can't kick the chickens off the Farm. Where are the chickens going to go? They live here."

"Not any more. Tell them, Justin." She elbowed her future brother-in-law.

Eddie's younger brother looked pained, but I suspected the pain came more from Krissie's orders than from her elbow. "I thought we could take some time to catch up first," he said.

Krissie elbowed him in the ribs a little bit harder, and he grunted from the impact. "There's no time for small talk. We don't have all day."

Justin rubbed his side. "Kelsey," he began.

When he said that, I knew I was in trouble. I'd known Justin just as long as I'd known Eddie—practically my whole life—and the younger of the two Cambridge boys rarely called me by my full first name. I was always "Kel" to them. Since he called me Kelsey, I took that as significant and a warning.

I nodded at him to go on.

"It's been brought to our attention that the chickens have hurt someone. Because of that, I have asked the court to make you remove them from the Farm. It's a public safety issue," he added apologetically.

I glared. "Who has been hurt by the chickens? They've been here all summer, and this is the first I'm hearing of a chicken-inflicted injury."

Krissie elbowed Piper this time. Her elbows were really getting a workout.

Piper's blue bangs fell over her eyes. "I have."

Benji stared at Piper in utter shock. I imagined my expression was much the same. A few feet away, Detective Brandon stood off to the side with a big grin on her face. I was happy to see that someone was enjoying herself.

I glared at Justin. "I didn't realize that best man duties include policing chickens."

"Come on, Kel," he said with the same whiny sound in his voice he'd had whenever Eddie and I wanted to go somewhere without him.

"Who wants to get rid of my chickens?" a voice bellowed from the side of the church.

Krissie yelped and jumped behind Justin.

"Uh oh," Benji whispered.

My thoughts exactly.

TWENTY-TWO

SHEPLEY, LOOKING EVEN MORE bedraggled than normal, came around the church with his nostrils flaring. Long strands of his gray hair fell out of his ponytail.

Gertrude, his large red hen, followed a few steps behind her owner. Her talons appeared longer than normal and her eyes were narrowed. They made a fearsome pair. I couldn't blame Krissie for jumping back to hide behind Justin.

"That's it!" Krissie squeaked. "That's the one that tried to peck me! And that's the one that got Piper. Isn't that right, Piper?"

"Gertrude did nothing of the kind," Shepley bellowed.

Krissie grabbed Piper by the arm. "Show them."

Piper's blue eyes went wide. "I—I—"

Benji folded her arms across her chest. "You didn't tell me that one of the chickens attacked you."

Out of the corner of my eye, I saw Detective Brandon cock her head ever so slightly, as if she was figuring something out for the very first time. I feared it was exactly what I didn't want her to know—that

Piper and Benji were a couple. I didn't want Benji any more involved in this, as far as the police were concerned, than she already was.

"You didn't tell me either," I interjected, hoping to deflect attention away from Benji's comment.

I felt Brandon give me an appraising look, but I refused to look at her.

"Can we see the injury, Piper?" Brandon asked in her strongest cop voice. It wasn't really a question. It was an order.

Perspiration beaded on the girl's brow. Although it was a warm day, I knew it had a lot more to do with the situation than the air temperature. Without a word, Piper lifted the sleeve of her short-sleeve dress and showed us her bare shoulder. There was a red mark there.

Detective Brandon stepped closer to take a better look. "That looks like an abrasion to me. How would a chicken do that, and so high on your shoulder?" She glanced down at Gertrude, who was pecking at the grass at Shepley's feet. "This must be a very special kind of chicken. Part ninja even? And I would expect to see a scratch or a puncture wound."

"The chicken didn't do it!" Piper cracked under the pressure.

"Ah ha!" Shepley cried, wagging his finger at her. "I knew she was lying. Gertrude would never hurt anyone."

Gertrude bent her neck and examined me with one chicken eye. I wasn't so sure about that.

"How did you get the abrasion, Piper?" The detective asked.

Piper dropped her head. "I got it when I ran through the woods."

"When you were running away from the scene of the crime," Brandon said.

Piper nodded, looking miserable.

Benji frowned. "Why would you lie about this? Don't you know how much trouble the Farm could get into if there were attack chickens? Don't you care about the Farm at all? Don't you care—"

"I think it's clear that Piper made a mistake and she regrets it," I interrupted, fearing that Benji would reveal too much.

"You lied to me!" Krissie, who'd been quietly seething up to this point, screeched.

Piper nervously brushed her bangs from her eyes. "You didn't give me a chance to say anything else! I tried to tell you."

Krissie sniffed. "You didn't try very hard. How can I trust a wedding planner who lies to me? I've half a mind to fire you on the spot."

"Now, Krissie," Justin said calmly. "If you fire Piper, who will you find to handle your wedding on such short notice?"

"She can't treat me like this!" Krissie cried.

Justin glanced at the expensive watch on his wrist. "Wow, look at the time. Since the whole attack-chicken thing was a false alarm, and thus I don't see any way that we can ensure you forcibly remove said chickens, I better head back to the office." He spun on his heel and bolted toward Maple Grove Lane.

Krissie took off after him. "Justin! Justin! Come back here!"

"Wow," Brandon mused. "He can really run."

"He ran track in high school. Sprinter," I said.

Brandon nodded. "I can tell."

The detective's cell phone rang and she removed it from her pocket. "Detective Brandon." She stepped away from us.

Shepley glared at Piper and then at me. "Are you going to just let her stay here after what she did?"

"Shepley, calm down," I said.

He leaned over and scooped up Gertrude, tucking her under his arm. "Someday, Miss Director, you're going to wish you hadn't pushed me so far." He stomped away.

I sighed. I would really have to grow a backbone and fire Shepley someday, but like everything else, it would have to wait until after the wedding.

Benji and Piper stood a little bit away from me, in the shadow that the church's steeple cast on the green. The pair was in a heated conversation. Tears rolled down Piper's face, and Benji's jaw was set. I bit the inside of my lip and told myself not to get involved.

Brandon joined me. "As much I would love to stay and see all the drama unfold, I have to go. The coroner called and has the report on Vianna's body. He'd like to share it in person."

"Did he tell you the extent of her injuries?" I asked.

She smiled. "Not something I'd share with you."

That's what I'd expected her to say, but it didn't make it any less annoying.

The detective headed toward Maple Grove Lane, then paused and said over her shoulder, "Nice try, attempting to hide from me that Piper and your assistant are a couple."

My face fell.

She grinned. "And that expression just confirmed it. Thanks for that." She turned back around and walked across the road.

I felt sick. A moment later, Piper ran in the direction of Maple Grove Lane as well. Benji remained rooted where she stood, staring at the front door of the church.

I wanted to go to her, but my own phone rang. I checked the display and saw that the call came from the Cherry Foundation. I should have expected this. I wanted to talk to Henry about what he knew about Vianna Pine, but per usual, he'd made the preemptive strike and contacted me first. As far as I knew, Henry had never had been in the military, but he probably should have been. He would have been great at strategy and sneak attacks.

"This is Kelsey," I said into the phone.

"Hello, I'm Henry Ratcliffe's secretary, calling from the Cherry Foundation. He'd like a meeting with you this afternoon at two o'clock." The female voice was prim and proper. I wouldn't have expected anything else from Henry's secretary. If he had his way, we would all be sent back to the era of *Mad Men*.

"That's great!" I said with all the fake cheer I could muster. "I'm so glad that you called. I'd like a meeting with him too."

"You would?" she asked. Not surprisingly, this didn't appear to be the reception that Henry usually got when he asked someone to a meeting.

"Yep, you bet," I said. "Tell Henry I'll be there with bells on."

"You really want me to tell him that?" she asked, sounding confused. "That you'll be there wearing bells?"

"Sure do. Thanks for calling." I hung up.

In the time that it had taken to answer the short call, Benji had left her vigil at the church and joined me.

"Who was that?" she asked.

"Henry's secretary."

Benji scrunched up her nose. "What did she want?"

"To set up a meeting between Henry and me this afternoon. Fine by me. I have more than a few questions for him. Are you two okay?" I asked, meaning her and Piper.

She sighed. "I don't know."

I opened my mouth, but snapped it shut when she shook her head.

Benji tucked a braid behind her ear. "You think Vianna died because of the inheritance?"

I nodded, understanding her need to move the conversation back to Vianna's death and away from her relationship with Piper. "It's the most likely motive for her murder I've come across so far. It has to be it. What I don't know is whether it was because someone wanted what Vianna was going to receive, or to keep what they already had, fearing they'd lose it when Vianna took over the Foundation."

"Like Henry," Benji said, catching on.

"Exactly, which is why I have to talk to him." I paused. "And I need to talk to Piper too."

Benji frowned. "Why?"

"Because Detective Brandon knows the two of you are a couple now, and, to protect Piper, I really need to know why she was in jail. I have to know, Benji. I think it's important."

Benji clenched her fist.

"I'm going to ask her to come to the cottage this evening so that I can talk to her."

Benji shook her head. "Don't."

"But—"

"Let me do it." She held up a hand. "I'll ask her to come. I'll come too. I want to hear what she has to say. I *need* to hear what she has to say."

I nodded. "All right."

Benji straightened her shoulders. "I'm going to go find Shepley. I need to apologize to him for what Piper did."

"You don't have to do that." I touched her arm.

She shook her head, and her long braids brushed her cheeks. "That's where you're wrong, Kel. I do." She walked off in the direction of Shepley's garden with her back straight, even though I knew her heart was half broken.

TWENTY-THREE

When I reached Maple Grove Lane, my Farm radio crackled. "This is Kelsey. What's up?" I paused. "Over."

"We have a situation," Judy responded. "Over."

There was always a situation on the Farm.

"What?" I asked.

"The sheep got out and they're inside the visitor center." There was a long pause. "Hey! Don't chew on that." And then there was static.

I groaned and broke into a run. A cluster of tourists stood outside the building. Some pointed at the sliding glass door that gave them a view into the main room.

"Excuse me," I said as I made my way to the front of the pack. The sliding glass door opened and I was greeted by a lobby full of bored-looking sheep.

Barton Farm had seven heads of sheep. They were all female. We didn't have a ram. When we wanted to breed the flock, we took our ewes to a farmer a couple of counties over. Between the oxen, draft horses, and all the other animals that lived on Barton Farm, I thought a volatile ram would put me right over the edge.

People claim that sheep are dumb. Perhaps that's true, but ours were escape artists. This wasn't the first time they'd made a break for it or unfortunately waltzed inside the visitor center. The cleaning crew that came in the evenings would not be excited about all the hoofmarks they'd have to scrub off of the pine floors.

Jason was trying to usher the sheep to the doors, but he wasn't having much luck. Judy stood beside the ticket booth. Her usually smooth hair was disheveled and she pulled at her bun. I had a feeling Judy would be asking for a raise after this week.

I hurried over to her. "How did they get in here?" I asked.

She shook her head. "Just like everyone else does. They pranced in through the doors. As to how they got out of the pen, I don't know."

Two seasonal employees stood off to the side, preventing the sheep from entering the cafeteria. For that I was grateful. If the animals went in there, or worse yet, the kitchen, everything would have to be scrubbed from top to bottom. It would force us to close food service down for the rest of the day.

Behind the staffers were a cluster of tourists watching the proceedings while eating popcorn and potato chips. Giddy smiles crossed all the faces. I don't know if they were more amused by the sheep in the visitor center or by the Farm staff trying to get them under control. I suspected the latter of the two.

"We need Tiffin," I said. "Judy, call my father at the cottage and ask him to let Tiffin out. Tiff will come straight here. He'll know the sheep got out. He might even be trying to escape the cottage as we speak."

"On it," Judy said, and went inside the gift shop to make the call.

Jason had four of the sheep clustered in one corner of the main room. With his arms out, he tried to herd them toward the doors that opened onto the Farm grounds. The largest of the sheep, Hollyhock, stared at him with a bored look on her face. It was almost as if she was asking him, "You're joking, right?"

Sweat dripped down the back of Jason's neck and onto the collar of his Farm T-shirt. I knew he wasn't sweating because of the sheep, but because there were so many people around watching him. I walked over and patted his arm. Under my breath, I whispered, "Try to relax. The sheep can sense your tension."

His Adam's apple bobbed up and down as he nodded.

A moment later, the sliding glass door opened and Tiffin barked. He didn't cross the threshold. He knew he wasn't allowed inside the visitor center when the Farm was open.

I clapped my hands. "Tiffin, come!"

With his tongue sticking out of his mouth, he ran toward me.

I pointed to the sheep. "Herd."

He lowered onto his haunches and barked at the sheep.

Hollyhock baaed loudly and eyed Tiffin. The corgi barked again, telling her that he meant business. Hollyhock head-butted another sheep as if to tell her to pay attention, and then she headed for the door with Tiffin on her heels.

As the remaining sheep saw their leader trotting toward the exit, they followed suit. Before long there was a line, seven sheep deep, marching out of the visitor center like they were always this cooperative. The Farm visitors clapped.

Tiffin led his flock to the pasture. Jason ran ahead, opened the gate, and quartered the sheep off on one side of the pasture, in a large pen, to keep them separated from the oxen. Mags and Betty liked to have their own space.

Finally, the onlookers dispersed and headed to other parts of the Farm. I gave a sigh of relief. I scanned the area for Jason, but he was nowhere to be found now. I couldn't help but wonder how the sheep had gotten free. If anyone knew, it was Jason, but he'd poofed. I would have to question him about this later. First, it was best to let him recover from being around all those people.

Betty and Mags looked on with their usual annoyance as I leaned against the fence. I spotted a scrap of white just on the other side in the field. Litter on the Farm? After checking to see where the oxen were, I climbed over the fence. My feet hit the pasture with a thud. As I drew closer to the scrap, I realized it looked like a museum tag. The white thread, which would have held it to the object, was still intact. I read Benji's careful printing: *J. B. 2013/5 flintlock revolver, c. 1810. Barton House.*

My hands shook. The tag was indeed a museum tag, and it had been attached to Jebidiah Barton's revolver.

In the back of my mind, I'd thought that the theft of the items in the trunk could be related to Vianna's murder, but I'd pushed this idea away. No one could know for certain when the items had gone missing, but now I knew it had to have been recent. I walked the grounds every day, and I would have noticed that tag in the grass. I should have noticed it even before this.

"How did this get here?" I asked.

The oxen didn't answer. They just stared at me and chewed their cud. I knew they must have seen who dropped it, but they weren't talking.

Was it possible whoever stole the revolver and other objects from the trunk had run through the pasture, and that was how he or she had dropped the tag?

I looked around again. On the other side of the pasture was our red maple grove and the Barton Farm property line. Beyond that was the state park, which was heavily wooded. Why would a culprit run out in the open like this? Why would they risk encountering Mags and Betty in the process? The oxen might tolerate Jason or me in their field, but there were few others they wouldn't charge.

I flipped the tag over in my hand. It didn't look any worse for the wear. There were some light water spots that I assumed were from dew, so it had to have been in the pasture for at least one night. Vianna had been murdered only the night before. We'd had a dry summer—I tried to remember the last time it had rained. The tag would have been in much worse condition if it had been rained on; clearly it hadn't been. I decided that if I checked when it last rained, maybe I could narrow down the time when the theft had occurred. At the very least, I could assume the theft was sometime after the rain.

I balanced the weight of the tag in my hand, and it felt like a block of lead. All I knew was that I would have to tell Detective Brandon about this, and it was a conversation that I knew well enough to dread.

TWENTY-FOUR

THE CHERRY FOUNDATION OFFICES were located in Cynthia Cherry's old mansion, which was tucked away in the Cuyahoga Valley only two miles from Barton Farm. The house was a formidable Tudor that looked better suited to the regal streets of London than to a patch of woods in the middle of Ohio.

Cynthia's father had built the home to show off his wealth, and Cynthia, his only daughter who'd never married, had lived in the mansion her entire life—from the day she was born until the day she died.

Every time I visited the mansion, memories of Cynthia and her kindness to Hayden and me came back in a rush. I didn't know how I would have survived my divorce if it hadn't been for her. I'd been a single mom, fresh out of graduate school, with a small son and no job prospects. During my interview for the director position at Barton Farm, she and I had hit it off and she'd hired me on the spot. I could never thank her enough for taking a chance on me. For that, I would be eternally grateful to her. And for that reason, I vowed to find out who had killed her grandniece. Cynthia would have loved Vianna with her whole heart, had she been given the opportunity.

But Maxwell had kept that from her. He and I had never gotten along—he was a pompous, selfish, and rude jerk. But Cynthia loved him, for all his flaws. It would have broken her heart to know that he'd kept his daughter from her all these years.

I couldn't think of a reason why Maxwell had done that. And now, with all three of them gone and the Cherry line ended, I would never find out.

At Cynthia's front door—because I would always think of the door as Cynthia's—I lifted the handle of the knocker and rapped three times. Almost instantly, the door opened, and Miles, Cynthia's butler, greeted me from the other side of the threshold.

After Cynthia died, the Foundation had laid off all of her in-house staff with the exception of Miles. At first I'd assumed Henry and the board had kept him because of the prestige a butler gave the Foundation. I later learned that Cynthia had given the Foundation no choice. In her will, she'd declared that Miles was to live out the remainder of this life at the mansion if he so chose. Since he was still there, I suspected he'd made the decision to stay.

"Hello, Miles," I said with a bright smile.

He stared down his long nose at me. Any time I met him, I was struck by his uncanny resemblance to Carson from *Downton Abbey*. It wasn't so much a physical appearance, but how he held his head high and kept his posture erect.

"Miss Cambridge," the butler said, with just enough disdain to make sure I knew he wasn't thrilled by my presence. He didn't make a move to let me inside.

"I have a meeting with Henry." I was still all smiles.

The butler pursed his lips together in such a thin line they all but disappeared from his face. After a beat, he stepped to the side and let me through.

I stepped into the foyer and the essence of Cynthia enveloped me, almost taking my breath away. There was no place I felt the loss of her as keenly as inside her eclectic home.

On the outside, the house was regal and stately. Inside, it was a hodgepodge that told the story of Cynthia's colorful life. She'd been a vibrant person and the interior of her house showed it. As an avid world traveler, each room of the home reflected one of her favorite places to visit. The foyer had a marble and mosaic floor and Athenian busts standing on pedestals, staring blankly into the space. The solarium was a Caribbean paradise, and the kitchen transported you directly to South America.

I was surprised that over the last year Henry and the Foundation hadn't made more of an effort to renovate the mansion more to their liking. Considering Henry's dour ways, I imagined that would include a lot of beige. Cynthia had not been a beige person.

I patted Miles on the arm. "Thanks."

He stared at the spot where I'd touched him as if a mouse sat there mocking him. "Mr. Ratcliffe is waiting for you in Master Maxwell's office."

I couldn't help but smile when he referred to the board chairman's office as "Master Maxwell's." I knew that along with Cynthia's eclectic décor, this must drive Henry crazy. I liked Miles better for it even though I hadn't liked Maxwell. "I know the way," I said.

He bowed and then strolled down the hallway.

I took the grand staircase two steps at a time to the second floor. At the top of the landing, I went right, in the direction of the west wing of the enormous house. When Cynthia and Maxwell were alive, Cynthia had lived primarily in the east wing and Maxwell in the west. The house was big enough that they could go days without running into each other if they chose. Maxwell, who was secretive even with his aunt, often chose that. Cynthia frequently complained about not seeing him enough even though they lived in the same house.

My sneakers made hushed noises on the dense carpet as I made my way down the long hall, up another set of stairs, and down a second long hallway to Maxwell's-now-Henry's office. The mansion truly was a maze.

To reach it, I first had to go through his secretary's office. The desk there was empty, much to my relief. The heavy dark wood door that led into the inner office stood open, and inside, Henry sat at Maxwell's expansive and expensive desk, poring over a sheath of papers. His head was bent, and it was clear that he didn't know I was there.

I suspected that Maxwell's office, with its masculine feel, dark wood, and leather furniture, was the one room that Henry would not choose to redecorate, along with maybe the library on the main floor, which was so British in décor sometimes I expected to find Prince Charles there drinking a cup of tea.

I knocked on the door frame.

Henry looked up from his papers. "Ahh, yes, Kelsey, please come in." He gestured at one of the two black leather chairs in front of his desk. "Have a seat."

I sat on one of the chairs and nearly disappeared. I wriggled my way out of the deep cushion and perched on the edge of the seat.

Sometimes being so small really was a bother. Henry made no comment on my struggle with the chair.

He glanced at the gold watch on his wrist. "You're twenty minutes late."

I folded my hands on my lap. "I had a sheep situation at the Farm."

"I see," he said coldly. "I sent my secretary out on an errand because I wanted us to have some privacy." He stood up and crossed the room, closing the heavy door with a resounding thud like the lid on a coffin. "I'd best close this so that we aren't interrupted if she should return earlier than planned." He walked back around the side of the desk and resumed his seat. "You must think I called this meeting because of the Pumpernickle wedding," he began.

I shook my head. "I assumed it was because Vianna Pine was Cynthia's rightful heir and now she's dead."

"Ahh, I should have expected you would find this out. Despite our differences, Ms. Cambridge, I have always appreciated the fact that you're a problem solver and able to get right down to business. I imagine you were the one who resolved the sheep situation on the Farm with little fanfare."

I didn't bother to reply to this comment. "I assume you knew of Vianna's relationship to Maxwell before the rest of the world did."

"Yes, of course." He leaned back in his chair for a moment before sitting up straight again.

"For how long?" I asked

He moved his stack of papers aside and set his elbows on the desktop. He pressed the tips of his fingers together in a steeple shape. It was a pose that I'd seen him do many times before. I wondered if he'd learned it in law school, as a posture that exuded authority, or maybe it was something he'd just picked up on television. The irony of the posture wasn't lost on me, considering how Vianna died.

"She came to me at the end of April with a letter from her dead mother. It said that Maxwell Cherry was her father and that she, Vianna, had claim to the Cherry family's fortune. Vianna's mother advised her daughter to contact the Foundation and claim her birthright."

"When did her mother die?" I asked.

"The end of last year."

That was around the same time that Cynthia died, I thought. "And she didn't approach the Foundation until April?" I asked.

"It wasn't until recently that she began to go through her mother's things, or so she said. That's when she found the letter." Henry pressed his lips together, as if just speaking of the letter put a bad taste in his mouth.

"Why didn't her mother tell her this when Maxwell died?" I asked. "He died over a year ago. She could have had her daughter claim her inheritance then, and she would have gotten to know Cynthia before she died."

Henry shrugged. "We may never know."

"So Vianna showed up with this letter, and that was it? You accepted her as the rightful heir?" I asked, even though I knew this wasn't true. According to Brandon, Vianna took a paternity test.

He flattened his hands on the desktop. "It was more than just the letter. She also had deposit records for her mother's bank account from Maxwell. The deposits varied in sum and were made sporadically, but the majority of them were from when Vianna was child. Her mother kept a file over the years. Apparently, it was in this file that Vianna also found the letter explaining who her father was."

"That was enough evidence for you." I concentrated on not falling back into the huge chair.

He smiled, as if he knew I didn't believe it could be. In this case, he would be right. "No. The Cherry Foundation is worth twenty million dollars, give or take a million on either side. Vianna wasn't the first, nor, I assume, will she be the last to come to us claiming to be Maxwell's heir. Maxwell had many liaisons in his life. He was no saint. More than one person with a fatherless sob story has claimed to be his biological child." He steepled his hands again. "I will admit that Vianna came with more proof than the others, but the Foundation still had to do its due diligence and have irrefutable proof that she was an heir."

"A DNA test, you mean," I said, inching forward in the chair again. The chair was like a great whale trying to swallow me whole. I sort of knew what Jonah had felt like now.

"Precisely." He smiled at me like I'd passed some sort of test.

"And?" I said, hoping to keep him talking.

"Since we always knew this was a possibility—someone crawling out of the woodwork and claiming to be an heir to Cynthia's fortune—we had both Cynthia's and Maxwell's DNA saved in a private lab. When Vianna made her claim, she and I went to that lab for the test. We just received the results on Monday."

The day before Vianna died.

"And..."

He frowned. "It was a match. Ninety-nine percent certainty. Vianna's mother told the truth. Vianna was in fact Maxwell's daughter."

"She learned that she was an heiress and a day later, died," I said.

Henry nodded. "I can see what you're thinking, and you're wrong. Her death isn't related to this in the least. She and I both

195

knew, but I hadn't yet told even the other members of the board. Not enough people knew to make it a motive to kill her." He leaned back in his chair. "I believe that the police have it wrong and the young woman's death was just an accident. She fell from the steeple when she made the foolhardy attempt to hang those lights. Her death was tragic and unfortunate, but there was no foul play there. I've told the police chief this."

"Why didn't you and Vianna tell anyone, or announce it that very day?" I asked.

He placed his elbows back on the top of the desk. "That was Vianna's idea, not mine."

I gave him a look.

He frowned. "It's the truth. She didn't want to overshadow Krissie Pumpernickle's wedding, and she knew it would impact her relationship with you as the director of Barton Farm. For all intents and purposes, she would be your boss when everything was sorted out. She thought it was best to wait until after the wedding and then deal with what being Maxwell Cherry's daughter meant."

Get through the wedding. That had been my motto of the week. I was surprised that it had been Vianna's too. Once again, it occurred to me that maybe we weren't as different from each other as I'd thought we were.

"If she'd told me, she could have forced me to hang those lights in the church steeple and she might still be alive," I pointed out.

"Perhaps." Henry shrugged. "It was Vianna's decision, but it has put me in a bit of trouble. Since I knew about her good fortune before the general public did, your police detective has gotten it into her head I might have had something to do with her death." His brow knit together.

I braced my hands on my knees. "You had as much to lose as I did if she'd taken over the Foundation."

"Be that as it may, I had nothing to do with it. Take my word for it."

I couldn't just take his word for that, or anything else really. "And how would we know you had nothing to do with the murder?"

He gave me a mirthless smile. "You can ask the New Hartford mayor. I was over at his house the night Vianna died. The mayor was there, as well as three other important men from the community."

"What are their names?" I asked.

He smiled. "Now, now, Kelsey, I've told this to the police. I have no need to give their names to you."

I glared at him.

He smiled. "So as you can see, nothing has changed, Ms. Cambridge. You're in the same spot as you were before. You run Barton Farm, and you answer to the Cherry Foundation Board and to me. You should feel grateful that the status quo was upheld."

I stood up. "Even if a young woman had to die to uphold it."

He shrugged as if it were of little consequence.

If I didn't dislike Henry Ratcliffe already, that would have done it.

I walked to the door and opened it. I saw the secretary's desk was still empty. I turned and asked Henry one final question. "Did Vianna have any children? Is it possible that a relative of hers could come out of the woodwork, too, and claim to the rightful heir?"

"No," he said firmly. "I checked."

I was sure he had. He wasn't going to let another heir wander onto his doorstep when he'd almost lost everything when the first one arrived. But the question remained, despite his protests to the contrary—had he gotten rid of Vianna to keep his position at the Foundation? He might have an alibi, but he also had more than enough money at his disposal to pay someone to do his dirty work.

I kept those thoughts to myself as I strode out of the office.

TWENTY-FIVE

I BLEW OUT A breath as I turned into Barton Farm's parking lot. It was late afternoon, and the Farm closed at five. It wouldn't be long before all the tourists were gone and the Farm was returned to the employees for another night. And the wedding was two days away. Even with everything that had happened in the last forty-eight hours, it appeared the wedding was a go.

As far as finding the murderer, I didn't know where to look next. Henry was a viable suspect, with the means and motive to hire someone to push Vianna out the bell tower window. But if Henry had hired someone, the killer could be anybody. It might not be someone Vianna had ever come across in her life, and I imagined a person who did that kind of work was very good at covering his tracks and disappearing after he'd collected his money. I supposed that Armin was a suspect too, because he'd loved Vianna and she'd rejected him, but it was hard for me to imagine Armin climbing up the ladder into the bell tower. I wasn't even certain he could squeeze through the hatch, and there was no way such a giant man could sneak up on someone.

And I had to admit to myself—even if I wouldn't to Benji—that Piper was as viable a suspect as Henry. She was Vianna's assistant. Armin said that she was in a way Vianna's protégé, and Vianna might have left her thriving wedding planning business to her. That was a serious motive. And I couldn't ignore that fact that Vianna was a difficult person to get along with. Maybe the wedding planner had pushed Piper too far and Piper snapped and in turn pushed her boss out the window. Detective Brandon would know if Vianna had left Piper the business. She would also know why Piper had a police record, but I doubted that she would answer either of those questions if I asked her for the information.

I rested my forehead on the steering wheel of my car for a moment, thinking that I must be missing something. There had to be another option. I straightened in my seat. I wasn't going to find that other option sitting in my car. I knew that.

I climbed out and waved to a group of elderly tourists as they piled into a van from a local retirement home. As the van pulled away, it revealed Chase leaning against his Jeep with his arms crossed over his chest.

My stomach tightened into a knot and I felt like my feet were stuck in a bucket of quick-dry cement. I couldn't move. I was experiencing a mixture of relief and annoyance at seeing him there—relief because I was happy to see him, but the relief and the fact that I wanted to lean on him annoyed me.

I didn't have to make a decision whether or not to move. Chase dropped his arms and walked over to me. He opened his arms wide, and as if my body had a mind of its own, I stepped into his embrace. He wrapped me in a warm hug that I wished didn't feel so good.

"How was your day?" he asked. His lips moved on the top of my head as he spoke.

I said the first thing that came to mind. "The sheep got inside the visitor center and caused a ruckus."

His chest rumbled with laughter against my cheek. "Was that all?"

"Oh, and murder," I said.

I felt him kiss the top of my head. "I wish I could make it all go away for you."

I felt my body tense. I was certain he felt it too. It was a reflex, one that I couldn't stop as much as I wanted to. I pressed my face farther into his chest. I wished that I could stay there forever and didn't have to worry about losing full custody of Hayden, my ex-husband's wedding, or murder. And as much as I didn't want it to, the sensation scared me. I didn't want to be dependent on a man. I'd been dependent on Eddie, and I couldn't face that level of betrayal again.

Chase tilted my chin up, forcing me to look at him. "What's wrong?"

"You know, dead bodies and stuff," I said. When all else fails, make a joke, Kelsey, I thought. It's what you're good at.

Concern crossed Chase's face. He let me go, and even with the warm summer sun on my back, I felt a sudden chill. I pushed the rush of feelings aside. Now was not the time for me to sort out how I felt about Chase. I could worry about that after the wedding.

I swallowed. "It's almost closing time, so most of the visitors will have left the village by now or are on their way out. I wanted to check out the church."

He sighed, as if he knew that was the best he was going to get out of me, and he would be right—at least for the moment, until I'd had time to think. I knew that at some point, Chase would no longer stand my delay tactics. He would want to know how I felt about him. The status quo wasn't going to work forever.

"All right," he said, gesturing in the direction of the village. "Lead on, Ms. Director."

I smiled at him, grateful that he didn't push me. I led him to the side gate that opened directly onto the Farm grounds. I knew if we went through the visitor center, I would become entangled in some small Farm emergency and would be lucky to make it to the church by dark. I did not want to be stumbling around the bell tower at night.

As we walked along the pebbled path, I waved at the smiling tourists passing us on their way to the exit. Chase waved to them too and asked what they liked most about the Farm, and I could feel myself relax as his normal good humor was restored.

When we reached the village side of the Farm, I saw that several of the seasonal employees were making their way across the street. They waved at us and whipped their cell phones out of their berry baskets and satchels. I suppressed a smile. It was hard for my staffers, especially the college kids, to keep their phones hidden away all day, as they must in order not to ruin the illusion of the Farm as it was in 1863. They were so eager to reconnect with the twenty-first century that they had to do it before they even reached the visitor center to clock out.

Cari, one of those college students, unbuttoned her waistcoat and said into the phone, "OMG, it was crazy hot today. Let's hit that Mexican place. I need a frozen margarita."

Chase laughed, and I knew he'd heard her too.

Finally, we reached the church. The crime scene tape was still across the front door, and above, the unlit twinkle lights dangled from the broken window in the bell tower. I walked up the three steps and removed the tape, scrunching it up into a ball in my right hand.

"Are you sure you're allowed to do that?" Chase asked, jogging up the steps to be at my side.

"The church will be released back into my care tomorrow morning. Taking a peek at its condition now won't make any difference."

"You're getting the church back that fast? How did you manage that?" He raised his blond eyebrows.

"I didn't." I looked up at him. "It was Henry Ratcliffe. He plays poker with the mayor."

"Ahh," Chase said, as if that explained it. Which of course, in a town of New Hartford's size, it did.

"Well, if Candy said that, it must be true," he went on. "She wouldn't let you in there if she had her way. Trust me on that." He frowned. "I'm surprised that she didn't tell me. I saw her not that long ago at the station. I dropped in to visit my uncle before coming here."

I grimaced, then quickly told myself I wasn't jealous of the beautiful police detective. Because feeling jealous was absolutely ridiculous. What a contradiction I was. I quietly mocked myself. I was unsure if I wanted Chase permanently in my life, but I was jealous at the prospect of him being with anyone else.

I unlocked the church door with the master key on my key ring. I stuck the key ring back into the pocket of my jeans and pushed the door open. It swung into the small vestibule. The space contained a single plain pew and a small table with a sign-in book and brochures with upcoming Farm events on it. Next to the table, two doors opened wide into the sanctuary.

I stepped inside the sanctuary. Golden summer light poured in through the clear glass windows onto the whitewashed pulpit and oak altar. The pews were plain and made of black walnut, a common tree in the valley at the time the church was built back in 1805. It had once been the First Congregational Church in a neighboring Northeast Ohio town. Now it was an artifact, like almost everything else on the Farm.

Thinking of the church as an artifact reminded me of the tag to Jebidiah Barton's revolver, which was burning a hole in my pocket. I knew I needed to tell Brandon about it, but it could wait until I checked out the church.

The sanctuary was plain, no frills, and in keeping with the Western Reserve style that the settlers of this part of Ohio had brought with them from Connecticut over two hundred years ago. There was no stained glass or Jesus hanging from the cross. A calm settled over me, as it always did when I entered the Farm's church. The serenity and lack of adornment soothed me.

In my mind's eye, I imagined nineteenth-century parishioners standing in the second row, hymnals in hand, the women in their bonnets and the men in three-button jackets.

"It's peaceful," Chase said, breaking into the moment.

I glanced back at him. I'd forgotten he was there. "It's hard to believe that murder could infest this place." I placed a hand on the back of the last pew. "I thought it would have been safe from harm."

"Nothing is completely safe," Chase said.

I looked back at him and met his gaze, and I knew that he spoke of much more than the church. I frowned and walked over to the door in the back right corner of the vast room. I opened the door and looked up the dark stairs leading to the balcony choir loft. The stairs were narrow, and I took care while walking up them. In the middle of the loft, a wooden ladder led up to the bell tower.

We always left the ladder down, so that the tourists could see up into the tower through the opening in the plaster ceiling. I realized now that I'd have to remove the ladder in order to ensure that something like Vianna's death didn't happen again.

Crime scene tape was wrapped around the ladder with the same enthusiasm as a teenager toilet-papering a house.

Chase walked around me. "I'll get it." He unwrapped the yards of tape.

After it was removed, I started to climb the ladder.

"What are you doing?" Chase asked.

I was about six feet off of the floor when I looked back at him. "What does it look like?"

He put his hands on his hips. "Didn't you say it was unsafe up there?"

"Well, yeah." I started to climb again. "But that won't stop me from checking it out, and at the very least, I have to remove those twinkle lights. Krissie won't want those as part of her wedding scenery now." I was halfway up the ladder at this point.

When I reached the top, I felt the ladder shift below me. I looked down to find Chase making his way up. I suppressed a smile and crawled through the hatch onto the bell tower's floor.

The floor of the tower was made of whitewashed pine boards. Sunlight crept through the three wooden-slatted windows and poured through the window with the broken slats. A folding step stool stood in one corner, and the middle of the tower was dominated by the one-ton church bell itself. The enormous brass beast was suspended in space by rope as thick as my leg and a network of pulleys.

Chase's head popped out through the hatch, reminding me of a groundhog making its first appearance in spring. With a grunt he climbed the rest of the way through the hatch. It was a tight fit for him, which only convinced me more that Armin, who was twice Chase's size, couldn't have pushed Vianna out of the window.

I walked over to the broken window. The police had been thorough when removing the frame. I didn't know if I should be happy about this or annoyed. After the wedding, I would have to get a carpenter up here to fix the window.

I peered down at the Farm grounds. It was a long way down. I swallowed. This was the last image that Vianna saw before she died. I reminded myself that it had been dark out when she fell. It must have felt like plummeting into a black abyss. Was that where she was now? I shivered as the dark thoughts crossed my mind.

The twinkle lights still hung from what was left of the window. Hanging on to the side of the tower, I leaned out and grabbed hold of them.

Chase groaned right behind me. "Will you at least let me do that?"

I scowled back at him.

He held up his hands. "I'm not suggesting it because I'm a man, if that's what you're afraid of. I just have longer arms. I won't have to hang halfway out of the tower to reach the lights." To prove his point, his leaned across my body, pressing into me, and grabbed the string of lights with little effort.

I wriggled out from under him and stepped back into the relative safety of the tower. "Okay, fine. Because you're taller."

He laughed. "Boy, you *are* stubborn."

I rolled my eyes. "Just a little."

That got a genuine smile from him.

Chase pulled the string of lights into the tower and wound them into a ball in his hands. "I wonder why Candy left these behind. I'd have thought she'd take them for evidence too. It looks like she took everything else."

"I was wondering the same thing," I said as I moved around the bell tower looking for anything out of the ordinary—for something that would give me a clue as to who had been in the tower with Vianna that night.

The enormous brass church bell dominated the space. I studied the rope and pulleys that held it in place. Because we weren't sure of the stability of those ropes and pulleys, we never rang the bell. It had been silent for decades, ever since the church was moved to the village from its original spot miles away. Getting the bell and tower assessed had always been a plan of mine as a restoration project for the Farm. Like so many projects on the Farm's land under my care.

I removed the notebook from my back pocket and made another note about the bell, reminding myself to make it a priority. I sighed. My To Do list grew longer every day, no matter how many things I might cross off of it.

As I wrote, I walked around the right side of the bell, opposite from the broken window.

"Oh, and be careful," Chase said, breaking into my thoughts. "Some of these boards look rotten."

As he said this, I tucked the notebook back into my jeans and took a step back, and my foot broke through the floor—taking the rest of me with it.

TWENTY-SIX

"KELSEY!" CHASE'S VOICE CALLED from what sounded like a long way away.

I groaned and rolled onto my side.

He peered through the opening above me. I blinked at him until his face came into focus. Worry creased his forehead. He was only four feet above where I lay.

"Are you all right?" His voice was tense.

"I'm okay." I touched the back of my head, where I'd hit it on the wooden floor, and started to sit up.

He held out his hand. "Don't. Stay put. You may have a concussion."

"I'm sure I don't. I didn't fall that far." I struggled to a sitting position and wobbled for a moment as the world tilted on its axis.

Chase made a sound that came out like a frustrated growl. "I wish you would just listen for once. I'm the one with medical training here."

I squinted at him and was happy to see there was only one of him. That had to be a good sign.

"Does anything hurt?" His voice softened.

I wiggled my toes inside of my sneakers. "Yes," I groaned. "In fact, everything hurts." As I said this, pain shot up from my right calf. I blinked a couple of times and looked down at my leg, which was bent at the knee. On the left side of my calf, blood oozed through my jeans. I swallowed and looked away. I didn't know if I was upset by the injury or by the fact that I would have to tell Chase about it, proving that he was right and I did in fact hurt myself. "Umm," I said.

"What is it?" His voice was sharp.

There was no way that I could hide this from him. "I think I hurt my leg. It's not that bad."

"I'm coming down there."

I waved my hands. "No, let me get out and then you can look at it."

"Please don't argue with me, just this once." With that, he carefully wriggled into the hole beside me. I covered my head, hoping that he wouldn't kick me in the temple. That certainly wouldn't help the dizzy spell that seemed to have come over me.

Gingerly, Chase knelt beside me. The space was tight and his chest was pressed up against my shoulder.

"I think this was a very bad idea," I said.

"Shhh," he said as he shifted his weight.

"Did you just shush me?"

He sighed. "From the amount of sass you're giving me, I predict you're going to live."

"Sass?" Now I was really annoyed.

He touched my leg above the blood stain, and I yelped.

He leaned away from me. "You're going to have to take off your jeans for me to see the extent of your injury."

"Are you crazy? I'm not taking off my jeans. There's not enough room to maneuver in here even if I wanted to."

"I wish I'd thought to bring my medical bag with me," he groused. "I could have cut your pant leg open and taken a look."

"These are my favorite jeans," I said. "I'm not going to let you cut them into pieces."

This made Chase laugh. "They're goners. You'll never get all the blood out of them. Just make peace with that."

He had a point. Unfortunately.

"We have to get you to a hospital." His tone turned serious. "You'll need a tetanus shot and probably stitches."

"I don't need a tetanus shot. I got one last year. Everyone who works on the Farm has to be up to date on their shots because of the work we do."

"Well, that's good to hear." He sounded a little relieved. "But you still need stitches."

I groaned. "I don't have time for this. The wedding is Friday. That's two days from now. Can't you just stitch me up and call it a day?"

"Kelsey, you could be seriously hurt. The wound could get infected."

"It won't under your care. I mean, you're an EMT. Patching up people is what you do."

He heaved a deep sigh. "I don't even know what to do with you anymore. You're impossible."

"No matter the intention, I'll take that as a compliment." I smiled at him.

"It wasn't meant to be," he grumbled.

"Too bad. Now will you help me out of this hole?" I shifted my seat and something poked me in my back end. "I think I landed on something."

"The hard wooden floor?" he asked.

"No, there's something else. Something pointy."

"Can you stand?"

"If you help me." I grimaced as I moved my injured leg. "I think I can."

"Hallelujah, you finally asked for my help. I should have turned on the video app on my phone to capture the moment." He grinned.

"It's an opportunity that won't happen again if you don't help me now."

Chase crouched beside me and put his hands under my arms. He started to lift me up.

"Ahh," I cried.

He froze. "Did I hurt you?"

"No," I lied. "You didn't." I bit down hard on my lip.

"I really don't think moving you is a great idea. We should call for help." His body tensed.

"What good is that going to do?" I asked. "I'll still have to climb down the ladder." I leaned heavily against him to avoid putting weight on my injured leg.

"I can carry you down the ladder." He didn't move.

"What are you, a caveman?" I snorted. "I know I'm small, but you can't just fling me over your shoulder and carry me down the ladder. I won't allow it."

"The climb might make your injury worse," he said. "And cave-men aren't so bad, are they?"

I ignored his cavemen comment. "I'll be fine."

He groaned.

"Now help me out of here. I want to see what I landed on."

Chase picked me up and placed me on my seat outside of the hole, then looked down. Now we were in opposite places from where we'd started. I was above Chase, peering down, and he was inside the hole in the floor, although he was standing so he was eye-level with me.

"What did I land on?" I asked.

Chase shook his head but dutifully crouched on the floor inside the hole again. "It looks like a cardboard box, and you pulverized it."

"Gee, thanks." It was just what every girl wanted to hear—that she crushed a box by sitting on it.

He lifted the box out of the hole, set it next to me on the bell tower floor, and climbed out. He sat on the floor next to me. I could feel his eyes on my leg. "Now can we go?" he asked.

"Not quite yet." I pulled the crumpled box a little bit closer to me.

"Did you know there was space under the bell tower floor like that?" he asked.

I shook my head and gritted my teeth against the pain in my leg. I didn't want him to know how much it hurt me. I knew he would insist that we go to the hospital right away, and I wanted to see what was in the box first. "If I knew, I would have looked in it a long time ago. Many of the buildings have surprises in them that we've discovered."

"Like the root cellar in the Barton House," Chase teased.

I couldn't help but crack a smile. It was his way of reminding me that he'd rescued me from another hole in the floor, once upon a time.

I lifted the right flap of the crushed box. Chase was right, I had all but pulverized it. I hoped that whatever was inside was still intact. There was a cotton cloth over the top of the contents. I pushed the cloth aside and my mouth fell open.

Chase leaned close to me. "What is it?"

"It's the missing artifacts from the Farm's storage."

"Missing artifacts?" he asked.

I nodded as I lifted an aged copy of *David Copperfield* from the box. "We discovered them missing the morning before Vianna died. After she died, I sort of put it out of my mind."

"Does this mean it could be related to her death?" Chase asked.

The book felt heavy in my hand. I didn't open it, since I didn't want the oils from my hands to harm the antique pages. I needed to have cotton gloves on in order to really take a good look at all the items.

"I don't know," I said honestly. "It seems kind of coincidental, finding them in the same place she was killed."

"Could Vianna have stolen these things?" he asked. "To do what with? Sell?"

"Vianna didn't need the money," I said.

Chase ran his fingers through his hair. "What do you mean?"

"That's right—you don't know the latest development." I went on to tell him about Vianna being the heir to the Cherry fortune and the Foundation.

He whistled. "That would have changed everything."

"Exactly," I said. "For the Foundation, for the Farm, and for me."

He peeked inside the box again. "Is everything there? Does it have everything you suspected went missing?"

"I hope so." I told him about the museum tag I'd found in the pasture earlier.

Chase frowned. "You're right. If that gun is missing, you've got to report it."

I riffled through the box's contents, taking a quick inventory with as much care as I could. Having gone over the spreadsheets when we'd reported the theft to the police, I knew everything that had once been inside that trunk. Benji, who'd cataloged the collection, would know even better than I what the artifacts looked like in detail.

I swallowed. One item was glaringly missing. "I can account for all but one thing."

"What's that?" Chase asked with trepidation.

I looked him directly in the eye. "Jebidiah Barton's revolver."

TWENTY-SEVEN

"Be careful," Chase called up to me as I gingerly swung my good leg over the side of the ladder and made the long, slow climb downward. Chase and the box of artifacts were already safely in the choir loft below. After much debate, we'd decided that it would be best if Chase went down the ladder first with the box, and I would follow. In case I fell off the ladder, Chase claimed he'd catch me or at least break my fall. I preferred not to put him to the test on that, so I took every step with caution, one painful rung at a time, but as I descended, I realized that my injury must not be as bad as Chase feared. I found I could put some of my weight on my hurt leg.

When I was four rungs from the bottom, I felt his hands around my waist, and he lifted me off the ladder and carefully set me on the floor.

He held on to my hand as I hopped in place.

I looked up at him "What's that smile for?"

He shook his head. "You look cute when you hop."

I narrowed my eyes.

"Now we need to get you to the hospital," he said in a serious tone.

"We can't do that now. I need to call Detective Brandon and tell her what we found. Like you said, this might be related to Vianna's murder, and it can't wait."

He groaned. "At least let's go to the cottage and take a look at your leg first. If it doesn't require stitches, I'll agree to your plan." He made a move to pick me up.

I hopped away from him. "I can walk. Thank you very much."

He arched his brow at me. "You're going to hop all the way across the Farm just to prove you can? You'll tire yourself out, and you'll need all your wits when dealing with Candy."

I had to admit he had a point. "Okay, fine," I said. "Lend me your arm just to get down the stairs."

Chase bent over and picked up the box, which really did look as if it had been run over by a semi. He tucked it under his left arm and held out his right elbow for me to grab.

I slipped my arm through his and he helped me step-by-step back to the sanctuary floor and then out the church door, only pausing long enough for me to lock up the building.

On his arm, I hopped down the church's stone steps and began the long walk to the cottage. I would never admit it to Chase, but by the time we reached Maple Grove Lane, I did sort of wish I'd let him carry me.

When we hobbled by the visitor center, Chase said, "Maybe we should take care of your leg in there."

"No," I said a little too quickly. "Let's go to my cottage. Judy has had enough excitement for one day. I'm afraid her seeing me like this would send her right over the edge."

He sighed, and we continued our way down the pebbled path into the sugar maple grove. When my cottage came into sight, I almost burst into tears at the joy of seeing it. I couldn't wait for a hot shower, a change of clothes, and to collapse on my own bed, not necessarily in that order. There wouldn't be time for any of that though. As soon as Chase said my leg was passable, I had to talk to Brandon and find out where this latest development in the case would lead me.

Hayden and Tiffin were playing tag in the tiny white picket-fenced yard around the cottage. My father, still in his cape, looked on from the front steps while reading what looked like a script. I had a feeling Hayden and I were going to have to practice new lines with him in the very near future.

Tiffin barked a greeting, and both my father and son looked up to see Chase and me at the gate. My father jumped out of his seat. "Kelsey, what on earth happened to you?" He gaped at my leg. "You're hurt!"

"It's just a scratch," I said, downplaying the injury.

"It's more than a scratch," Chase said.

I gave him a look.

He shrugged, as if to ask what I was going to do about it.

"What happened?" Dad asked.

I gave my father the short version about my accident, and then Dad looked at Chase. "What's in the box, and why does it look like it got ran over by a train?"

"Kelsey landed on it," Chase deadpanned.

"Thanks," I muttered. I would have pushed him for that comment if my leg didn't hurt so much.

Chase grinned as if he knew I wanted to push him. "Let's go inside and take a look at that leg."

Hayden's face creased in concern. "Mom, you have blood on your pants."

I held my hand out to Hayden. "Don't worry, buddy. It looks a lot worse than it feels."

We all went into the house, and Chase set me on a kitchen chair. He then put a second chair in front me and put my leg on that. Dad handed him a pair of scissors, and Chase carefully cut into my jeans from the cuff up. He was right—the jeans were goners. When the fabric was cut away, he cleaned the wound with rubbing alcohol that Dad had found in the medicine cabinet. I winced as the alcohol stung something fierce.

Hayden folded his hand into mine. "Maybe you should go to the doctor. Wouldn't you make me to go to the doctor if I was hurt like that?"

Chase raised his eyebrows at me while he continued to tend the wound. "The kid has a point."

I patted Hayden's cheek. "You're right. I would make sure that you were all checked out and okay, and that's what Chase is doing here. Chase is as good as a doctor. He saves people's lives every day." I pleaded with Chase with my eyes. "Right, Chase?"

"That's right," Chase said, jumping in. "Your mom will be fine. She might walk funny for a couple of days, but that's no big thing."

Hayden looked from Chase to me and back again, and the worry in his small face cleared. "Okay." He turned to me. "Mom, since you're okay, can I watch a show in your room?"

I sighed. "Sure, you can watch a show."

My son gave me a fist pump in the air and ran up the stairs with Tiffin on his heels. Frankie followed at a much more sedate pace.

After Chase wrapped gauze around my wound, he said, "You're lucky. The cut isn't that deep. You probably don't need stitches."

I grinned. "Told you. I was right."

He shook his head. "One of these days, Kelsey Cambridge, you aren't going to be right. I hope you'll be able to handle that."

"But not today," I said, struggling to my feet. "I'll just go change my clothes and then call the detective."

"Need any help with that?" He wiggled his eyebrows.

I swatted at him. "No."

What seemed like a long time later, I hopped back downstairs in a clean T-shirt and running shorts. With my injured leg, it had taken me much longer to change than normal. I saw my father and Chase sitting side by side on the couch. The moment I stumbled down the last step, they were both up and out of their seats. I held up a hand. "I'm fine. I'm fine."

Dad smiled and sat back down, but an expression I couldn't read crossed Chase's face. I didn't take the time to stop and try to figure out what it was. "I need to call Detective Brandon and tell her what we found in the bell tower."

"I already did that," Chase said.

"What do you—"

My questions were cut off by a knock at the door, and without waiting for anyone to answer, Detective Brandon stomped inside. "Are you withholding information from me, Kelsey Cambridge? I could have you thrown in jail for tampering with evidence."

"Tampering with evidence?" I yelped. "You wouldn't *have* this evidence if Chase and I hadn't found the box—it would still be missing. Your officers have been in and out of the church a dozen times today, and you didn't find it."

"You took it from the crime scene!" Her face was bright red. "You should have called me from the church. Now you've moved it, and any clues to how it got there have been ruined."

"I think those were ruined when Kelsey landed on the box," Chase said dryly.

I scowled at Chase and gave him a you-are-not-helping look. He smiled in return.

"And you!" Brandon glared at Chase. "You know better. What do you think your uncle will say when he hears about this?"

Chase's cheeks flushed. "He'll say I did the right thing because I was more worried about Kelsey's injury than a stupid box."

The detective glanced down at my bandaged leg. "She looks fine now."

Chase glared at her in return. "Because I took care of her."

"You're so good at taking care of things, aren't you, Chase?" she asked as her pretty lips curled back into a sneer.

My father whistled. "Okay, stop it, all of you."

The three of us stared at my father. His cape, draped over his shoulders, gave him a regal air, or at least it would have if he hadn't been wearing a T-shirt and jeans underneath.

"What's done is done. There's no going back to before," he said.

"Is that Shakespeare?" Chase asked.

Dad grinned. "No, but it should be. I just made it up."

Detective Brandon threw up her arms. "I don't have time for this. You all have seemed to forget that I'm in the middle of a murder investigation. I have to get out of here. Where's the box? I'll take it back to the station to examine it and look for fingerprints."

Chase pointed to the mangled cardboard object on the table.

"Are you sure Kelsey and not a refrigerator landed on it?" Brandon asked.

I rolled my eyes. This crushing-the-box thing was never going to go away, I could already tell.

The detective removed gloves from her jacket pocket and slipped them on. She opened the box and peered inside. "Is everything here? Everything you reported missing? I assume that you looked through it?"

"I did look inside, yes," I said.

She raised her eyebrow. "So, is everything there?"

I swallowed. "You have the spreadsheet of contents that Benji made, but I did notice one thing missing right away."

She looked up at me.

I removed the museum tag from my shorts pocket and held it out to her. "Jebidiah Barton's gun is missing."

TWENTY-EIGHT

AFTER BRANDON LEFT WITH the box of artifacts, Dad went upstairs to check on Hayden, leaving Chase and I standing in my living room together. I started picking up the toys that Hayden had scattered around the house and tossing them into my son's toy basket in the corner of the room.

"Brandon is right," I said. "We should have called her from the church so that she could properly catalog the evidence."

"Kelsey," Chase said with a sigh. "You were bleeding."

"The evidence was more important." I picked up a yellow truck.

He shook his head. "Than you bleeding to death? I don't think so."

I tossed a truck into the basket. "I have to find that gun. I don't know if it works anymore, but someone could get hurt."

Chase came over to me and held me by my upper arms. "Would you just be still for one moment?"

I looked him in the eye. "I have to fix this."

"I can help," he said.

I shook my head. "I don't know how you can. I've messed every-thing up, and I have to fix it."

"I can help," he repeated.

I met his gaze. "You can't. Benji—this Farm—it's all my respon-sibility. I need to take care of it myself."

He dropped his hands from my arms. "You don't want my help. You want to do everything on your own. Is that it?"

My brow wrinkled. "It's my job. Everyone at the Farm trusts me to handle this. They rely on me to take care of things. I'm ultimately responsible for everything that happens here, so I have to fix this."

"You don't get it, do you?" He ran his hand through his blond hair. "I want to be there for you, and you just push me away over and over again. I don't deserve that, Kelsey. I really don't."

"That's not what I'm saying." I frowned.

He folded his arms. "What are you saying?"

I opened and closed my mouth a few times, but I didn't have an answer for him.

"Your silence is answer enough." He leaned forward and kissed me on the cheek. "Goodbye, Kelsey."

"Goodbye?" I asked, but by that point Chase was already walking out my front door.

I went to the door and watched him walk down the path. Half of me wanted to run after him; the other half was relieved. I knew that I'd taken it too far this time. I'd put my wall up too high, and he was tired of trying to climb it. I knew he was walking away from me and might never come back. If he didn't come back, I had no one to blame but myself, but at the same time, I wouldn't or couldn't take back what I'd said. The Farm was my responsibility, and I was the one who had to make things right again. I needed to do it on my own. If Chase couldn't accept that, then our relationship was doomed. I sighed. I would handle all that after Krissie's wedding. I could handle anything after the wedding.

I closed the cottage door. Benji and Piper would be arriving soon to discuss whatever Piper's past crime was. I was looking forward to seeing Benji in particular. I knew that even with everything that had happened, my assistant would face the discovery of the missing artifacts with a logical mind.

My phone rang. I hobbled over to the kitchen counter and picked it up. My leg hurt, but the only person I'd admit it to was myself. I checked the phone's screen, and Benji's image smiled back at me.

Dad came down the stairs. I noticed he'd finally removed the cape. Now he fit the image of small town grandpa a little better.

Before I could utter a greeting into the phone, Benji said, "Kelsey, we can't meet you at the cottage tonight."

"Why not?" I couldn't keep the disappointment from my voice. There was so much that I needed to talk to her about.

She took a deep breath. "Because Piper has been arrested." There was a pause. "For Vianna's murder."

"Piper's been arrested?" My eyes went wide as I looked at my father. Dad mouthed, "Go."

That was all the encouragement that I needed. "Benji, I'm on my way. Tell Piper not to talk to the police."

"It's too late. She already has. She's already told them everything." She sounded as if she was about to cry.

Before I could ask Benji what "everything" was, she hung up.

The entire drive to the police station, I had my hands on the steering wheel at ten and two in a death grip. I worried over what Benji meant with her last comment. What could Piper be confessing to the police? Was she confessing to the murder? Had she killed Vi-anna? The very idea made my stomach turn, and the reason for that was Benji. My assistant and friend was my primary concern. I cared what happened to Piper, but only as far as it had an impact on Benji. I'd always viewed Benji as a little sister, and I couldn't, I wouldn't, let her be hurt.

The New Hartford police department was located in a large municipal building near the center of town, not that far from Armin's flower shop. It seemed like I'd gone to see Armin so long ago—I could hardly believe it was just that morning.

I parked in one of the diagonal spaces in front of the building. This late in the evening, with no events going on downtown, there were plenty of parking spots from which to choose. I jumped out of the car and ran up the wide cement steps to the front door as fast as my injured leg would allow. The soles of my shoes slipped on the red, polished stone floor. An ornate receptionist desk stood empty in the middle of the room with a giant brass chandelier floating above it.

In front of me, behind the receptionist's desk, were glass doors that led into the mayoral and city administrative offices. To my right was another set of doors that led into the state park offices, and to my left were the doors I was looking for—the police station.

Detective Brandon smiled at me as I stepped through those doors into the hallway of the station. There was a small wooden folding table in the middle of the hallway, covered with brochures reminding people of the consequences of DUIs and not remembering to buckle your seat belt. To my left, I spotted Benji in my peripheral vision. She was in some kind of a waiting room.

"Kelsey, I wish I could say that I'm surprised to find you here," the detective said. "But that would be a lie. What are you doing in my station?"

I walked up to Brandon, refusing to allow her to intimidate me. "*Your* station? I imagine that Chief Duffy wouldn't want you to call it that."

The detective's perpetual frown deepened, as did the lines around her mouth.

"I'm here because I heard Piper was arrested." I folded my arms. "This must be some kind of mistake. I know she didn't do anything wrong."

Out of the corner of my eye, I saw Benji stand up and move to the waiting room's doorway. She held onto the door frame as if her life depended on it.

Detective Brandon chuckled. "She didn't do anything wrong? You're so trusting at times, Cambridge, it's quite amusing."

"What do you mean by that?" I asked.

"Your innocent Piper isn't as innocent as you believe. The girl has a record. When I arrested her today, it wasn't her first arrest. She's an old hat at this."

"And what's her past arrest for?" I asked.

Brandon glanced over her shoulder at Benji, who had a gray cast to her face. "I have to return to Piper now. I'm sure Benji will fill you in on all the particulars."

"I have only one more question," I said.

The detective snorted. "I seriously doubt that you have only one more question, Kelsey Cambridge."

She was right. I always had more than only one more question, but I wasn't going to tell her that. "The twinkle lights in the steeple," I said.

"What about them?" she asked.

"Why did you leave them there? It seems they would be important evidence for the murder." I studied her face as I spoke.

She knit her brow together. "They are in fact evidence, which is why I didn't leave them there. They're in the evidence room. What kind of incompetent police officer do you think I am?"

I'd never thought of Brandon as incompetent, which was why I'd been so surprised when Chase and I found the lights still hanging from the window in the bell tower. I thought back to the times I'd looked up at the church that day, and I realized that I actually didn't remember seeing any twinkle lights there after the police had removed the window frame. I certainly would have noticed them, as would all of the officers who'd been crawling around the grounds since last night.

"Cambridge, is that all?" the detective wanted to know.

I nodded. I wasn't sure why, but I didn't want to tell her about the mystery lights.

She started down the hallway, but then stopped and turned. "Despite screwing up the chain of evidence, you provided us with a very helpful tip by finding that box in the bell tower, Kelsey. Thank you for that. I suppose you can say that you solved yet another murder. Let's all hope it's your last." She continued down the hall.

I watched her go, feeling like Judas collecting his thirty pieces of silver.

Benji emerged into the hallway and ran to me. She threw her arms around me. "Kelsey! I'm so glad you're here. I was losing my mind sitting in there all alone." She stared down at my leg. "What happened to you?"

"A minor accident. It looks worse than it is. I'm more worried about you." I hugged her back. "You need to tell me what's going on. Do you finally know what sent Piper to jail before?"

Benji let go of me with a sigh. "We'd better sit down."

I followed her back into the waiting room. The seating options were slim. We had our choice of some uncomfortable-looking wooden folding chairs that looked like they harkened back to the 1950s and a long, flowered couch. Benji chose the couch, so I sat next to her. I fell so deeply into the couch that my feet no long hit the floor.

"Let me help you," Benji said, and she pulled on my arm until I sat on the edge of the sofa and my feet were firmly on the ground.

"Thanks." I adjusted my seat, careful not to fall back into the sofa a second time. "Now tell me what's going on."

"Piper stole those artifacts that went missing from the storage room. She admitted it to the police. Detective Brandon made her crack."

"The detective can be very persuasive," I said.

Benji folded her hands on her lap. "She's done this before."

"What do you mean?" My pulse quickened.

She stared at her hands. "When Piper was a freshman in college, she was an intern for an interior decorator and she got caught stealing jewelry from one of the houses the decorator was working on. The police discovered that she did it several times, from several homes, and she even sold some of the jewelry before she was caught."

"And that's what she wanted to do with the artifacts?" I asked.

Benji nodded miserably. "Since they were found in the bell tower, the police—or at least Detective Brandon—believe she killed Vianna to keep her crime hidden. The detective's theory is that Vianna caught Piper in the act of hiding the artifacts, and Piper killed her to protect her secret."

"So by finding the artifacts, I got her arrested." I said this barely above a whisper.

Benji held up her hand. "I don't blame you. Don't worry about that. I know you had to tell the police what you found." She clenched her hands together. "But I'm telling you, whatever wrong Piper did, she didn't kill Vianna. She's not capable of that. I know it."

"Did Piper tell you why she began stealing?" I asked.

Benji shifted uncomfortably in her seat. "She said she did it to help pay her school bills. She said those were the only times she stole—well, until she stole from the Farm."

Had Piper ever heard of school loans? I kept this thought to myself.

"Did you know that Piper had a history of theft?" I asked.

Benji shook her head. "I knew she was keeping something from me recently. She'd been acting strange, but I never expected for it to be this."

"How'd she know about the artifacts?" I asked, even though I already suspected I knew the answer. I needed to hear it from Benji.

My assistant hung her head. "I showed her where they were. It's all my fault. I wanted to impress her with how the trunk opened. You know, with the sequence of levers you can push to open it without a key. I should have never taken her down into storage. I know non-employees aren't allowed down there, and it's for a reason—because stuff can go missing like this. Even when the items turned up missing, I refused to believe it had been her, even though I think I always knew that it was."

"Why did she hide the artifacts in the bell tower?" I asked.

Benji squinted at me as if the answer pained her somehow. "That's my fault too. I told her no one ever goes up there. This was before Krissie got it into her head that she wanted lights up there. I guess Piper thought it would be a safe place to stash the artifacts until she could sell them."

I pondered the missing revolver. "That was her only plan for them?"

"I can't think of anything else she'd do with them." Benji rubbed her forehead. "She doesn't understand how museums work and didn't realize that the trunk's items had very little monetary value. It wasn't like she was going to make any money on the black market with Jebidiah's watch. There are hundreds out there just like it, and Jebidiah wasn't Abraham Lincoln or anything. He was just your average middle-class farmer in Ohio."

"Then why steal it?" I rested my elbows on my knees.

Benji scrunched up her face. "That's my fault again. I might have given her the idea that the items were more valuable than they actually are." She frowned. "Piper is so upwardly mobile. She has all these great big dreams of being a big-time wedding planner, making ridiculous amounts of money doing it. I guess I didn't want her to think the career I'd chosen, to be a historian, was lame. I'll never make the money she will someday."

"It's better to be happy than rich," I said. What I didn't add up was that Piper's career wasn't going anywhere as long as she was in jail.

"Okay, we've got another mystery," I went on. "What happened to Jebidiah's revolver? It should have been in the trunk too, but it wasn't. I found its tag in the oxen field."

Benji's brow shot up. "You did? I suppose it could have fallen off the gun when Piper was moving the box." She bit her lip. "The revolver was in there when I showed Piper the artifacts. About a month ago, I think."

"Was that the last time you saw the inside of the trunk?" I asked.

She wouldn't meet my eyes. "Yes. Piper must have remembered how to open the trunk to get into it." She studied the linoleum floor.

I put my hand on her shoulder. "Benji, I'm not going to scold you. You've learned your lesson from this times ten."

She nodded. "God knows I have."

"What are you going to do?" I asked. The question could apply to so many things for her, but I knew she understood what I meant when she answered.

"I don't know." Her voice was tight. "Piper betrayed me by taking those artifacts. She knows how important preserving history is to me, and Barton Farm, and you. But I love her. I can't help it. I don't know what I'm going to do." She looked at me with tears in her eyes. "What should I do?"

"You need to decide that for yourself." I gave her a sad smile. "You need to decide if what you and Piper have—despite what she's done—is worth fighting for. I can't tell you what to do."

She wrapped one of her braids around her forefinger. "Was it worth it for you and Eddie?"

I shook my head. "I wanted it to be, but no, it wasn't."

"For you and Chase?" she asked more quietly.

I thought of Chase walking out of my cottage just a few hours ago, and perhaps walking out of my life all together. "I don't know yet."

She nodded, as if happy I'd given her the honest although not simple answer. "I don't know yet either."

I touched her arm. "You don't have to make any decisions now. Let's just get through this, and then you'll have time to think."

She nodded, but she looked so crestfallen that it broke my heart. "What if the police are right? About, well, about everything?"

Maybe Detective Brandon was right and Vianna had been killed in order for Piper to protect her theft. The saddest part was, Benji was correct that the items in the trunk had little or no value outside of Barton Farm.

That meant Vianna's death had been even more pointless.

"Come back and stay at the cottage tonight," I said. "It might help you not to be alone."

"I'll be fine." Benji wiped tears from the corners of her eyes. "Don't worry about me, Kelsey. I'll be in to work tomorrow. I know you'll need my help with the final wedding preparations, and I imagine Krissie will expect more from you, now that Piper—well—now that Piper can't help."

"Just because she stole those things doesn't mean she killed Vianna." I gave her a hug.

"That's nice of you to say, but how can you know? I want to believe that's true."

"I thought you believed she's innocent," I said.

"I do. At least, I think I do." Benji stared at her hands. "I heard you ask the detective about a string of twinkle lights in the bell tower."

"I did. Do you know anything about that?" I asked.

She wouldn't look at me. "Piper put them there after the police left the Farm."

I blinked at her. At least one mystery was solved. "Why?"

"She wanted to do it in honor of Vianna. Like a memorial or something. That's why I don't believe she could have killed her. I was with her when she did it. She wanted to do it alone, but I insisted on going with her."

I couldn't help but wonder if Piper wanting to hang up the new twinkle lights had been a ruse to return to the bell tower and remove the artifacts from their hiding place. Benji insisting that she go with her had foiled Piper's plan. But I didn't share any of these suspicions with Benji. She already had enough worries about Piper without me adding to the list.

"But what if I'm wrong?" Benji asked. "What if she put that string of lights up out of guilt? I thought I knew Piper, but I've learned she's lied to me several times about big things. What else has she been lying about? Does she not really love me?"

Chief Duffy's wide form filled the doorway. "Candy told me you were in here."

I stood up.

He gave me an apologetic smile. "You should both go home. There isn't anything else you can do tonight."

"What about a lawyer for Piper?" I asked.

"A public defender has been called in for the girl. It doesn't look like she can make bail, so we'll hang on to her for the time being."

My stomach turned. I knew, with all the evidence mounting against her, Piper was going to need the best legal counsel she could find.

TWENTY-NINE

THE NEXT DAY, THURSDAY, went quickly. Benji was on the Farm grounds bright and early as promised. Krissie and her parents were too. The Pumpernickles were overjoyed that it looked like Vianna's murderer was safely behind bars and they could get back to the business of planning the wedding. With both Vianna and Piper out of the picture, the brunt of the wedding details had fallen on me, and Benji jumped right in, helping any way that she could. I understood that she needed to work to keep her mind off Piper. By the end of Thursday, the arrangements were well in hand, or so I thought.

The morning of the wedding was clear and bright. I checked the weather forecast on my phone while still lying in bed. It was going to be hot. The temperature was predicted to hit the high eighties by late afternoon. The reenactors I'd conscripted to participate were going to melt in their wool uniforms. At least with everything that had happened in the past few days, Krissie had finally given up on the idea of full-scale battle reenactment.

Chase was going to be one of those reenactors, in his Union medic uniform. Or, that's what he'd agreed to do back when I first asked Chief Duffy if some of his regiment could put in an appearance at the wedding.

I sighed and rolled out of bed. The day had to start whether or not I was ready for it.

Twenty minutes later I was in the kitchen, double-checking my extremely long list for the day, and Hayden came flying down the stairs.

"Dad's getting married today!" he shouted at top voice.

I smiled at him. I was relieved that despite all the arguments and ugliness between Krissie and me, Hayden had been spared knowing about it. He was genuinely happy to see his father get remarried.

Dad stepped out of his cupboard bedroom, fully dressed, cape and all, for the day. Underneath the cape, he wore jeans and a Union army flak jacket. His white hair was brushed back from his forehead pompadour style.

I pursed my lips. "Is that what you're wearing to the wedding?" Usually I didn't much care what my father wore, but I knew that Krissie would.

"Sure thing," he said with a wide grin.

I groaned. I knew it would be a complete waste of time to argue with him. If Krissie wanted my father to change, she would have to take on that battle herself.

"The wedding is at six," I said. "But be sure to bring Hayden over to the village side much earlier than that." I flipped through the agenda clipped to my wedding-day clipboard. It wasn't lost on me that this was the agenda Vianna had made before she was killed. "Krissie would like Hayden at the church by three."

Dad poured coffee into a mug from the carafe. "Don't worry, I'll take care of Hayden. You handle everything else."

When Dad said "everything else," he really meant it. I flipped through the agenda one more time and with a final sip from my coffee, got up. The sooner I faced this day, the sooner it would all be over. I said goodbye to my son and father and headed through the door with Tiffin on my heels.

My corgi ran ahead of me when he spotted a squirrel up the pebbled path. While I walked, I went over all I had to do before the ceremony began. With any luck, the vendors would already be setting up in the village. At least I knew the reception tent had been put up the day before.

Despite everything I had to do, thoughts of Benji and Piper and of Chase weren't ever far from my mind. I'd thought several times of calling Chase after I got home from the police station Wednesday night, but I'd stopped myself every time I picked up my phone. After the wedding, I reminded myself. I would sort this out after the wedding.

The visitor center came into view, and I saw Benji sitting on the top of a picnic bench outside of it. She had two coffees in paper cups on the table next to her. She stared out into the pasture, where the oxen grazed at a leisurely pace. They weren't in a hurry. They never needed to be. I couldn't help but envy them a little.

Tiffin forgot the squirrel and barked. He took off down the pebbled path, ready to greet his friend.

Benji jumped off of the table and greeted my dog, giving him scratches behind the ears and under his chin. Although much taller than I was, she looked so small squatting on the path beside my dog. Her wide smile that was always present was nowhere to be found. It was as if even her many black braids had also lost their bounce. Piper's arrest had taken a toll on her. It pained me to see it.

I stopped in front of them on the path. "Any news about Piper?"

She shook her head. "I tried to call her public defender, but he didn't answer his phone." She frowned. "It's not even eight yet. I know it's too early to expect any news."

"What about her family? Have you talked to them?"

She shook her head. "That's the thing. Piper doesn't have any family. Her mom died when she was younger, and she hasn't spoken to her father in years. Everything she's done, she's done completely on her own."

"What about your family?" I asked.

She grimaced. "No. I want to sort out how I feel about all this first. Then I'll talk to them."

I opened my mouth to protest. Benji's parents had always supported her in everything. I didn't believe that this would be any different.

Benji held up her hand. "Let's just get through the wedding, okay? The police aren't going to let Piper out today. She can't make bail, and I can't afford to spot her."

"I could help," I said.

She shook her head. "I can't let you do that."

"Okay," I agreed. "Let's just get through the wedding."

She nodded. "Thanks."

Benji and I headed over to the village. When the church area came into view, I was happy to see the rental company carrying tables and chairs into the white reception tent.

"Looks like this will go off after all, Kel," Benji said. "You did it."

I smiled. "We did it, but let's not say that just yet. The bride has yet to arrive."

"Right," she said.

By late afternoon, the caterer was there with his staff, setting up the chaffing dishes for the food. Civil War reenactors in full uniform milled about, chatting with the tourists who were on the grounds until the wedding guests arrived. I had yet to see Krissie or Eddie. I knew Krissie and her bridesmaids were getting ready at a swanky hotel just outside of New Hartford. Even though I'd yet to see her, text messages from her were coming in fast. She asked about every little detail. I finally stopped checking my phone. I hadn't heard a peep from Eddie. I could only assume that was a good thing.

Benji was inside the tent, going over the last-minute details of the menu with the caterer. I was proud that she was able to set her personal problems aside and focus on the wedding. Despite the mistake she'd made in showing Piper the artifacts, she would make a stellar museum director someday.

I surveyed the scene, looking for places where I could help. Armin and his staff—minus the guy he'd tossed out of the flower shop—carried boxes of flowers into the tent. They had already decorated the church, which was full to bursting with flowers. Everything seemed to be in order. Across from me, Laura waved from the front door of Barton House. I waved back, but stopped mid-wave as Henry Ratcliffe came up the pebbled path.

I took a deep breath and went over to meet him. "Henry, I'm surprised to see you here so early."

He scanned the grounds. The church doors were wide open, allowing passersby a view of the inside. Flowers and ribbons hung on the ends of the pews and enormous vases of daylilies stood on pedestals at the front. The tent was dressed up too. The side facing the church was open, and we could see the portable dance floor being pieced together and the tables set with golden cutlery and white, gold-rimmed dishes. Everything was perfect and lovely, just how Krissie had envisioned it. Just how Vianna had planned it. It was sad that she couldn't see the end result of all her hard work.

"I stopped by at the Pumpernickle family's request to make sure preparations were complete. I see you have everything well in hand, Ms. Cambridge," he said in his droll voice.

"You expected me not to?" I folded my arms.

He smiled. "I knew you would do just as well as Vianna. I wasn't concerned. Vianna was a complication that we didn't need." He brushed his hands together as if dusting them off. "I think we're all better off not having to worry about her anymore."

Armin came out of the reception tent just as Henry said his last comment. He dropped the empty box he'd been carrying onto the grass and stomped toward Henry. "What did you say about Vianna?"

Henry pulled his neck back like a turtle retreating back into his shell. "Who are you? I don't have to answer you."

Armin pulled his arm back and, before I could warn Henry, popped the older man in the nose. Blood sprayed and Henry cried out in pain. I jumped back to avoid being hit by blood spatter. If the cracking sound I'd heard was any indication, I guessed that Henry's nose was broken.

Armin shook out his fist and walked away as if nothing had happened.

"That had to smart." Drunk Lincoln tucked a silver flask into his coat pocket and strolled by with his top hat under his arm.

"I'll sue you!" Henry managed a muffled cry through his hands.

I scooped up Henry's glasses, which had been knocked off by the punch, and I slipped them into his suit pocket as Laura moseyed over.

"That was kind of amazing," Laura said. "The wedding hasn't even started yet and there's already a fistfight."

I gave her a look.

Henry moaned.

"Can you take him back to the visitor center and get him cleaned up?" I asked Laura. "I really should stay here and supervise."

"Sure," she said good-naturedly. "Come on, Henry." She waved him in the direction of Maple Grove Lane.

He mumbled a reply.

"If you want me to understand you, you'll have to speak up," she said in her best teacher voice.

Henry followed her to the pebbled path.

"Laura, he might have to go to urgent care to get that nose looked at," I said.

"I'll call him an ambulance if need be," she replied over her shoulder.

I shook my head.

As Laura walked away with Henry in tow, I heard her say, "Don't get too close to me. I can't have any blood on my shirtwaist. It's really hard to get the stain out."

Benji ran by with the box of wedding programs.

"Benji," I called after her. "Can you take that flask away from Drunk Lincoln, please?"

"On it," she said with a smile.

I sighed. This wedding just might kill me after all.

THIRTY

AFTER THE WEDDING CEREMONY was over, Eddie and Krissie ran out of the church hand in hand, Eddie carrying Hayden on his shoulders as he ran. Krissie positively glowed, making a gorgeous bride in her lace and tulle ball gown. Eddie was handsome in his light gray suit and yellow bow tie, and Hayden was adorable in his outfit that was a mini-version of his father's. They looked like the picture-perfect family. I tried to be happy for them. I tried not to care. I failed. I didn't want to be with Eddie, not anymore, but I would be lying if I said that I wasn't at least a little jealous of the happy trio.

Laura wrapped her arm around me. "You'll have your day again, Kel."

"What are you talking about?" I asked, blinking at her.

"I saw how you watched Eddie and Krissie during the wedding. You'll have that again too." She looped her arm through mine.

"I don't miss Eddie, if that's what you think." I squeezed her arm.

"I know that." Her lip curved into a smile. "He and Krissie deserve each other." She laughed. "I'm just saying, you'll have a family again like that if that's what you want."

"That's the problem. I don't know. I thought I was happy with the Farm, and with just Hayden and me, until…"

"Chase?" She raised a single auburn eyebrow.

I shrugged. "I think we broke up, although neither of us has said so definitively. It's something else I'll have deal with after the wedding, and I want to help Benji too. She's convinced Piper didn't murder Vianna. If that's true—and I think it is—then I have to find out who did it. There is still a killer loose on my Farm."

Laura sighed. "For once worry about yourself first, okay?" She nodded in the direction of the pebbled path. "You need to take care of that."

I followed her line of sight and saw Chase standing in the middle of the path in his reenactor medic uniform. It was the first I'd seen of him since he'd walked out of my cottage two nights before. "Did you know he was here?" I asked.

She shook her head. "He must have just arrived. He wasn't inside the church during the ceremony. I know that for sure. I was in the back."

A knot formed in my stomach.

Laura gave me a little shove. "Go talk to him. I think you owe both of you that."

I nodded, knowing she was right, and now that the wedding itself was over, I was feeling less stressed. Everything was in place for the cocktail hour and reception. The photographer was already coaching the wedding party on where he wanted them to be for photos. Everyone knew what they were doing. Vianna had made sure to hire all the right and most professional people. It wasn't until I'd seen the wedding go off without a hitch that I realized how good she'd been at her job. That knowledge made her death all the sadder.

I looked back at where Chase had been standing and saw that he was gone. I headed in that direction until I ran into Eddie, who was alone.

"Kel, you got a minute?" he asked.

"Do you need something? Is everything okay?" I looked around for Krissie and wondered what must have gone wrong for her to send Eddie over to talk to me. "You don't want to miss your pictures."

He smiled. "Do you always assume there's a crisis needing to be fixed?"

I forced myself to relax. "No."

Eddie cocked his head. He'd known me longer than almost anyone else there, with the exception of my father.

"Okay, fine, not all the time," I admitted.

He laughed. "That's more like it. I just wanted to thank you. The wedding has been perfect. Krissie is so happy. I can't thank you enough."

"It wasn't just me. Vianna did most of the work."

He nodded. "And Vianna too."

"I'm glad to hear that everything went as Krissie hoped. You make a beautiful couple." This was the truth. Eddie and Krissie were stunning together. They were a much better match than Eddie and I had ever been.

His smile widened. "Thank you. The Lincoln reenactor was a nice touch. How did you pull that off?"

"I have my ways." I glanced inside the tent and saw Lincoln talking to several of Krissie's guests. He swayed slightly as he spoke. I needed to remind Benji to keep an eye on him and to keep him away from the bar.

Eddie laughed again, sounding as happy as I'd ever heard him. "I know you do. You're a miracle worker. You always have been."

I shifted my feet, eager to continue my search for Chase. "If that's all…"

He placed a hand on my forearm. "It's not. I just want to let you know that Krissie and I have agreed not to petition the courts to change the terms of the custody. I think the fact that we were all able to work together on this wedding proves that we can communicate and overcome obstacles outside of the court system. I realized today that this would be a much better way to handle it for us, and most importantly for Hayden."

I blinked at him, trying to digest what I'd just heard. "And Krissie agreed to this?"

"Yes. She just wants me to be happy." He beamed with a wedding glow. "She makes me so happy."

I found myself smiling because he did look happy, and I was relieved that my smile didn't come with a twinge of regret.

"I know this is the best thing for Hayden," Eddie went on. "For him to live here on the Farm most of the time. He wouldn't be happy with Krissie and me. I know that."

"Thank you. I'm relieved to hear it." I suspected that the custody issue would come up again between us, but at least for the moment, I could catch my breath.

Hayden waved at me from the dance floor, where he was dancing with Krissie. He looked adorable in his tuxedo, and I had to admit, Krissie was the most stunning bride I'd ever seen.

Hayden waved at me. "Mom, come on! Dance with us!"

I shook my head, but Eddie heard our son too and grabbed my hand, pulling me onto the dance floor with him.

The four of us—Hayden, Krissie, Eddie, and I—stood in a circle and danced. For better or worse, we were all a family now because of the little boy gripping my hand with all his might. And for just a moment, it felt right.

THIRTY-ONE

It was time for the father-daughter dance, and I was able to slip away from the reception tent. Outside, I took a deep breath. I couldn't wait to tell Chase that my custody worries were over, but I still needed to find him.

"This should have been our wedding," a female voice said on the other side of the tent.

Chase laughed. I recognized his laugh immediately. He said something in reply that I couldn't make out.

I walked around the side of the tent just in time to see Detective Brandon and Chase kiss. And it wasn't a little peck on the cheek, either.

I sucked in a breath. I felt like I'd been punched in the gut. I'd been wrong about Chase. I'd been wrong about him all this time. He was just like every other cheater.

Chase pulled away from the detective and saw me standing behind her with my mouth hanging open. I snapped it shut and turned around, fleeing around the corner of the tent.

I heard his footsteps coming after me as I ran behind the church, where I'd be out of the wedding-goers' line of sight. I didn't want anyone to see my face until I got my emotions under control.

In my mind, I was back in the awful morning when Hayden was just a toddler and I learned of Eddie's affair. I'd never felt so small and alone in my life. I wasn't going to let that happen again. At least I'd found out what Chase was really like before I made the mistake of allowing it to go too far.

"Kelsey." Chase stopped a few feet behind me. "Kelsey, please turn around."

I ran a hand over my face, willing myself to regain my composure.

"Kelsey, please."

I took a deep breath and turned to face him.

His reenactor rifle hung from his belt. He was in that outfit he'd worn when I'd first met him nearly a year before, when he'd played dead on the pasture-turned-battlefield for the Farm's Civil War re-enactment. For some reason, that made facing him like this now that much more painful.

"It wasn't what it looked like," he began.

I folded my arms. "Tell me what it looked like."

He ran his hand through his thick blond hair. "Kelsey..."

I turned to go. "I have get back to the wedding. The ceremony may be over, but there's still a lot to be done. We haven't had the toasts yet or cut the cake."

"Wait." He grabbed my arm.

"Let me go," I hissed. I refused to make a scene at the wedding, which Krissie would hold against me for years to come.

"She kissed me!" Chase cried. "I swear. It wasn't my idea."

"You didn't exactly jump away, from what I saw." The words popped out of my mouth before I could stop them.

"Kelsey, that's not fair. You just showed up at the wrong time. You don't know what happened before that." His hand was still on my arm.

"I do. I heard her say that this should have been your wedding." I swallowed. "Meaning hers and yours."

"Then you didn't hear what I said to her before that." He was still holding onto my bare arm. As much as I didn't want it too, my skin tingled under his grasp.

"Let me go. We can discuss this another time. It's Krissie and Eddie's day. Let's not ruin it with our own drama. I don't want to ruin it for Hayden either."

"Listen to me." He sounded so desperate that I met his gaze for the first time since he'd caught up with me. I saw naked hurt in the chocolate brown eyes that I'd thought I knew so well.

"Yes," he said. "Before you got there, Candy said she wanted to get back together with me. She told me that she still loves me."

I swallowed again and wondered if he was telling me this with the intention of hurting me more.

He stared at me, locking me into place with his eyes. "But I told her that it was never going to work. I told her that I love you."

The flirty, jokey Chase I knew was gone. In his place was a desperate man, trying to tell me the truth. Even so, I couldn't hear it. His words just came like another blow.

"You have a funny way of showing it," I said.

I knew that wasn't the reaction a man wanted to hear when he told a woman he loved her, but it was my knee-jerk response. Chase wasn't the first man to tell me he loved me, and the first time hadn't ended well. Why would this be any different?

His face fell. For the briefest moment, I felt a twinge of regret. Despite that, I couldn't stop myself from saying, "You told her that you love me, but you've never said it to me. Don't you see that as a problem? Shouldn't I have been the first to know?"

His cheeks flushed red. "I would have, if I knew you'd be willing to hear it. I think this reaction right here is a perfect example why I haven't."

"What's that supposed to mean?" I snapped.

"You won't let me love you. You won't let anyone love you. Ever since the moment you and Eddie split, you put a wall up around you so high, no one has any chance of getting over the top of it. God knows I've tried, again and again, only to fall on my face. I'm done with that. If you can't give me what I need, I have to give up."

"What you need?" My eyes narrowed.

"Yes," he said. "Everything in this relationship up until this very point has been about you—making you comfortable, going at your pace. It's never been about me for one second."

His words sucked the air out of my lungs as if they had some sort of vacuum attached to them. Before I could recover, he said in a quiet voice, "Kelsey, one of these days you're going to have to let someone in. We aren't all going to betray you like Eddie did. Unfortunately, that's something that you have to figure out on your own, and I can't help you." He turned and walked away, leaving me alone at the corner of the church.

It wasn't until I touched my cheek that I realized I was crying.

I couldn't remember the last time I'd had enough tears well up in my eyes to spill over onto my cheeks. It must have been when my mother died. I couldn't remember crying when I'd kicked Eddie out of the little bungalow we'd shared downtown. I brushed the tears from my cheeks. Eddie hadn't been worth crying over, not like my mother had. And apparently, not like Chase was. Half of me wanted to run after him, but the other half of me was frozen in place because I was afraid what those tears might mean.

A bang came from inside the church, relieving me of making any decision at all. My duty as the director of Barton Farm was calling. I suspected that one of Krissie's wedding guests had drunk too much and stumbled back inside. I knew that I should have locked the church after the reception began.

I walked around the building and up the three stone steps to the front door.

There was another bang inside as I stepped over the threshold that led into the sanctuary. Rays of scarlet and ochre light poured into the large room through the western-facing windows, casting their glow on the worn wood of the pews and the unadorned altar in the narthex.

The flowers and bows that had been draped over the ends of the pews were still there. Some of the petals had fallen to the polished pine wood floor. At least they'd waited until after the ceremony to fall. I didn't think Krissie would have tolerated one petal hitting the wooden floor before she said "I do."

I scanned the sanctuary, and since it appeared empty, I began to wonder if I'd imagined the banging. Maybe I'd made it up to avoid running after Chase. If that was the case, my mind was playing a cruel joke on me. I turned to leave the building to go find Chase. I needed to talk to him—to tell him I was sorry and that I loved him too.

As I took a step toward the door, something poked me in the back.

"Don't move," a voice hissed in my ear. I recognized it immediately as Shepley. "I have a gun on you."

As he said this, everything came into focus. Piper was innocent. Benji had to be told this so she wouldn't throw away her relationship like I just had. The problem was, after killing Vianna, would Shepley have any hesitation in killing me? I seriously doubted it.

He ushered me to the open door that led to the stairway to the choir loft. "You're going up there."

"To the bell tower?" I asked. "You have to be joking. I'm not going up there with you."

I knew with my whole heart that it was Jebidiah Barton's gun that was digging into my back. Shepley must have taken it from the tower where Piper had hidden it with all the other artifacts.

"I said go," he snarled.

I snorted a laugh. "There's no way you can make me." I wondered if this was how he'd gotten Vianna into the bell tower. Perhaps she hadn't gone up there on her own to string the lights, as we'd all assumed.

"Yes, I can." He dug the barrel of the gun painfully into my spine, so hard that I was afraid that he might push it through my back and out the other side. Still behind me, he grabbed the back of my left arm so tightly I was certain he'd left a bruise. He forced me to move forward, toward the stairs to the choir loft.

I frowned at the stairs. There was still no way I was going up there. There wasn't enough money in the world to make me climb those stairs, and then the ladder, with a deranged gardener.

Then I heard a voice.

"Mom?" it called, from the top of the bell tower.

My heart stopped. I sprinted up the stairs to the choir loft.

THIRTY-TWO

I GLARED BACK AT Shepley lumbering up the stairs after me. "What's Hayden doing up there? I know you're capable of a lot of terrible things, but I didn't know that child endangerment was one of them."

He let go of my arm. "I can't help it if he wandered in here."

Before I could argue with him, Hayden's pale face appeared in the hatch above. "Mom, are you coming up? Shepley said he'd ask you to come up here. You can see the whole wedding from here, it's so cool!"

I smiled at him. "Hey, bud. What are you doing up there?"

He frowned. "I just wanted to see what it was like." His voice trembled. "I know I'm not supposed to be up here."

He wasn't, but this wasn't the time to discipline my child. I had to get him out of the church and away from Shepley as soon as possible.

Hayden's voice floated down to us. "Shepley said I'd get a bird's eye view. I could see everything down below like a bird flying in the sky, and he's right!"

"It's okay, bud. I need you to come down though."

Shepley jabbed the gun into my back again. "No. You're going up."

"Not with Hayden here. This changes everything," I said in a sharp whisper.

"I know it does. It means that you'll actually follow my directions." His hot breath was on my neck.

"I—"

"Do you want your son to see his mother get shot? Because I can arrange that," he hissed in my ear. "Those nightmares will haunt him for the rest of his life."

My heart rate doubled in speed. Of course that was the last thing I wanted to be imprinted on my son's memory. "I thought you cared about Hayden," I hissed back. "You've always been kind to him. How can you do this to him?"

The gun on my back quivered. "I do care about the boy, but I care more about getting out of here than anything else. Now get up that ladder or I'll give your son a nightmare that he'll never forget."

He said it with so much menace that it turned my stomach. I'd always known Shepley was disgruntled, hard to please, and a difficult person, but I'd never thought him to be cruel. In that moment, threatening to kill me in front of my son, he was cruel.

I put my hands on the rungs. Hayden waved at me from the hatch. I smiled at him as brightly as I could as I began to climb.

As I crawled through the opening, Hayden met me, and when I was standing, he threw his thin arms around me. "I'm sorry, Mom. I know I shouldn't have come up here. I just wanted to see it, is all."

I hugged him tight, tighter than I normally would.

Shepley came up the ladder, and I placed my body between him and Hayden. "Hayden and I need to go back down," I said. "His father will be wondering what happened to him."

Shepley had the antique revolver in his hand, but he pressed it against his right hip. "Might I have a word, Kelsey?"

I saw the hand with the gun in it twitch. I kissed the top of Hayden's head. "Hayden, why don't you stand over there for a moment?" I pointed to the other side of the giant bell. "Be careful of the hole," I warned.

"How did that hole get there?" my son asked.

I smiled. "The bell tower is old, so who knows." Now was not the time to tell him that I'd fallen through the floor. "Just stay as far away from that hole and the open window as possible."

His smooth brow wrinkled. "Mom, what's wrong?"

"Nothing is wrong, honey," I said. "Shepley and I were just looking over the church after the wedding to see what has to be done to clean up." I cleared my throat. "You stand over there for a moment, and I'll talk to him. We shouldn't be long and we can go back to the party. Have you had any cake yet?"

"No," he said in a small voice.

I smiled at him as brightly as I could. "Well then, we'll get you an extra-large piece. I know one of the tiers is double chocolate."

Some of the fear left his eyes. "Double chocolate?"

"Oh yes," I said. "Krissie asked for a chocolate cake."

His heart-shaped face broke into a grin, and he walked to the other side of the bell as I'd instructed him to do.

With Hayden's view blocked by the enormous bell, Shepley raised the gun and pointed it at me again.

"You have to let Hayden leave," I hissed. "He knows nothing, and he's just a little boy."

Now that the gun wasn't digging into my back, I could see for sure that it was the revolver Piper had stolen.

"Shepley," I said in a voice that sounded unusually high for me. "Why don't you let Hayden go down the ladder? Please?"

"Mom, can I come over there now?" Hayden peeked around the side of the bell.

I shot Shepley a look, and he hid the gun behind his back. Maybe he had a tiny piece of his heart left.

Hayden came around the side of the bell. "Can we have cake now?"

I stepped in front of him, again putting my body between Shepley and my child. "Sure, buddy. We can have cake. Let's go back down the ladder."

Shepley stepped in front of the hatch, blocking our way. "Hayden, you can go down and have cake, but I have to talk to your mom for a little bit longer."

My heart rate kicked up again. He was going to let Hayden go. That's all I wanted. I wanted my son to be safe.

Hayden frowned. "I have to go down the ladder alone?" His eyes were the size of saucers. "It's really far down. Mom needs to come with me."

"She can't," Shepley said, leaving no room for argument. I felt the barrel of the gun return to the small of my back.

I squeezed Hayden's hand. "Don't worry, buddy. I'll be down just as soon as Shepley and I are done talking. It won't take long."

"Then can I wait with you?" he asked.

I shook my head. "No, I think you should go down and get started on that cake. Be sure to save me a piece."

Hayden stared at me uncertainly. I put the most reassuring smile on my face that I could manage. If my son's expression was any indication, it wasn't very convincing. Hayden looked down the ladder and then shuffled back. "Mom, will you go down with me? It's really high."

"Your mom needs to stay up here with me to talk over a few things," Shepley repeated.

Hayden's lower lip trembled. "But what if I fall?"

I felt myself begin to shake. What was worse? To have Hayden climb down the ladder alone and possibly fall, or be shot? Neither were good options. "You won't fall. I promise you. It's just one rung at a time. I'll watch you climb down—just keep your eyes on my face as you go." Sweat trickled down my back.

His lower lip trembled. "I can't."

"Sure you can," I said, taking a small step toward him. Shepley came with me, and I continued to feel the barrel of his gun in my back. "Remember all the times you climbed the big ladder in the visitor center to help string lights for Christmas? This isn't any different than that. You're a pro at that. Just keep your eyes on me as you make your way down."

"It's a lot bigger than the ladder in the visitor center."

I nodded. "That's true, but you're a lot bigger now too. I know you can do it. You climbed up here. It's not different from going back down."

He looked from me to the hatch and back again. He nodded as if to himself, like he'd come to some sort of decision. "Okay." His voice was quiet but firm.

I gave the tiniest sigh of relief. Now that Hayden had agreed to climb down the ladder, I had to make sure that he got down safely. I would give my right arm if it meant Shepley would let me go down with my son, but I knew that wasn't going to happen.

"You can do it, buddy. It's one rung at a time," I repeated.

"Are you sure?" His eyes were so trusting that it broke my heart. I imprinted them on my memory, just in case this was the last time I would see them.

I felt tears burn in the back of my eyes, but I wasn't going to let Hayden see me cry in this moment. He would never go down the ladder if I did. "Yes. Trust me."

"Okay," he said in that still, small voice again. Carefully he grabbed the ladder and swung his right leg, followed by his left leg, onto the top rung. I watched as he took the first step down. The ladder never wavered and he visibly began to relax. With his eyes fixed on me, he took another step downward. "It's not so hard." The light and cheer had returned to his voice.

He stopped in the middle of the ladder, breathing hard.

"You got this, buddy. You can do it. You're halfway there."

He stared up at me with his father's eyes and I suddenly was transported back to when Eddie and I were children, when we were just two young kids with skinned knees and sunburns running loose in New Hartford all summer long. Along with Justin, we'd gotten into a mess of trouble. The day Eddie got stuck in a manhole, he'd looked at me with that same fear, asking me for help. It was then, I think, that I fell in love with him, although I was too young to even know what that meant. I'd wanted to rescue Eddie. I'd always been a rescuer. I wanted to rescue Hayden in this moment as well.

I licked my lips. My tongue felt impossibly dry. There were so many people down below who could help us if they only knew that we were in trouble, but I couldn't risk calling out for help if I wanted to keep Hayden safe.

I held my breath as he made it all the way to the bottom. With two rungs left, he jumped to the choir loft floor. "Mom, I did it." He waved at me.

"Great job, buddy." Every muscle in my body went limp, and the tears I was holding back threatened to spill over again. "Go get a big piece of cake. Remember to save me a big one!"

"Okay!" he cried, and he ran for the stairs. A moment later the sanctuary door slammed after him with a resounding thud.

I moved toward the broken window.

Shepley pulled on my arm. "Where are you going?"

"Can I at least go to the window to make sure he makes it to the reception tent all right?" I asked.

"Fine," Shepley snapped.

To my relief, I saw Hayden skip into the reception tent. He was safe. That was all that ever mattered.

Shepley yanked me back from the window, and I fell to the floor at the foot of the bell.

THIRTY-THREE

PAIN SHOT THROUGH MY injured leg. I remained on the floor for a moment and rubbed my elbow where I'd landed on it. I had to think of a way out of this situation. I could jump out of one of the steeple windows, but that hadn't ended well for Vianna, so I discarded the idea. The ladder was the only feasible way out. Yet Shepley stood between me and the ladder, and I knew that even if I made it out the hatch, I would be a sitting duck for Shepley to shoot me as I made my way down.

"Stand up!" Shepley ordered.

I struggled to my feet. "Why did you kill Vianna? Was it over the garden? I told you to ignore that letter."

He glared at me. "It's not just a garden, or the letter. It's my whole life. She had the power to take away my whole life."

As he said this, I knew it was the truth. Either by fate or by his own doing, Shepley had never found anything else but the garden to comfort him after the loss of his family. But why hadn't he felt reassured when I'd told him not to worry about Vianna's letter?

"I don't know how Vianna could have taken away your garden," I said cautiously.

"Because she was the heir. She was the Cherry heir," he spat.

"You knew that?" I tried to keep my voice level.

"Of course I knew."

I blinked at him. "But how?"

He sniffed. "I heard her telling that assistant of hers. The girl with the blue hair."

"How did you overhear their conversation?" I asked, stalling. What I needed right now was time, and maybe a miracle.

"I wanted to talk to her about her order to remove all the plants from the grounds for the wedding. That's when I heard her talking to the blue-haired girl."

So that was what had cost Vianna her life. If she'd never placed the letter in Shepley's mailbox, he'd never have gone looking for her, and would never have overheard her talking to Piper. Vianna would still be alive.

As if he read my mind, Shepley said, "What was I supposed to do? Let her take away everything I've worked for these last twenty years? Is that what you expected me to do?"

"You killed her to save the Farm?" I asked.

"It's *my* Farm."

I didn't see much point in arguing this point with him, especially since he was holding a gun. Artifact or not, the gun might still be able to put a hole in me, and I really wanted to avoid that. "But we talked about it," I said in the calmest voice I could manage. "I said to ignore her order. I care about the Farm too. Don't you think I would fight for it? This place is important to me too."

"What could you have done? Cynthia Cherry's will was clear. The control of the Foundation would go to her nephew Maxwell, and if he were gone, any children he might have. Everything you've done since Cynthia died would have been for nothing. You should be thanking me for getting Vianna out of the way."

I refused to believe that. "Even so, I could have talked to her. I could have done something. There's always more than one way."

Shepley laughed. "You're one to talk. The Foundation tricked you into planning your ex-husband's wedding, and that wouldn't be the last demeaning task they'd make you do once Vianna was in charge."

As he spoke, the music picked up below, as if to remind us that the wedding was still in progress and that everyone in the safety of the reception tent was having a wonderful time. The music was a fast song. Shouts and cries of delights rose from the dance floor.

I thought of Hayden, and I thought of Chase. How long before he'd come looking for me? *Would* he come looking for me at all, after the terrible fight we'd had? I didn't know that I would, in his place. But that might just be the difference between Chase and me. Our differences were a chasm too wide to traverse, yet I realized, standing there with death just one bullet away, that I wanted to see if we could make it across the chasm.

Shepley began to pace. "Vianna had a plan for us all. I heard her tell the girl with the blue hair that. She was going to change every-thing. She was going to get rid of everything I've worked for." He stopped midstride and pointed the gun at me. "After my family died, I vowed to myself that I wouldn't allow anyone to take anything from me ever again. I'm not going to lose this Farm."

The anniversary. The anniversary of the death of his family had been the day Vianna died. It all started to make even more sense.

"Don't get any ideas about getting away," he said. "Put your hands in the air where I can see them."

I did as I was told, but I kept talking. "I don't understand why you're doing this now, Shepley. You don't need to do this. Vianna is dead and Piper has been arrested. You got away with the murder."

He steadied the gun with his other hand. "I heard you telling Laura you're determined to find out who the real killer is. I knew I had to get rid of you. I know you. You don't give up. Just like me."

I didn't want to be "just like" Shepley. I wanted to be nothing like Shepley. And I needed to get out of there. The gardener was becoming more desperate by the second.

My eyes flicked in the direction of the bell. Below it was a long rope that the sexton would have pulled to notify the town that the church service was starting, or to warn the townsfolk of a fire nearby. It was used as a beacon and as a warning.

It was just what I needed.

The rope was only two feet away from me. But would it work? I wondered. The bell hadn't been rung in decades, and I could make things much worse if I ended up pulling it from the rafters.

"What are you looking at?" Shepley snapped.

I stared at him. I couldn't let him know my plan, no matter how unlikely success might be. My eyes fell on the gun in his hand.

I wrenched my eyes away from the gun and moved them to his dark eyes. Shepley's gaze had never been welcoming, but at that moment, it was downright deadly. He was capable of murder. I knew that. He'd killed Vianna. He'd had enough rage in him to attack her and push her through the window. Now he was brave enough to kill me in cold blood.

"I know you lost your family," I began. My arms were tiring from holding them in the air, but I didn't dare let them fall. I had no doubt that Shepley would shoot me. He'd wanted to for years.

"Don't talk about them." He choked out the words.

"I know it was an accident. I know you tried to get them out." I did my best to keep my voice even.

His breathing was ragged. "I did try." His eyes glazed over. "But the fire was too hot. The flames too big. I heard their screams." He pressed the heel of his left hand to the side of his head. "Do you know what that's like to hear the dying screams of your wife? Of your child?"

A chill ran down my back. "No. It must have been horrible."

"It was worse than horrible. It was hell."

I believed him.

"My only solace is these gardens, these flowers, and that woman wanted to take that away from me. I couldn't let that happen. Don't you understand?" His voice was almost pleading now.

"Did you tell Vianna that?" I asked.

"Yes. I saw her go into the church with the lights. I knew she was planning to hang them in the bell tower. I followed her."

"Did you see anyone else?" I thought of Piper, arriving at the church around the time Vianna fell.

"No," he snapped. "I figured it was my best chance to reason with her. I didn't come here with a plan to kill her. I was only going to tell her why she was doing the wrong thing, how she was ruining what Cynthia built."

I swallowed. "How did it go?" Since Vianna was dead, I could take a wild guess, but I needed to buy time so that I could find the perfect moment to grab the rope.

"I tried to reason with her, but she laughed at me. She said that I would be the first to go after she was given control of the Foundation. She said she had the proof that she was Maxwell's daughter, and that she and the Foundation would make a joint announcement after the wedding."

Vianna's proof was the paternity test, I thought.

"You should be happy I got rid of her. She said that if it weren't for the stipulation in Cynthia's will that allows you to be the director, and live here, she'd fire you too. You really should be grateful."

I shook my head. I knew this was true, but it didn't make what Shepley did right. "Still, she didn't deserve—"

"Don't tell me what she deserved!" He bellowed. "I don't care what people deserve. Did I deserve to lose my family? Did my wife and my—" His voice caught. "Did my wife and my daughter deserve to die?" He lifted the gun and held it level with my chest.

My mother had always told me that if you're going to make a mistake, err on the side of compassion. That's what I'd always tried to do in my life and my work. Perhaps it was why I'd gotten into so many scraps.

Standing there with Shepley holding the gun level with my chest, I thought of the many times I'd had grounds to fire him, the many times that I'd erred on the side of compassion and given him one more chance. Was my compassion for this tragic and angry man now my undoing? Had I been too nice? Had my mother's advice led me astray?

All I knew was I wasn't going to die at the hand of the gardener. I couldn't let that happen. Hayden needed me. I wasn't going to let my son lose his mother so young, like I had. I knew what that was like. I knew the personal cost of it. I couldn't leave him to be raised alone by Eddie and Krissie.

"No," I whispered. "They didn't deserve it. Many terrible things happen that shouldn't, but they do."

He held his hand steady. The gun didn't waver. "And your death will be just another one."

I couldn't wait any longer. I lunged for the rope, grabbed it, and fell on my back on the floor, pulling on it with all my weight.

The bell rang, and the sound reverberated in the tower and inside my head. Below, the music stopped and we could hear shouts. Just like back during the Civil War, the bell had worked—it had called for attention, called for help.

I let the rope slip from my hands, and the bell rang again on its back swing. The ringing. I would never get that sound out of my head.

"What have you done?" Shepley screamed. "You shouldn't have done that!"

I crawled backward, scrambling to get away from him. The rough boards dug into the heels of my hands. Through the broken window, I could hear the wedding guests' shouts. At least if I died up here, Shepley wouldn't get away with murdering either Vianna or me. Everyone would know what he did.

"Kelsey! Kelsey!" Chase's voice floated up from the sanctuary floor.

Shepley stared at the hatch and then back at me. I rose to my feet. My back throbbed from where I'd landed on it, but I ignored the pain. I had to get up. If I was to be shot, I wasn't going to take the bullet lying down.

The ladder groaned, and I knew that Chase was coming up.

"Chase," I shouted. "Shepley is up here, and he's got a gun."

I heard Chase swear. "I have one too."

I knew he was lying. Chase was an EMT. He didn't carry firearms, and his reenactor pistol wasn't going to do much more than give a burst of smoke and a loud crack.

Shepley glared at me. "You leave me no choice."

He was going to shoot me. I knew it. He was going to shoot me, and Chase would have to be the one to find my body.

Instead of pointing the revolver at me, though, he held it to his temple. "It doesn't matter anymore. I don't have anything else to lose."

"Don't!" I screamed.

But I was too late. There was a burst of smoke and flame as he fired the kill shot.

I covered my face with my hands. I couldn't watch. I didn't want to see Shepley dead on the floor at my feet.

He screamed in pain, and I dropped my hands from my eyes to see him writhing on the floor. Dead men don't scream.

Chase leapt through the hatch and scooped up the revolver. "It misfired. This thing probably hasn't been fired in a hundred years. The flint is brittle. It wouldn't be my first choice of suicide weapon. There are much more reliable guns."

I stared at him. He must have literally flown up the ladder when he heard the gun blast.

Before I could say anything, Detective Brandon's head poked over the edge of the hatch. "What's going on up here?"

Shepley groaned on the floor. His cries of pain turned to whimpers. Chase handed the gun to Brandon, hilt first, as she climbed off the ladder. "He shot himself with this, but it misfired."

Brandon held the gun with two fingers, aware of fingerprints, I was certain. "The missing revolver, I assume."

I could only nod.

Chase went over and knelt next to Shepley. The gardener wailed as he rocked from side to side.

"Stop rolling around," Chase ordered. "I can help you."

Finally, Shepley stopped moving. Brandon looked at me.

"See, Piper didn't kill Vianna," I said, finding my voice again. "You need to call the jail and let Piper go." I gave her a condensed version of what had happened.

As I explained, Officer Sonders' head appeared in the hatch. He didn't come all the way up, just looked at the detective and awaited instructions.

"He's badly burned on his forehead," Chase said. "I need my medical kit. It's under the cake table in the reception tent, and you need to call for an ambulance. He needs to go to the hospital."

Brandon nodded to her officer, who disappeared back down the ladder.

"I was going to see them. I need to see them," Shepley moaned.

"See who?" Brandon asked. Her voice was as sharp as a razor.

Shepley glared at her but refused to answer. I knew that answer and said, "His wife and daughter." I didn't even mask the tears in my own voice.

Chase looked up at me. There was something in his expression I couldn't read, but I knew for sure that I wanted to. Maybe that was the most important realization I made that day.

EPILOGUE

THE POLICE AND EMTs who were called in to deal with Shepley graciously worked around the wedding. Even so, I winced every time Krissie glanced in the direction of the church. Happily, she appeared to have hit the Civil War-era ale a little too hard at her reception and was a tad too tipsy to care about anything much. The last time I saw her, she was dancing the "YMCA" with Abraham Lincoln and having the time of her life. As it turned out, Honest Abe had some moves.

I stood just outside the reception tent, keeping an eye on both the police moving in and out of the church and on the wedding festivities. Eddie joined me.

"Thank you," he said in a quiet voice, barely above a whisper. "Thank you again for what you did for Krissie. For all of this. I know it was hard, and that you didn't want to help her, but I'm so grateful you did." He swallowed. "I know we don't always agree on things and most of the time it's my fault. I know that I treated you badly. I just wanted to say I'm sorry. I'm starting over with Krissie, and I pray I don't make the same mistakes with her that I did with you."

I glanced at him out of the corner of my eye. Maybe Eddie had been hitting the ale pretty hard too. I wasn't going to argue with him—he had in fact ruined our marriage. If it hadn't been for his affair, I was certain I would still be married to him and as in love with him as I was on the day of our wedding. But there was no going back in time to ask for a do-over. In my experience, do-overs were never granted because I certainly would have asked for more than one.

"Eddie!" Justin popped his head out of the tent. "It's time to collect your bride and leave. Your chariot awaits."

I patted his arm. "Go on. Your bride is waiting."

He smiled. I realized in that moment, as Eddie walked away from me and toward Krissie, that he really loved her. Despite all her irritating flaws, he still loved her.

That was the funny thing about love, I decided. No one else outside that unique relationship could understand it. No one knew what it was like to be that couple together or how they felt about each other. At best, outsiders could guess, they could recommend, they could even warn, but it was really up to the two people in the middle of it to decide if it was worth it, just like I'd told Benji at the police station. Eddie and Krissie had decided it was worth it, and for their faith in what they had together, I wished them all the luck I could spare.

I walked around the side of the tent so I could watch them go. They walked arm in arm to the Farm's carriage, which was being pulled by Scarlett the mare. One of the Confederate reenactors sat in the driver's seat. I knew he would drive them to the end of the Farm property, to where a limo waited that would drive them on to their honeymoon.

The wedding revelers threw birdseed at the couple as they headed down the pebbled path to the carriage. Abraham Lincoln blew Krissie kisses. Krissie squealed with delight, and the high-pitched sound made me smile.

An hour later, after the police and wedding guests were gone, the caterer and rental company staff swooped in and began to clean up. My Farm staff and I also pitched in. I think everyone was ready to go back to a normal life around Barton Farm. The sooner the evidence of the wedding was gone, the sooner that would happen.

I went around the tables, collecting linens and dropping them into a basket. My father sidled up to me. He was still wearing his cape, of course. "Hayden is tucked into bed. The little guy was plum tuckered out. I left Jason with him to babysit."

I smiled. "Thanks, Dad. He's had quite a day."

"You've had quite a day too." He folded up chairs and leaned them on the table for the rental company to collect.

I began to shake as I realized how close I'd come to losing my son. Had Shepley made another choice, Hayden could have been killed.

My father noticed, as fathers do. "Oh, my girl." He wrapped his arms around me. "You're safe. Hayden is safe."

I took a deep breath and straightened up. "Thanks, Dad."

He smiled. "I think your mom was looking out for you and Hayden."

My heart ached at his comment, but I thought he just might be right. Then I felt my father studying me. "What?" I asked.

"I don't mean to be nosy, but I am your father. Is everything okay with you and Chase?"

I sighed and dropped another cloth napkin into a basket to be laundered. "I don't know." After the police took Shepley away, Chase had left without a word to me. I thought I might have ruined whatever chance I'd had at a happily ever after.

"You know," my father mused, "Tennyson once said, 'The vow that binds too strictly snaps itself.' He wasn't just talking about wedding vows. Look at Shepley. He vowed that he would never lose everything again, and now he's on his way to prison."

I studied my father. I should have known that he would recognize the root of my problem with Chase, and that it was my vow not to be hurt again. The vow I'd secretly made to myself was the culprit that had torn us apart.

"Kelsey! Kelsey!" Benji called from outside the tent.

I dropped the basket on the table and ran out, wondering what it could possibly be now. Wasn't my ex-husband's wedding and being held at gunpoint enough for one day?

"Look!" Benji pointed into the dark.

I could just make out the shape of Piper and Chase walking down the pebbled path.

"She's here," Benji whispered.

I wrapped my arm around her waist. "What are you going to do about it? Have you decided?"

She looked down at me with tears in her large brown eyes. "She's worth it."

I smiled. "Go."

Benji started toward Piper, but stopped. "But what about you and Chase?"

"He's worth it too," I said.

She grinned, then turned and ran toward Piper. She crashed into the other girl and threw her arms around her. Their laughter and shouts of joy could be heard all over the Farm.

Chase walked toward me at a much slower pace. I met him on the path. "Thanks for bringing Piper here," I said. "As you can see, Benji is thrilled."

He grinned. "It was the least I could do. I was at the police station doing some paperwork and offered her a ride. This is where she wanted to be." He gazed down at me. "This is where we both wanted to be."

I looked at the ground and then back up at him. His features were half cloaked in darkness. The only light came from the work lamps the caterer had set up and the moonlight, which peeked out from behind a cloud. Even in the semidarkness, I could see there was a smile on his face.

"I'm sorry," I began. "I was afraid, and I—"

He put a finger to my lips. "I'm sorry too." And then he kissed me.

ACKNOWLEDGMENTS

Special thanks to everyone at Midnight Ink for supporting this series, especially acquisitions editor Terri Bischoff and production editor Sandy Sullivan. You gave me the opportunity to combine my favorite things, mystery and history. I will always be grateful to you for that.

As always, love and gratitude to my super agent Nicole Resciniti. I could not have this career that I love without you. You are the best cheerleader an author can have and the best friend a girl can have.

Thanks also to my beta reader and assistant Molly Carroll for her insightful and humorous comments on the novel when it was a work in progress. Special thanks to Suzy Schroeder and Derrick Ranostaj for assisting in the historical research of this novel.

Love to my family, Andy, Nicole, Isabella, and Andrew, for always supporting my life as an author.

Finally, to my Heavenly Father: this year you surprised and stretched me again. Thank you.

© Sara E. Smith

ABOUT THE AUTHOR

Amanda Flower, an Agatha Award–winning mystery author, started her writing career in elementary school when she read a story she'd written to her sixth grade class and had the class in stitches with her description of being stuck on the top of a Ferris wheel. She knew at that moment she'd found her calling: making people laugh with her words. She also writes mysteries as *USA Today* bestselling author Isabella Alan. In addition to being a writer, Amanda is a public librarian in Northeast Ohio.

www.amandaflower.com